AF580690

# The Summer That Changed Us

Jami Albright

Copyright © 2026 by Jami Albright

All rights reserved.

No part of this book may be reproduced in any form or by any electronic or mechanical means, including information storage and retrieval systems, without written permission from the author, except for the use of brief quotations in a book review.

This is a work of fiction. Names, characters, places, and incidents are either the product of the author's imagination or are used fictitiously. Any resemblance to actual persons, living or dead, events, or locales is entirely coincidental.

Edited by: Serena Clarke

https://www.serenaclarke.com/editing/

Proofread by: Donna Rich

donnarich@me.com

Cover Design by: Deborah Bradseth Designs

https://www.dbcoverdesign.com/

# The Summer That Changed Us

At fifty, Hope Hall has done everything right. She earned a PhD, built a career, and held her marriage together with determination and stubborn denial.

When her life publicly unravels, Hope returns to her hometown in Texas, and the loud, loving, opinionated family who never quite understood her. Surrounded by her four sisters, who make everything bigger, messier, and usually a public spectacle, she expects the chaos, the old grudges, and small-town rivalries that always seem to involve toilet paper and bail money.

What she doesn't expect is June—her wild, fearless sister, who has spent a decade giving cancer the middle finger. But you can only run from the devil for so long, and what's coming for June may be the thing Hope's family can't survive.

Told with sharp humor, messy love, and the kind of honesty that sneaks up and wrecks you, ***The Summer That***

***Changed Us*** is a deeply moving, laugh-through-the-tears story about sisters, second chances, and what it really means to show up when it matters most.

*For Joni*

*The way you lived your life after cancer taught me how to live my life after your death. You are with me every day and in every word of this book.*

*I love you, sister.*

# Chapter One

How much damage can a canapé do, if hurled at someone's face?

That's the question I'm pondering while I track my as-of-tonight ex-boss to the front of the room to give some asinine speech, full of empty platitudes in my honor. She's a moving target, so I'd need to factor that into my calculations along with wind speed, range, and how much her perpetual smooching will slow her down.

A woman should not feel this miserable while being celebrated. Right?

But here I am, fifty years old, standing in a restaurant full of people raising glasses in my honor, disoriented by how fast my life has crumbled to pieces.

Holloway Preparatory High School is calling it an early retirement party.

I call it the end of the one thing I knew I was good at. The thing I've always been proud of. I wasn't just a teacher. I was an educator at the most exclusive private school in Dallas, but I'm not anymore.

*If only I'd tried harder to stay relevant.*

*I should've spoken up when I saw things changing.*

*Why couldn't I go along to get along?*

This is a fun little self-destructive game I like to play. But figuring out what I did wrong is imperative, if I'm going to land the professorship position I've applied for at The University of Texas.

I want that job for many reasons. Stability, relevance, legitimacy, to validate my whole damn life. Because who am I if I'm not doing my life's work at the highest level possible? Also, rubbing it in Holloway Preparatory High School's face would be truly satisfying.

My ex-boss, Principal Susan Bounds, holds her champagne glass with both of her dainty hands and clears her throat. "Thank you all for being here tonight to honor Hope on her early retirement."

Hope. Not Dr. Hall. In fact, she's never once acknowledged the fact that I hold a PhD in English Literature.

"I know I speak for everyone here when I say that we are all going to miss you terribly at Holloway Prep. Twenty-five years as an educator." Susan shakes her head. "Girl, you've been doing this almost as long as I've been alive. Also, you never did give me your secret to looking so good at your age," she says with an innocent giggle.

I do not miss the jab.

The canapé I'm holding is burning a hole in my hand.

*Drop the canapé, Hope. And no one gets hurt.*

The awkward laughter that skips through the room like an uncoordinated three-year-old tells me that my coworkers didn't miss it either.

"We wish you much happiness in your retirement. I can honestly say that the AP English classes just will not be the same without you, Hope." Susan's smile is as fake as mine.

The silence in the room seems to crest and hang in the air like a giant quote bubble waiting for text.

*Why is it so quiet?*

I turn my attention to my colleagues, hoping for some context clues, and every eye is on me. Oh, crap. They're waiting on me to respond.

I make sure the *it's fine, I'm fine, nothing to see here,* smile is still firmly in place, and say, "Thank you so much, Principal Bounds." I turn my attention from the woman I won't miss to the people who I will, my fellow teachers. "I can say with 100%certainty that my life is better because of Holloway Prep, you all, and of course, the young lives we've all had a hand in shaping. It's been the honor of my life to work beside you all." It's the truth. It's also all I've got. So, I do the only thing I can think of to get me out of this situation. I lift my drink to the room and say, "Go, Huntsmen."

"Go, Huntsmen," the crowd echoes.

There's another beat of awkward silence, as if my audience expects me to say something inspirational or optimistic about my future. I won't. I'm not that good of a liar. I've also exhausted all the contrived excitement I'd managed to muster.

"Well," Principal Bounds says. "Thank you, Hope. Best wishes from us all." She turns to the crowd. "Thank you all for coming tonight. Be sure to sign Hope's card before you leave."

*Is it over? Please, God, let it be over.*

My muscles begin to uncoil fractional inch by fractional inch, as the partygoers gather their things and head for the door. If I can survive the next few minutes, then I can... what?

Move on?

Start over?

Hide and lick my wounds?

"Whatcha gonna do with all your free time, Hope?" Clyde

Anthony, the AP Calculus teacher, who's never been able to read a room, asks.

I briefly consider blasting him with the truth. *Well, Clyde, the plan was for me and my husband, Ian, to travel and rediscover each other, but he left me nine months ago because "he couldn't live like this anymore," four months after he convinced me to retire. So now I have nothing, and I'm scared out of my freakin' mind.* Instead, I say, "Oh, you know, this and that." It's a stupid answer for a stupid question.

*Good Lord, Hope, you're an absolute delight tonight.*

My phone buzzes, and I check the screen. It's a text from my younger sister, June. Thank you, God, for a reason to walk away from this conversation.

"Thanks for coming, Clyde. Excuse me." I hold up my phone. "My family's texting." I make my way to the door, step outside the banquet room in the restaurant where the party's being held, and open the text.

*You are coming home this weekend, right? It's the trivia championship at The Rusty Bucket. We need all the help we can get. Also, I miss you.*

My guilt at not making the forty-minute drive from Dallas to my hometown of Bonedalia, Texas, is why I text back.

*The highway runs both ways, little sister.*

Her response is immediate.

I bark a laugh. June is the funniest person I know, and she doesn't take crap from anyone, including me.

*So are you coming???*

I text back.

*I'll be there. How are you feeling?*

My phone buzzes in my hand. This time her text includes a video.

*Yay! Watch the video.*

The thumbnail of the clip is of June and a bunch of high school girls in baseball uniforms. I click the video and immediately hear the girls chanting, "Coach. Coach. Coach." Then June hops into frame doing the Griddy, feet skipping, arms swinging, and the classic "dance face" that women over thirty wear when they're dancing. She goes out of frame, then comes back moonwalking. Then, much to the delight of her team, she ends the performance with the splits.

I pound out three letters on my phone.

*OMG*

She responds.

*Not bad for a woman with incurable cancer, huh?*

Classic June. She's always refused to ever believe that this disease she's lived with for nearly ten years is more than an inconvenience.

I text.

*Impressive. How are you feeling?*

Her answer is immediate.

*I'm fine.*

I purse my lips and type out another message.

*How are you really?*

I watch the three dots dance until her reply comes through.

*I've been having some headaches. I'm assuming that's from the new chemo.*

All thoughts of my miserable night flee, and I immediately go on high alert. My fingers fly across the keyboard of my phone.

*What'd the doctor say?*

*What's the name of the chemo?*

*Do you have any other symptoms?*

*Were you told this would be a side effect?*

I wait for her response, my anxiety ticking up with each dance of dots on the screen.

*Holy cow, you went from 0 to overprotective big sister faster than I thought possible. Simmer down, Crazy. I'm fine. Of the three small tumors that metastasized to my brain, two are gone, and one is only the size of a mustard seed. It's good news.*

If it's such good news, why do I feel like I just got into a foot race with a tiger? But I can't say that to her, so I send.

*It is good news. Sorry. I'll see you tomorrow.*

Her reply is three red hearts. My response comes easily.

*I love you too, trouble.*

I slip my phone back into my pocket, then realize she never answered my question about her doctor. I pull out my phone to text her back, but stop when I glance toward the hostess desk of the restaurant. The glass of champagne and two appetizers I managed to ingest during the party threaten to make an reappearance. My vision blurs, then clears, but the scene before me doesn't change.

Ian.

His salt and pepper hair peeks out from under his gray cowboy hat and brushes the collar of his light blue denim shirt. He's thinner than he was the last time I saw him, but it looks good on him. In fact, he looks better than I've seen him look in a long, long time. Damn his eyes.

*What's he doing here?*

He turns to speak to someone next to him. I can't see who he's talking to from my vantage point. The grin he gives the person he's with causes the skin around his eyes to crinkle at the corners and smile lines to form parentheses around his mouth. Instead of aging him, these signs of time passing only make him look better.

The fifteen-year-old girl who fell head over heels in love with him, and believed we'd be the source of each other's ridiculous happiness, curls into a ball and wails like a baby for the future lost. I want to shake that silly girl and remind her that she did everything, became whatever he wanted, and still it wasn't enough. She wasn't enough.

Anger slams into me like a Mac truck. The ferocity with which it hits me is confusing, until I realize, he's happy. It's clear that he's exactly where he wants to be.

And I'm just here, frozen in this no-man's-land between what my life used to be and what it actually is. And hanging over all of it is June saying she's having headaches.

Then Ian's companion comes into view. My phone slips from my fingers and clunks against the floor, like an off-key note in a life that's fallen completely off its axis.

He's on a date.

The foreign phrase bounces around my skull as the truth comes into clear focus—the closure I thought this night would bring isn't happening.

This year isn't over.

It's still veering out of control.

# Chapter Two

Nothing's more pitiful than a grown woman hiding in a public bathroom stall from her ex-husband and his girlfriend, but here I am. My intention had been to run as far and as fast away from the scene I witnessed, but instead of heading for the front door, I ended up in this 3 x 5 box.

Girlfriend.

I say the word a few times to see if I can clear the bitter taste from my tongue.

I can't.

Marcy Williams. His employee.

The woman I told him he needed to watch out for ever since she started working at the dealership three years ago. But he insisted, INSISTED that she was nothing more than a good employee.

The image of him holding out his hand to help her take the two steps down from the hostess stand to the restaurant floor blisters the place where my memories live, and it's sure to leave a scar.

The assault of emotions pummeling me makes it impossible to grab hold of one and identify it. All I know is that my ex-husband appears to be moving on with his life, and I'm... not.

I press my head against the metal partition, ignoring the fact the surface is a petri dish. Communicable diseases are the least of my worries right now. The metal is cool on my overheated skin. Unfortunately, it does little to calm the death march shuffling through my gut, dragging behind it the dregs of any secret hope of reconciliation with Ian.

The realization that the loss of that hope is at the core of my breakdown is unwelcome. I thought I was past wishing he and I would find our way back to each other, but apparently, I am not.

I breathe through the misery, trying to gain some rational perspective, but I can't do it alone.

I grab my phone from where it rests on the toilet paper dispenser, pull up my best friend, Carrie's, and dial, but hang up before she can answer because someone enters the bathroom.

The sound of happy humming fills the air. I can't remember the last time something so joyful and carefree came out of my mouth, like fairies dancing on buttercup petals.

How nice for her.

I get a glimpse of the woman's profile through the crack in the stall door. Are you kidding me?

Marcy.

Anger replaces every living molecule in my body. Not because she's here with Ian, but because she has inserted herself into my well-deserved freak-out. It doesn't matter that she has no idea I'm in this stall. She doesn't belong here. This is my breakdown, and mine alone.

The humming ends as she stops in front of my current

hiding place, but she's not looking at the stall or the sinks. She's facing the full-length mirror on the wall.

I have to admit that she's lovely. Young, fresh, lovely...

And, pregnant?

My breath comes in harsh, heavy, ugly huffs as I watch her raise her shirt and lovingly rub her barely-there bump. Her smile is so blissful and full of hope that even I want to linger there in that joyful place with her.

I'm unable to grasp what I'm seeing. My processing ability resembles an old television trying to find a signal with rabbit ears. One second, the image of Marcy is there, the next it's lost behind the static filling my brain.

After several moments of admiring her growing child—Ian's child?—she washes her hands, dries them, resumes humming, and leaves.

It's a miracle I'm still upright. My body has gone completely offline. I'm numb from the neck down. I'm a floating head with one word clanging against my brain.

*Pregnant.*

*Pregnant.*

*Pregnant.*

I can't believe this is happening.

My phone buzzes in my hand. I answer the call without thinking. "Hello." The word is little more than a breath of air.

"Hope?" It's Carrie. "Did you call?"

"Yeah, it was me." I still can't get the volume of my voice beyond a sigh.

"Why are you whispering?" she whispers back. "Also, aren't you supposed to be being celebrated right now?"

"I am—I was."

"Where are you?" she asks. "It's all echoey."

"In the bathroom stall."

"Oh, okay." She chuckles. "I thought something was wrong."

"Something is wrong."

"Did something happen at the party?"

"No, it was fine." I sniff back angry tears.

"So, what's the problem?"

I try to speak, but my words won't make it past the bubble of sour emotion filling my throat. Finally, I manage, "Ian just walked in with Marcy Williams."

"To your party?"

"No. To the restaurant."

"Like on a date?"

"I don't know. Maybe. They went to a table with other salespeople from the dealership."

"So, you don't know if it was a date."

"They came in together, Carrie." I'm no longer whispering. "He held out his hand to help her down the steps from the hostess area. It was quite gallant."

"Jack hasn't said anything about him dating anyone." Jack and Ian have been best friends, brothers really, since they were in the sixth grade.

"Would Jack tell you if Ian asks him not to?"

The silence on the other end of the line is so loud that it hurts.

"He might not." Carrie's voice is thick with concern. "Are you going to be okay? Do you need me—"

"She's pregnant."

"What? Who?" Carrie asks.

"Marcy. She came into the bathroom. I saw her bump through the crack in the stall door." I should probably be concerned with how dissociated I am from this conversation.

"And you think it's—"

"Ian's."

"Hope, no. He couldn't..."

"Of course he could father a child, Carrie." I let my head fall back, and study the divots on the tiles in the ceiling. "All he had to do was find someone with a fully functioning reproductive system."

The door to the bathroom opens again. "I need to go." I'm back to whispering.

"Um... Okay. We'll talk—"

I disconnect before she can say anything else and stare at the door of the stall without seeing it. I rub my hands over my aching belly. My fingers slide over the estrogen patch stuck to my lower abdomen. Another reminder that the clock on having a child has run out—not that it matters anymore. The medically necessary hysterectomy took care of that years ago.

I never imagined a future without Ian that included him becoming a father. I guess I assumed our childlessness was something we'd always share.

But no.

That title is mine alone.

# Chapter Three

The next morning, I'm in the car headed to Bonedalia to see my family. I check my reflection in the rearview mirror, hoping some color might migrate back into my cheeks during the short drive. Unfortunately, so far I'm just as pale as I was last night, when I stepped out of that bathroom stall.

I try to shove the events of the previous evening from my mind. It doesn't work. Sweat beads on my upper lip, and I turn the AC down and adjust the vent to blow on my face.

My phone buzzes. I glance at it and see that it's another text from Carrie. It's the fourth I've ignored.

I jump when it rings. I guess she got tired of being snubbed.

I push the button and answer. "Hey."

"Hey, I've been texting you."

"Yeah, sorry. I'm driving," I lie. Well, I am driving, but that's not why I haven't answered her text. Best friends are great until they're worried about you, but you don't want to talk about the thing they're worried about.

"Oh, that's right, you're headed home." A baby wails in the

background. "Hang on." She's back on the line in a few moments. "Sorry, Regina and Caleb are here with the baby."

*The baby. Really, God?*

"How is the princess?"

Carrie laughs. "She's perfect, of course."

Despite everything, my lips pull into a grin. "Of course."

Carrie's daughter Regina just had her first child a few months ago, and Carrie has been in a constant state of bliss ever since.

I'm happy for her, I really am. I'm also jealous as hell.

The worst part of infertility is mourning someone you will never hold. An identity and a life that were never yours.

I know my friend's not flaunting her children or grandchild in front of me, but she'll never be alone.

I will.

I am.

And the unfairness of it all abrades every part of my soul.

"I wanted to check on you and to tell you that Jack says he doesn't know anything about a baby."

"Carrie—"

"Before you yell at me, I made him swear not to say anything to Ian."

If it were any other couple, I'd be worried that Jack wouldn't keep his word, but I'm confident that Jack will do as Carrie asked. "Okay. But that doesn't mean anything."

"I think it does. If she's already showing, then she's far enough along that Ian would've said something. Hope, you know he would've told Jack."

I stretch my neck from side to side. "Maybe."

"Hope."

"Maybe that's true." I puff out a breath that makes my bangs flutter. Yes, I got bangs. That should've been the first warning that my life was in free fall. "The thing is, I don't want him back. Or I don't want the Ian he's become—unreliable, selfish, distant. Marcy can have that guy. I am better off without him. I've been without the old Ian for a long time."

Carrie's silent on the other end of the line, but the accusation comes through anyway.

"I don't."

"I still think if you had forced the counseling issue, you two could have, still could, work things out."

The thwack of the sun visor being slapped into the upright position fills the car. "I asked him to go to counseling."

"But you didn't bring it back up when he said he'd think about it. One honest conversation between the two of you might've turned things around."

"I shouldn't have had to bring it back up. He should've wanted to fix our marriage, too." I hate that I'm yelling. But I gave my marriage everything I had, even after Ian stopped participating. I gave, and I gave, until I finally gave up.

"I'm not blaming you, Hope." Carrie's voice is calm and steady. "I'm always team Hope."

"I know. I'm sorry I yelled at you."

"It's okay. You're due a good bitch session."

"I made you cuss." Carrie never cusses. "My work here is done."

"Ha-ha. I cuss plenty... in my head."

"That's hilarious." The laughter is the pressure valve release I've needed. "Thanks for that."

"Anytime."

The billboard welcoming me to *Bonedalia, Home of the Fighting Longhorns* comes into view. "I'll call you when I get settled in at Mom and Dad's. We'll set up a time to get together."

"I'll see you at the Rusty Bucket, right?"

"Oh, yeah, the trivia championship. June is fired up about

it. She practically threatened death if I didn't show up." And after last night, June is about the only person who could lure me back to this small town and my family.

I love my people, but they're a lot to manage.

Carrie chuckles. "I get it. This is serious business. We have a good team, and it'll be even better with you added to the roster."

I flick on my blinker to change lanes. "Carrie, it's trivia night, not the Olympics."

"Hey, city girl, first prize is unlimited wings for a month at the Rusty Bucket. Also, the bragging rights alone are enough to get a better table at the diner."

"You sound like June. If you tell me that you've recently TP'd the Fowler's house to mess with their game, then I'm performing an intervention."

Carrie laughs. "I have not. But you do have to admire your sister's ability to hold a grudge. What was she, sixteen, when Marjorie Fowler made out with her boyfriend at the homecoming after-party?"

"Fifteen." I shake my head. "And don't remind me. I'm still not over her and Dad's clandestine mission to defile the Fowlers' Halloween decorations."

"Putting the Fowlers' giant skeleton on their flagpole, like a stripper, then placing the other skeletons around the pole with dollar bills in their hands... pure genius."

I can't help the smile that pulls at my lips. "They're ridiculous."

"How's June's treatment going?"

The heaviness in my gut, temporarily lightened by the amusement from remembering Dad and June's antics, is back in full force. "It's going well. Of the three small tumors that metastasized to her brain, two are gone, and she says one is only the size of a mustard seed. It's good news."

"So why do I hear worry in your voice?" Carrie asks.

"It is good news, but I... I don't know. Her original cancer has been so well maintained and treated for so long that I think we all got a little complacent. Plus, with everything happening in my life, I took my eye off the ball and wasn't checking on her as much as I should've."

"Hope, I know you like to manage things, but you can't control her cancer. You do know that, right?"

"Of course, I know that," I say, but I actually don't know any such thing. As soon as I get up to speed on June's treatment and condition, I'll come up with a plan to get her back to at least where she was before the cancer metastasized.

"Hope—"

"Oh, for the love..."

"What?"

"My dad is driving down Hamilton Street on his riding lawn mower."

"That doesn't sound safe."

"Oh, don't worry, he has one of those orange caution flags that stick up in the air on the

back. So, he's fine." The sarcasm oozes off every word. "Carrie, cars are starting to pile up behind him. I've got to go." I disconnect, not quite believing the scene before me.

A traffic jam on my hometown's main street is a rarity, but a nearly eighty-year-old man driving a riding lawn mower, going a whopping fifteen miles per hour, will do it. A few cars are passing him, but the others are falling in behind him like they're playing a game of redneck follow the leader.

I tap down the stewing resentment in my chest. Why am I always the one who has to point out the ridiculousness in my family? If my sisters were here, they'd think this stunt was hilarious.

So, saving my father from himself falls to me.

I drive in the second lane to catch up with him. Not too hard, given his current rate of speed. Once I'm even with the lawn mower, I honk.

He looks over and surprise colors his sweaty face. It's a sweltering Texas day, with the temperature easily reaching ninety-five degrees outside. Great, not only do I have to worry about him being run over, but now I have to get him off that thing before he collapses from heatstroke.

He grins and waves, like he's not the grand marshal in a hometown hillbilly parade.

I gesture for him to pull over.

He ignores me.

I gesture again.

He still ignores me.

He's always been good at that.

I'm about to honk again, but then someone behind me lays on their horn. In my rearview mirror, I can see a line of cars behind me. Crap, now I'm part of the spectacle.

The horn blares behind me again, and this time, they mean business.

A glance over at my father. The set of his jaw tells me trying to stop him is a fool's errand, so I say a prayer of safety to the lawncare gods and speed up.

The last thing I see in the rearview mirror, before I make the turn onto the road that leads to my parents' home, is that the number of cars behind my dad has doubled, and now the unmistakable blaze of red and blue flashing lights has joined the procession.

# Chapter Four

I pull into the parking area in front of my parents' house. It sits on ten acres, not huge, but big enough for a small barn and a tank—or pond, as my city friends call it—where we fished and swam as kids.

My sisters and I spent more days than I can count dangling our feet from the dock, giggling, playing, fighting, and making up. As teenagers, Carrie and I spent nearly every summer night staring at the stars, talking about boys and dreaming of the ones we just knew we couldn't live without.

Speaking of boys we couldn't live without, it was also where Ian and I got up to things that teenagers probably shouldn't but inevitably do. The desperation and yearning of young love should come with a warning label.

*Caution: Won't last forever.*

Like a child touching a hot stove, I quickly yank my mind off that line of thinking. And slam the door on those memories. Nothing good comes from reliving things in the past.

Before I exit the car, my mom is coming out of the house. Her brunett hair is cut short, curled, and backcombed within an inch of its life. I notice she holds the railing and carefully places each foot on the steps, and something in my chest constricts.

This woman and my father loom large in my memories as athletic, active, vibrant people. They're getting older, and there's nothing I can do to stop it.

I step out of the car. "Hey, Mom."

"Hello, baby." Her slim arms go around me, enveloping me in the loveliness of her vanilla and roses scent, a place I could happily live for the rest of my life. My muscles uncoil for the first time since I saw Ian with Marcy last night. "How was your drive?" she asks.

I reluctantly step out of her embrace and open the back car door to retrieve my overnight bag. "Fine, until I got to town and saw Dad driving down Hamilton Street on his riding lawnmower."

She shakes her head and grins. "He loves that new lawnmower."

Her response doesn't surprise me. My mom thinks my dad is it, and there ain't nothin' *iter*. It would be adorable if it didn't drive me crazy. "Why is he driving it through town? Is it even street legal?"

"He says he likes the wind in his hair." Mom chuckles, and I think my head might explode.

"Mom, he's bald."

Her laughter is deep and rich, rolling from her like a bubbling stream I want to bathe in. "You know how he is when he gets something in his head."

Oh, I know how he is, and so does my therapist. Years of therapy, and I still have to remind myself that he's not the thoughtless man I grew up with anymore. He's softened, and I've forgiven him, but some days...

"That can't be safe."

Before Mom can answer, the roar of a lawnmower engine and the whoop of a police siren interrupt us. We turn to see Dad cruising up the driveway with the local law following.

Dad pulls the mower next to my car and swings his leg over to dismount the thing.

Now that the police cruiser is closer, I can see that Officer K.P. Sikes is behind the wheel. She was on my little league baseball team, where Dad was our coach.

K.P. exits her car and walks toward us.

Dad waves like he's seeing her at the grocery store, not like she's followed him home with lights and sirens. "Thanks for the escort, K.P., but I'm fine as frog's hair. How's your daddy?"

"He's just fine." Officer Sikes adjusts her utility belt. "Mr. James, I wasn't escorting you home. I was trying to pull you over."

"Pull me over?" Dad looks from K.P. to my mom. "Why?" The man is truly shocked by this news.

My hands go to my hips. "Why?" I motion to his current means of transportation. "You can't drive your lawnmower through the middle of town. What were you thinking? You have a perfectly good truck to drive."

He narrows his eyes like he's lining up a target. "I do, thanks to Ian."

Bullseye.

Before I can answer, he turns back to K.P. like he hasn't just taken a swipe at me. "I put a caution flag on it, so the other cars could see me." He says it as if it's the most reasonable thing ever.

The good officer's lips twitch, but she gains control before she smiles. "I understand, but you can't use your lawnmower as a personal vehicle."

"Can you believe this malarky, Marie?" he asks my mom.

Mom shakes her head. "I was worried about you taking it to the store, Russ."

He sucks his teeth. It's the dismissive sound he's perfected over the years, when it comes to dealing with my mom, my sisters, and especially me.

I've always been the fly in my dad's ointment. The one who points out the thing everyone else pretends not to see.

His attention goes back to Officer Sikes, and he holds his hands out with his wrists together. "Go ahead then, K.P., slap the cuffs on me."

K.P. lowers her head and shakes it back and forth slowly. When she looks up, humor is shining in her eyes. "I think I can let you off with a warning this time, Mr. James. As long as you promise not to do it again." She tilts her head in question.

It takes him longer than it should to answer. "I guess I can agree to that."

"Thank you, Coach. I only want you to be safe."

The use of "coach" seems to soften him up. He nods. "Well, thank ya. You be safe out there too, K.P."

The officer does smile now. "I will." She turns her attention to me. "It was good to see you, Hope."

"You too, K.P." I set my bag down. "I'll walk you to your car."

"Are you in town long?" she asks.

"Just for the long weekend." I glance back at my parents. My mom is helping my dad remove the flag from the mower. "Thanks for not giving him a ticket."

"Honestly, I'm not sure what I'd even write him up for. Mowing the streets of Bonedalia? Killing the ozone layer?" She chuckles.

"Noise pollution?" I smile and shake my head.

She opens the door to her cruiser and then slides into the car. "Take care, Hope."

"You too." I step back so she can make the three-point turn to exit.

Then I head back toward the house. My parents have already gone in, and they've taken my bag with them. My dad's way of apologizing for his Ian comment. I'm certain of this. It's what he does. He offends, then tries to make it up to us, without ever addressing the issue.

Pausing on the porch, I blow out a breath and stretch my neck from side to side.

I hear laughter coming from inside. No matter the insanity out here, I know my family, and there's always more to come.

That thought fills me with both dread and a tinge of excitement. I am a product of these people, no matter how hard I've tried not to be.

# Chapter Five

I swing open the screen door and move into our front room, and am immediately assaulted by a tennis match blasting at full volume from the TV. My fourteen-year-old niece, Chloe, and fifteen-year-old nephew, Max, are huddled together on one of the sofas, laughing at something on their phones. I can hear June and my youngest sister, Babe, in the kitchen with my parents, talking loudly. It's impossible to know by the volume if they're in a knock-down, drag-out fight or in total agreement. The Jameses are yellers—you have to put eyes on us to know what's really going on.

We yell when we're happy and excited.

We yell when we're angry.

We yell when we're bored.

I've spent the better part of my adult life training this particular trait out of my DNA. It's been a battle and taken years of strict discipline, but I can proudly say that I rarely if ever yell, for any reason. I didn't even yell when Ian left.

*Maybe you should've,* an ugly, accusatory voice taunts.

What would've been the point? He'd made up his mind.

I drag my thoughts from nine months ago to the present and my family. They're currently discussing whether or not a lawnmower should be allowed to be used as a personal vehicle.

"I don't see what the big deal is," June says.

Of course she doesn't. She and my dad are always on the same side of any argument, unless they're arguing against each other. And on those rare occasions, we all run for the hills.

"I can see how it would be a safety issue, but I also understand why you're upset, Dad," Babe, ever the peacemaker, says.

Babe is the youngest. That's not her real name, of course, but she's never gone by anything but "Babe" or "The Baby" her whole life.

"Hope. I didn't see you there," June says.

"I'm here." It's an effort to infuse my voice with cheerfulness. I'm fighting to keep the muscles around my mouth upturned to hide my shock at June's appearance. For the first time in ten years, she looks truly unwell.

She's recently shaved her head because the new chemo regiment she's on has caused her hair to fall out. That's never happened before. The contrast between this fragile-looking woman in front of me and the June I know is disorienting.

She once won a "Ms. Honky-Tonk" contest with a bloody towel tied around her head. Before the contest began, she got into a fight with another girl, and the woman hit her in the head with a beer bottle, opening a deep gash in June's forehead. Babe, June's unwilling partner in crime, tried to get her to go to the ER, but she refused. The title of "Ms. Honky-Tonk" came with a $300 cash prize, and she needed the money to make rent. So, she borrowed a towel from the bartender, competed her little, bloody, honky-tonkin' heart out, and won the damn thing.

The wound required sixteen stitches. So, yeah, fragile is never a word anyone would use to describe June.

Still, the pocket of anxiety that's lived behind my breastbone since she was first diagnosed with non-smoker's lung cancer swells, and for a few heartbeats, I can't draw breath. I cling to the mantra I've used for the last ten years and hang onto it for dear life. *There's not a world where June doesn't exist.* The pressure eases with every repetition.

"How long are you stayin'?" Babe asks me.

I open the fridge and grab a bottle of water. "Until Tuesday."

"So, you're staying for the Memorial Day Parade?" June asks. "We're takin' the Fowlers down this year."

"That's right." Dad holds his fist out for June to bump.

"You two..." I shake my head and pat my purse. "I've got the bail money right here."

Everyone, including my dad, laughs. The pleasure I feel coloring my face is stupid. It's pathetic that something as small as a chuckle from this old man is like a cool rain on a sweltering August day. I'm still a daughter who wants her daddy's approval.

I clear my throat and level June with a stern look that she doesn't take seriously at all. "I hope I don't have to use it."

June grins. "That's up to the Fowlers. Right, Dad?"

He winks at her. "That's right."

Every year, the city of Bonedalia has a Memorial Day float contest, and Dad and June go head-to-head with their nemesis, the Fowlers. They used to rope the rest of us into participating, but their competitiveness was too much. So, a couple of years ago, we all boycotted and refused to join them in their madness.

The pressure in my chest shoves against my ribs when I notice June rub her temples. "Does your head hurt?"

She immediately drops her hands to the table. "A little."

*There's not a world where June doesn't exist.*

*There's not a world where June doesn't exist.*

*There's not a world where June doesn't exist.*

"More than a little if the circles under your eyes are any indication," Mom says.

June shrugs but doesn't confirm or deny Mom's assessment.

I want to press her, but I know that look. She's done with this conversation. I glance around. "Where are your husbands?" I ask my two youngest sisters.

Before they can answer, Grace and Joy, sisters two and three, burst through the front door, and they're in the middle of a huge argument. A natural state for their relationship.

"I saw the text on his phone," Grace shouts.

"Why did you have his phone?" Joy slings back.

Grace crosses her arms defiantly. "That's none of your business."

"He. Is. My. Business," Joy shouts.

I meet June's gaze and she rolls her eyes. "It's the Jimmy Jenkins saga, episode one million."

I drop into a chair at the kitchen table. "I can't believe the two of you are still fighting over that man."

"Shut up, Hope," they say in unison.

June laughs. "Damn, Hope. I think that's the only thing they've agreed on in their lives."

They both give her the stink eye.

Jimmy Jenkins has been an issue for these two since high school.

I rest my chin in my hand. "It boggles my mind that two beautiful, accomplished women would fight over a man like Jimmy Jenkins."

June, who never misses an opportunity to malign the man, says, "I saw him at the grocery store last week. He was wearing his usual uniform—a tank top and cut-off jean shorts—but instead of his rainbow flip-flops, he was barefoot." She trains her eyes on Joy and Grace. "Did I mention we were at the grocery store?"

Babe snorts a laugh, then tries to cover it with a cough.

I turn back to my feuding sisters and point to June. "This is the man you're still fighting over?"

"You don't know him like I do," Joy says.

Grace plops down in a chair like a petulant child. "I know him better than you, and she's right. He has depth."

Dad barks a laugh. "Depth? Damn, Grace. The man's as shallow as a rain puddle."

"Russ," Mom warns.

June shakes her head in disgust and murmurs, "Ridiculous."

I know how she feels. "Can you at least agree not to fight around June? She has a headache."

It's like a switch flips. Jimmy Jenkins is immediately forgotten, and all their attention is on June.

"What's wrong?" Grace asks.

Joy pushes Grace out of the way. "How long has it been hurting?"

Grace nudges Joy over. "Have you taken anything?"

"Do you need to lay down?" Joy asks.

"Thanks a lot," June mouths to me.

I sign, "You're welcome."

The front door opens, and Clay, Babe's husband, walks in with Aaron, June's husband.

"Something smells good," Clay says.

"Mom's making dumplin's." Babe smiles at her husband like she hasn't seen him in months.

Clay goes to my mom, picks her up, and spins her around. "That's why you're my favorite mother-in-law, Marie."

My mother's laughter fills the kitchen. Once Clay puts her

down, she slaps his shoulder. "You're a nut. Now get everyone to the table."

"Yes, ma'am." He turns and yells, "Y'all come eat."

Mom shakes her head. "I could've done that, Clay."

His unapologetic grin makes my mother laugh again. She turns her attention to me. "I made a great big salad and grilled some chicken for you, Hope."

"Oh, you didn't—"

"You too good for chicken and dumplin's?" It's an accusation from my dad, not a question.

I shove down my irritation. "No. I love chicken and dumplings, but if Mom has a grilled chicken salad, then I prefer that." I'm very disciplined with my diet. I don't eat a lot of fats and carbohydrates. He knows this. He's just trying to pick a fight.

Mom jumps in before the conversation gets out of hand. "Of course she's not, Russ. But I know that Hope prefers healthier options." She takes my chin in her hand affectionately. "And it's no trouble to grill a chicken breast." Her warm lips press against my forehead.

"Thanks, Mom."

She winks at me and goes back to the stove.

Aaron bends to kiss June. "Hey, babe, how are you feeling?"

She grins up at him. "Right as rain, baby. Right. As. Rain."

One side of his mouth kicks up. "That's what I like to hear."

Irritation scrapes against my insides. I love my brother-in-law, but he's in denial about June's cancer. My whole family is. It drives me crazy. In their defense, they take their cues from June, and she is the reigning queen of denial.

I've always known the truth of the severity of her cancer. That's where the pocket of anxiety comes from. I've never shared what I know with the rest of my family. June made it clear from the beginning that she didn't want statistics or a prognosis. Her attitude is that she'll decide how she lives, and cancer won't have anything to say about it. My irreverent, brave, delusional sister has looked cancer in the face for ten years and dared it to do its worst. She's always believed it wouldn't beat her. And she expects that same defiance from all of us.

I admire her for her attitude. I wish I were more like her. Her courage in the face of such an uncertain future has always humbled me. She's a fighter in more than one sense of the word.

Within minutes, we're elbow to elbow around my parents' oversized farm table.

"How's the job hunt, Hope?" Clay asks.

The food I've eaten sours in my stomach—touchy subject. Leave it to sweet, oblivious Clay to ask. I wipe the corners of my mouth with my napkin. "It's going. I've applied for a professorship at the University of Texas but haven't heard back from them yet."

"Hook 'em," he says around a mouthful of food, grinning.

"Hook 'em," I say in return.

He shovels another forkful of dumplings into his mouth. "You let us know if you need any help, you know, financially." He whispers the last word, like if he says it aloud, I might ask for a loan on the spot.

I bite the inside of my cheek to keep from smiling. "Thank you, Clay, but I'm good for now. Remember, Texas is a fifty-fifty state."

"Must be nice," my dad says from the other end of the table. The words are varnished with the slightest tinge of nastiness.

There he is. This is the man I'm used to dealing with.

I pull on the armor I'm accustomed to wearing around him and give him my sweetest smile. "It is. And to think, if my marriage hadn't imploded, I wouldn't have that good fortune."

He makes that teeth-sucking sound again. We've never been close. He's never tried, and I gave up trying a long time ago. So, we coexist for the sake of our family.

June gives me a look. I give her one right back. She and Babe have never understood my low-level animosity toward our father. But they grew up with a very different Russ James than Grace, Joy, and I did. By the time they came along, he'd mellowed. Plus, it is no secret that June is his favorite. I don't begrudge her that, but she'll never be able to see things from my perspective. That's okay. We can agree to disagree about our dad.

"Speaking of your ex, he said he could get me a great deal on a new truck," Clay announces.

"Ian?" I don't know why it comes out as a surprised question. I only have one ex, but hearing his name here, at my family's table, feels like he's popped up like a rusty, off-key jack-in-the-box.

"Yeah, I called to get his advice on what kind of truck would be best for the kind of driving I do, and he volunteered to give me his owner's discount." Clay shakes his oblivious head. "That Ian, he's a good guy."

Well, this isn't awkward at all.

"Aunt Hope, can Uncle Ian get me a car too?" Max, Graces's 's son, asks.

Okay, now it's definitely awkward.

I jack the corners of my lips up and pin them in place. "You should definitely ask him, honey."

"I want a car too," Chloe yells.

"Eat your dinner, Chloe," Joy says to her daughter.

"But—"

"Eat."

"Hope, you're still coming to trivia night, right?" June to the rescue.

I relax my phony smile and grin at her, hoping my gratitude for the save shows. "I wouldn't miss it." I look around the table. "Is everyone going?"

"All the grown-ups are going," Max says in such a put-upon way that the adults laugh.

Ian-free conversation resumes, and I have never been more grateful for anything in my life.

The muscles in my neck have just begun to relax when Clay points his fork at me and says, "You know, it's a real shame you and Ian couldn't make it work, Hope. He's the kind of guy you can really count on."

The emotional bomb he's lobbed my way takes pieces of my soul with it as it explodes. I glance down, shocked to see I'm not bleeding out all over the table.

"Did y'all hear the latest about the Schwartz twins?" June asks.

Clay sits up straighter. "Is it juicy?"

June grins. "Oh, yeah."

Clay claps his hands and rubs them together. "Then I'm all ears. Those two have been nothin' but trouble, since we were in high school. Also, two grown men shouldn't still be wearin' matchin' clothes. I don't care if they are twins. It's unnatural."

June winks at me, then starts in on a truly ridiculous story.

Within minutes, my family's forgotten about me and are laughing and gossiping about people I don't know, which was of course June's plan.

What would I do without her?

I hope I never have to find out.

# Chapter Six

Trivia night at the Rusty Bucket isn't in danger of becoming a recruiting ground for Mensa anytime soon. The questions are mostly pop culture references and local happenings, and there's even one about who the Bonedalia cheerleaders were in 1985. Surprisingly, Joy and Grace work together to get that one.

Baby steps.

We're a large group. Of course, the joke in town has always been that my family travels in a pack because there are so many of us. Carrie and her husband, Jack, have also joined us.

I'm seated next to Carrie, but my gaze keeps involuntarily going to June at the opposite end of the table. She's the same ol' June—loud, brazen, hilarious as ever. That should ease my mind, but something seems off.

Carrie bumps my shoulder and whispers, "She seems good."

"Take that, losers!" June shouts to the four people next to us after we get the current question correct.

I laugh along with everyone else. I shake off my concern

and chalk it up to my overprotectiveness. "She does. But if she's not careful, we're all going to be brawling before the night's over. And I didn't wear my brawling shoes."

"That girl is too much," my mom adds. Affection coats each word like melting whipped cream rolling down the side of a hot fudge sundae.

"How long was the boat tour supposed to be on Gilligan's Island?" asks Mr. Langdon, our quiz master and the retired chemistry teacher from Bonedalia High School.

"Three hours," I shout.

"Correct," he says.

June jumps to her feet and points at me. "That's my brilliant big sister!"

It didn't take a lot of brain cells to answer that question correctly. But I raise my beer into the air and accept the compliment. "And that's my troublemaking little sister."

June dips her chin. "Guilty as charged."

Grace throws a handful of popcorn at June. "Sit down, trouble."

Aaron pulls June into his lap and kisses her. It isn't a little peck on the lips either. It's the kind of kiss that leads to things that happen behind closed doors, which prompts the surrounding tables to throw more popcorn our way.

After another *not safe for public consumption* kiss, June returns to her own chair and yells at the popcorn throwers, "Y'all better be glad I'm a lover, not a fighter."

Our fellow patrons laugh and hurl more snack food at us. They all know how untrue her declaration is. She's probably fought at least one person at each table before.

I soak it in. It's been a while since I've felt this kind of contentment and belonging, even with my own family.

"Alright, settle down," Mr. Langdon says into the mic. "The next question is a tough one, so put your thinking caps on." He clears his throat. "Where were the Declaration of Independence, the Constitution, and the Bill of Rights stored during World War II?"

There's a long, long silence. All the teams are working together to come up with the answer, including ours. Several suggestions are batted around the table, but none of us feels confident enough to answer the question.

The room has gone quiet, except for the murmurs from some of the teams.

Mr. Langdon taps the mic. "Anyone? Anyone? Bueller?"

More silence.

"It appears I've stumped you—"

"Fort Knox." The answer comes from the back of the room.

Mr. Langdon points. "Correct. Give the cowboy in the back twenty points."

Everyone turns to see who the responder is.

Time stops, then stutters back to life. It can't be.

*Marcy.*

*Pregnant.*

*Baby.*

"Ian!" Clay yells and waves.

Ian grins and begins making his way to our table.

The pressure in my head increases with every step he takes toward us.

"What is he doing here?" I whisper to Carrie.

"I don't know." She looks at Jack. "Did you know he would be here?"

Jack shakes his head. "I told him we were coming tonight, but I had no idea... I'm sorry, Hope."

Sweet Jack. "It's fine, Jack. We'd inevitably see each other at some point." I just didn't think it would be at the Rusty Bucket on trivia night.

I force my gaze away from Ian as he glides through the

room, shaking hands with people at nearly every table. Ian Hall is still Bonedalia's favorite son.

"Join us, Ian," Clay, head groupie in the Ian Hill fan club, says.

"I'm sorry," Babe mouths.

I shake my head. "It's fine," I mouth back. Though it's anything but fine. I'm spinning out and trying to hold it together. I have no idea what I will say to him.

*How's your pregnant girlfriend?*

Except for Clay and Jack, Ian is met with a cool reception, even from my dad, who's always thought Ian hung the moon. When Ian shakes his hand, Dad doesn't stand or look him in the face, just unfolds one arm from where they're crossed over his chest and holds his hand out, then recrosses his arms when Ian moves on to greet the others at the table.

My mom, Grace, Joy, and Babe give a mumbled hello when he greets them. In that moment, I've never loved my family more. We might fight and go after each other, but if you come for one of us, then you have to deal with all of us. It's the James way.

Well, except Clay, who is still gushing over Ian.

Ian turns his attention to June. "You're lookin' well, Bug." Bug is the nickname he gave her when she was little. Since then, that's all he's ever called her.

June leans back, hooking her elbow over the top rung of her chair, and looks him up and down. "What the hell are you doing here, Ian?"

Babe spits beer, and my mom says, "June Elizabeth."

"What?" June asks. "I'm only asking what everyone else is thinking."

"It's fine, Marie. It's a fair question," Ian says. "I came to town to help Mom with a few things around her house today. Jack said y'all'd be here, so I thought I'd pop in to say hello." He shoves his hands in the front pockets of his perfectly fitting jeans. And believe me, being forced to acknowledge that fact chaps my behind.

June puckers her lips and nods. "Okay." She flings her arm into the air and waves in mock enthusiasm. "Hello, Ian." Then she crosses both arms over her chest. "We've all said hello. Now you can leave."

He seems unfazed by her rudeness, but I know he isn't. June is his favorite person in the world. They've been close since we started dating when she was five, and he's always doted on her, so her disdain has to cut deep.

He shifts his attention to me. "Hi, Hope." He pushes his hat back on his head and grins, and for one achingly familiar moment, he's the man I married.

"Ian." I'm shocked I can get the word through the anger and heartbreak choking me. How dare he intrude on the first happy night I've had since he left?

"Have a seat, Ian," the clueless groupie says, pulling up a chair.

"Clay." Babe digs her elbow into his side. Poor guy. There's probably a permanent elbow-shaped groove in his ribs.

"Naw, I can't stay." Ian focuses on me again. "Hope, I found a few things of yours at Mom's. I boxed them up. If you want to come to the truck to get them—"

"No."

"Oh, okay, I can drop them by the house—"

"No."

"What should I do with them?" The little "1 1" lines form between his brows. I know that look. He's irritated, and that gives me a ridiculous amount of pleasure.

I hold his gaze but don't answer.

June snorts. "I think what she's trying to say is you can shove them up your—"

"Get rid of them."

"What?" Ian asks.

I stand. "I said, get rid of them. I don't want them."

"But—"

I push my chair in and lean on the back of it. "I don't want anything from you. There's nothing you have that I want, Ian. Nothing. So burn them." I turn my back on him and make my way to the bathroom.

As I walk away, June shouts, "That, ladies and gentlemen, is my badass big sister."

# Chapter Seven

When I return from the bathroom, there's a commotion at our table. My family is out of their seats and gathered around where June was sitting. I don't see her, but I can see Ian's cowboy hat in the middle of the upheaval.

Oh, Lord, I hope June didn't actually hit him.

Moving quickly through the crowd, back to my family. Some people are standing on their chairs to get a better look. Mr. Langdon is no longer on the stage but joined the throng surrounding the turmoil.

When I get close, I see Mom and Babe are crying, and June is slumped over in Aaron's lap.

I elbow my way through the spectators. "What happened?" I don't mean to yell, but that's how it comes out.

"We don't know," Joy says without taking her eyes off June.

"She was fine, then she grabbed her head, cried out, and..." Grace motions to June.

I move to Aaron's side. "Did she pass out?"

My brother-in-law doesn't answer. All of his attention is on stroking June's back.

I take his shaking hand and repeat my question. "Aaron, did she pass out?"

His dark, terrified eyes are glassy. "I... I don't know. She won't say anything."

I crouch down so I can see June's pale face. "Hey, Junie." I rub my hand over her fuzz-covered head. "Can you hear me?"

"Yes." Her answer is barely audible.

"Can you tell me what's happening?"

"Head," is all she says.

"It hurts?"

"So much." All the life seems to have drained from her face, and she's limp in Aaron's lap. "Help me, Hope," she breathes.

I've never heard June sound so helpless and desperate. "Should we go to the hospital?" I ask, dreading her answer.

"Hospital?" Aaron asks. The word seems to have jarred him from his stupor. "Naw. She's okay. She'll be okay. She doesn't need to go to the hospital. Do you, baby?"

I should not hit this man. I should not. He's as terrified as the rest of us. But I really do want to.

"Let's let June decide what we need to do," I say as patiently as possible. I look back at my sister. "What do you say, Junie?"

"I think..." She cries out as pain rips through her again. "I think we should," Babe says through tears.

"I think The Baby's right, huh, Junie?" I ask again.

"Yes," she breathes. "But don't tell her I think she's right."

Something between a laugh and a sob chokes me. "It's our secret." Then I look at Aaron. "We need to call an ambulance."

He's shaking his head before I finish the sentence. But then June begins to moan in agony. He bends to kiss her head. "Okay."

Grace goes into commander mode. "Carrie, call the ambulance. Clay, pay the bill. We'll all settle up later. And somebody get Mom a chair." What would we do without level-headed, drill sergeant Grace?

"I'll get the bill," Ian says.

"Thank you," Grace says with zero emotion.

My dad pulls out his wallet. "I'll take care of it."

"Russ, put your money away. I've got it." The tone in Ian's voice indicates that he's tolerated what he considers acceptable disdain but is now tired of my family's foolishness.

My father's pale blue eyes find mine. There's a question there, but I'm not sure what he's asking. Permission to let Ian pay, if I have the situation under control, if June will be okay, or some combination of all three. The sheer helplessness in his posture causes a foreign emotion to well up in my chest. It feels like sympathy. I don't like it. And I certainly am not ready to examine it, so I just nod.

The paramedics are there in minutes. I look up to see Rick Stokes moving purposefully toward our group with a defibrillator in his hand and a large medical bag slung over his shoulder.

I lean toward June's ear and whisper, "Junie, Rick Stokes is striding toward you like you're the only woman alive. It's your dream come true."

"Woohoo," she says pitifully.

Rick was her crush all through middle and high school. Like driving by his house hourly, following him around like a puppy, *I'll show you my boobs* kind of crush. But Rick wasn't interested. When he came home from college with a boyfriend, we all understood why. Though June never got over her infatuation.

The dreamy paramedic crouches down next to my sister. "Hey, June. Can you tell me what's going on?"

"Oh, you know, still trying to get your attention." Her attempt at humor is encouraging. Surely, it can't be that serious if she can still joke.

He opens his bag. "I'm flattered as always, but you know my heart belongs to another." He pulls out a blood pressure cuff. "Can you sit up for me, sweetheart?"

"I don't think so," she whimpers.

"Okay, we'll do this in your handsome husband's lap." He winks at her. "That sounded as dirty as I meant it to."

A grimace of pain follows the weak grin she gives him.

"It's okay, babe," Rick says gently. "Once we get you into the rig, we'll start an IV and give you the good drugs. You'll be feeling no pain shortly."

I stroke June's head again. "Hear that, Junie? You get the good drugs."

Aaron continues to mutely rub June's back with a trembling hand.

Rick must notice he's crashing out because he says, "Aaron, can you give Dustin here some information about your wife?"

"Um... sure." Aaron turns his attention to the other paramedic, but his eyes remain glassy, and he keeps losing focus as Dustin asks the questions.

When it's clear that Aaron isn't up to the task, Grace jumps in and gives the paramedic the information he needs.

After what seems like forever, they gently lift my sister onto a gurney.

"Which hospital?" Rick asks Aaron.

"Um..."

"Reece Medical," Grace says.

"Thank you," a shell-shocked Aaron says to her. "I don't know what I'd do without you."

She dips her chin once, clearly uncomfortable with the compliment.

"We'll meet you there," Rick says, then they wheel my sister to the waiting ambulance.

My family stares after them, all in varying degrees of upset and confusion. How has this happened? My vibrant, kickass sister was just giving my ex hell, then...

Strong hands knead my shoulders. My body melts into the touch before I can stop it. Warm breath feathers across my face. "Come on, I'll give you a ride to the hospital."

Ian.

He's no longer my safe harbor. I hate that I forgot that. By the force of will, I stiffen my spine and step out of his reach. "No."

"Hope you can't drive yourself. You're too upset," he says in the confident tone he's always had.

Joy loops her arm in mine. "Hope, you can ride with us." To Ian, she says, "Thank you for taking care of the bill."

"It's not a problem." He takes his cowboy hat off, smooths his hair back, and then replaces it. "I can drive you all."

"That's not necessary. Our family's got it," Grace says from my other side, *You're not family anymore* like a flashing neon sign over her head. Babe steps in front of me, with her back to Ian, and says, "Jack and Carrie have their Suburban out front; we'll ride with them. Clay's taking Mom, Dad, and Aaron. Let's go."

I duck my chin and walk out with my pack at my back, shielding me from the pain behind me.

I only wish there were someone to shield us all from the unknown ahead.

# Chapter Eight

Hours later, with June released into Aaron's care and instructions to follow up with her doctor, we're on our way home. I'm riding with Mom, Dad, Clay, and Babe, who promptly fell asleep in the backseat of the Suburban the minute Clay pulled out of the parking lot. That's what an adrenaline crash will do to you.

I'm jealous. I wish I could escape this nagging fear that something is very wrong. My stomach churns at the stink of the emergency room still clinging to me, like I've showered in antiseptic and desperation. All I want is to wash it and this night away, but I know that while I can get rid of the hospital stench, the scenes from this night are carved into my memories.

"What did the doctor mean, he doesn't know why she's in so much pain?" Mom asks. The frantic confusion in her voice only feeds the secret panic brewing in my mind.

"He said there wasn't anything they didn't expect to see on the MRI, Marie," my dad says. "In fact, two of the tumors are gone, and the other one has shrunk to nearly nothin'."

"And why didn't they keep her for monitoring?" Mom isn't

letting it go, and I don't blame her. None of us has ever seen June that helpless and fragile.

I pull one leg into the seat and turn to face her. "They didn't keep her because they gave her a choice whether to stay or not, and you know she's never going to willingly stay in the hospital."

Clay laughs. "I would've made the same decision. I hate hospitals." He grins at me in the rearview mirror. "Babe and I have that in common."

Despite the unease rolling off Mom and saturating the air, I smile back. Babe is a notorious germaphobe.

"But why did it happen?" Mom practically yells then glances over her shoulder to the sleeping Babe and lowers her voice. "I don't understand."

She needn't bother. When Babe's asleep, nothing short of a bomb going off will wake her.

"I'm no doctor, Marie, but the MRI results sound like good news," Clay volunteers from the driver's seat.

With all my heart, I want to agree with him, but something about June's ashen face has my heart in a vise and stifles any hope that this isn't a serious development.

I clamp my lips together, afraid anything I say will betray the party line of *June's just fine*.

"You saw her, Marie. She's back to her normal self, if not a little high." Dad chuckles. "She probably got too hot tonight."

"Yes." Mom latches onto this theory like it's the last ounce of oxygen in the room and she's fighting for her life. "That could be it. It was definitely hot in the Rusty Bucket tonight." Her smile's unsteady, but it holds. "I bet you're right, Russ. She just got too hot."

I'm torn between feeling guilt, because I'm so annoyed that they can't see this incident could be a sign that something is seriously wrong, and relief because the lines of distress have left her sweet face.

Hell, maybe they're right. Maybe she did get overheated. I desperately want them to be right.

*There isn't a world where June doesn't exist. There isn't a world where June doesn't exist. There isn't a world—*

I can't.

I just can't pretend that this was simply an overheating situation. I clasp my trembling hands in my lap so Mom won't see how rattled I am.

*I can't imagine a world without her.*

*Who are we, if she's not here?*

*We do not function without her.*

"What do you think, Hope?" Mom asks, but it's clear by the pleading in her eyes that she wants me to agree with them.

I cannot break her heart.

And I don't want my parents to feel the same terror that's taken up residence in every cell of my body.

So, I do what's expected. "Dad might be right."

Carrying the certainty that something has forever changed after tonight feels like treachery.

"See there, Marie, even Hope agrees with me, and she's the smartest of us all."

The statement jerks me out of my despair spiral. "What?"

He shrugs. "You've got a lot of smarts. We all know it."

The pleasure that breaks over me is stupid. I'm a fifty-year-old woman with a PhD. I'm confident in my intellectual abilities, but to hear him say it... I have no idea how to respond, so I go with what's familiar. "That's what I've been telling you for years."

He laughs.

Laughs.

He glances back at me and grins. "That you have, girl. That

you have." There's not an ounce of meanness in his tone, and I resist the urge to check for cameras. Surely, I'm being punked.

Dad shifts his attention to my brother-in-law. "Clay, whatcha got going tomorrow?"

"I'm going over to Wells to pick up a load of railroad ties. Babe wants me to put in some raised flower beds in the backyard. I should be back around three. Why?"

"I need help cleaning out the gutters. Those damn trees are sheddin' like crazy."

"Happy to help. I'll call you when I'm headed home," Clay says.

My dad claps him on the shoulder. "I'll provide the beer."

"Oh, good. Just what y'all need if you're going to be on the roof." The words are out, and I hold my breath, expecting my father to clap back.

But he doesn't. Instead, he grins over his shoulder and says, "Life ain't worth livin' without a few risks, Hopey."

Hopey?

What is happening?

My dad never jokes with me unless it's at my expense.

Wading into murky water, I say, "Well, in that case, why don't y'all try it blindfolded too?"

He chuckles. "Maybe next time."

I glance over at my mom, and my heart takes another nosedive. She seems not to have heard any of the conversation. She's staring out the window, chewing her thumbnail. So maybe I haven't alleviated her fears after all.

I open my mouth to say something that will make her feel better, then close it. What would I say?

It's going to be alright?

I don't know that.

The only thing I'm sure of is that if June's as sick as I think she is, none of us are prepared for what that means.

# Chapter Nine

"Ian texted to check on June this morning," Carrie says the next day at my mom's kitchen table.

I sip my iced tea, and it hits my stomach like acid. "Did he?"

"BFD," June says.

"BFD?" Mom asks.

"Big fu—"

"June Elizabeth Phillips, you watch your mouth." Mom's wagging her finger at my sister, but I can see the smile at the corner of her lips.

June grins. "I'm just saying. He hurt Hope and made his decision. He isn't part of this family anymore. He's lucky I wasn't in fightin' shape, or I would've given him more than I did last night."

I ignore what she said about Ian and zero in on what I suspected. "So you weren't feeling well before the pain hit?"

She picks at the salad Carrie brought for lunch. "I could tell something was off, but I figured it was the radiation making me feel weird."

"Have you felt off like that before?" I venture the question, fully prepared to be shut down.

"A few times over the last couple of weeks, but it went away. But last night..." She places her hand on the top of her head. "It was like my brain was trying to split through my skull."

I'm back to controlling my expression. It takes all my concentration to respond with only casual interest. "So weird."

"I still can't believe the doctor couldn't tell you what was wrong," Carrie says.

"Russ thinks it was the heat." Mom regurgitates the excuse from last night, but I can tell she believes it less today than she did last night.

"Yeah, that was weird, but the drugs they gave me more than made up for the lack of diagnosis." June pops a bite of salad into her mouth. "They were, indeed, the good stuff. Plus, I got to stare at Rick Stokes for the whole ride to the hospital."

"He is pretty," Carrie says.

"Sooo pretty," she agrees.

"Marie!" my dad calls from the back of the house.

"In here."

"I need some help," he says as he walks into the kitchen and hands my mom a tube of some kind of ointment.

She stands and takes it from him. "Turn around," she instructs. He complies and pulls the waistband of his pants down a few inches, exposing the top of his butt cheek.

"My eyes!" June yells.

"Y'all," I cry. "Not in front of Carrie." Thankfully, Carrie can't see the butt cheeks from her place at the table.

"It's fine," she says, and takes another bite of her salad. She's been around my family enough to be completely unaffected by their antics.

"You know"—Mom grins like she's about to tell us the

juiciest secret—"rubbing ointments and creams on each other's ailments has become our foreplay."

I cover my eyes with my hand. "Oh, good Lord. One, I didn't know you knew that word, Mom, and two, ew."

She gives me a look. "Hope, how do you think the five of you got here?"

"I don't think about it. Ever!"

Dad pulls his pants up, slaps my mom on the butt, and winks.

Carrie giggles, and June covers her ears and rocks in her chair. I'm too stunned to react.

Mom's laughter sings through the kitchen as she moves to the sink to wash her hands, but she never takes her eyes off June. Her entire existence hangs in the balance of how June acts from one minute to the next.

June's phone rings. "Hello," she says. "Oh, okay. Why?"

The seriousness in her tone gets all our attention.

"Alright. Will they call me to schedule, or do I— Oh, you already scheduled it. Okay, I'll be there on Tuesday. Thank you. Bye."

She hangs up and stares at the phone.

"What was that?" Mom's words are brittle as dried bark.

"It was my doctor's office. Dr. Rogers wants me to have another MRI before my appointment on Tuesday."

"But you had one last night," I say.

She looks up. Her face is smiling, but her eyes are not. "The one last night was without contrast." Her shoulders move up then down. "Dr. Rogers wants one with contrast."

"So does that mean the one from last night is useless in diagnosing what's going on?" I swallow to get rid of the sour taste on my tongue.

"I... I don't know." June pushes her phone away, as if the farther it is from her, the less offensive it is. "But... I'm sure it's fine." And with those four words, she flips the internal switch that only she controls, and any worry we glimpsed on her face is gone.

I'd give anything to possess that same switch. I do not.

This is how she's lived for the last ten years, deciding that things will be fine. It's an admirable, if not delusional, way to live. But maybe delusion is the only way you get from day to day when you have incurable cancer.

I sip my iced tea and ask as nonchalantly as possible. "Do you need us to go with you?" I don't want to overstep, but I want to be there.

"Let me talk to Aaron. If he can get off work, then he'll take me."

I stab a cherry tomato in my salad. "Okay, well, let us know."

"Your dad and I are going," Mom says, with all the authority and privileges that come with birthing five children.

"Damn right we are," Dad agrees.

June nods but doesn't say anything, while her gaze slides back to her phone.

"Well, I'd better be going," Carrie says, and stands.

Mom takes her hand. "Thanks for lunch, Carrie."

"Anytime, Marie." She turns her attention to my dad. "I hate that I'm going to miss the rest of the striptease, Russ."

His cheeks flush red, and he smiles. "I save all my stripteases for Marie."

"Okaaay. I just threw up in my mouth," June says.

A relieved laugh bursts from me. "Same."

"Y'all stop, or Carrie's never going to come back," Mom says.

"Not a chance, Marie," Carrie tells her, and leaves through the kitchen door.

"Enough of this chitchat," Dad says. "I'd better get to work."

"What work?" I ask.

"I'm going to get started on those gutters."

"Dad, Clay said he'd help you. You've got no business getting up on that roof by yourself. You're nearly eighty years old, for heaven's sake." I try not to yell, but from the look on his face, I don't succeed.

"Girl, I've been doing hard work longer than you've been around to tell me what you think is best for me." He grabs his ball cap and shoves it onto his bald head.

"I'm just saying—"

"You're saying I'm too old to take care of my home."

"No. That's not what I'm saying." But it kind of is. Still, he has no business being on that roof.

Dad and I are in one of our famous standoffs. Neither of us is willing to back down. We both know what happens next, and it's not pretty.

"Dad, before you do that, will you check the oil in my car?" June asks around a mouthful of salad.

It takes a minute for him to answer. He drags his furious gaze away from mine, and his features transform instantly as he looks at his favorite daughter. "Well, you know I will."

She holds up her keys. "You're the best."

He takes them. "Tell you what, I'll take it to be detailed too. That alright with you?"

"You really are the best daddy." She flutters her lashes at him.

He rolls his eyes, but the delight brightens his weathered face.

A familiar jealousy rears up inside me. I'm embarrassed by the ferocity of envy burning through me over the ease of June's relationship with this man who I've always found so difficult and aloof. I've never understood why it's so easy for her and so hard for me. Am I that unlikable... unlovable?

"Be back in a bit. Marie, if Clay gets here before I get back, have him start on the front gutters." He leaves without another word.

I watch him walk out as the adrenaline from our argument drains away. My gaze slides to June.

She shrugs. "You just have to know how to handle him."

I want to say a million things, all in my defense, because I wasn't wrong. But I keep my mouth shut and leave the room before I say something to my sick sister that I can't take back.

# Chapter Ten

Cuttin' Up salon is a monument to a time when women got their hair done weekly and slept with toilet paper wrapped around their heads to maintain the backcombed style until their next visit.

The placard on the door of the building, which is Patty Patton's converted garage, proudly declares that Cuttin' Up has been around since 1975. Patty isn't the original owner, her mother Patsy was, but Patty inherited the business when her mom passed.

The Pattons had a thing for "P" names that sound confusingly the same. Patsy's husband's name was Palmer and their son is Paul. Naming conventions in a small town are something else I have never been able to understand.

Take our family. Mom gave the first three of us virtue names —Hope, Joy, Grace—then switched to months of the year for the younger two. Babe's real name is April. Though June could have benefitted from a name a little more virtuous, or possibly a fruit of the Spirit. Self-Control James has a nice ring to it.

Mom flips up the visor after checking her lipstick in the hidden mirror. "I really appreciate you driving me to the beauty shop, Hope."

"It's not a problem." If I'm being honest, I was looking for an excuse to get out of the house. After my earlier interaction with Dad and June, I need time to regroup. I have several more days to get through here in Bonedalia. I need to pace myself if I'm going to make it.

Not to mention the second MRI. I can't shake the feeling that everything hinges on the results of that test.

"Are you thinking about June needing a second MRI too?" Mom's question is so unexpected that I don't have time to consider lying.

"Yes."

She has a death grip on her purse in her lap, with her gaze fixed on the front door of Cuttin' Up. "What do you think it means?"

"I don't know, Mom." It's as honest as I dare be.

"I'm so glad you're here, Hope."

"I am too, Mom."

"And about your dad..." She shifts her body so that she's looking at me. "You know he loves you, right?"

I bite down hard on all the things I want to say, and reply, "Dads love their kids." It's a nonanswer. Her sad smile tells me she didn't miss how I sidestepped the question.

Over the course of my life, she has insisted that my father loves me and is proud of me. But my reality hasn't always reflected that assertion. If I had a dollar for every time she said, "You know your daddy's proud of you, he just can't show it," I'd have a lot of dollars.

I grab my purse from the floor of the backseat, then open my door. "We're going to be late for your appointment."

She must sense that I'm done with this conversation, because she says, "Patty will have my hide if I'm late."

The smell of perm solution with just the slightest undertone of mildew hits me the minute I walk through the door. For some people, the combination would be odorous, but not me. Some of my best memories with my grandmother were made here at the Cuttin' Up. I loved sitting quietly with a Dr. Pepper and a bag of peanuts while Memaw and Patsy gossiped.

They never lowered their voices or used code. They spoke freely about the details of the Martinsons' divorce—she cheated because he spent all their money—the trouble the Grandberrys were having with their hoodlum son—he was caught egging houses in the rich part of town—and why the junior high school principal quit her job without notice—she'd found out the elementary and high school principals, both men, were making nearly three times what she was making. They had a real hard time understanding that last one. The woman should be glad she had a job, and what did she expect. Those men had families to support. Even at eleven, I knew there was a flaw in that argument.

I learned two things during those visits. One, peanuts taste better if you pour them into your Dr. Pepper. Two, bad behavior results in people spending a good part of their day gossiping about you. I vowed never to be on the receiving end of that kind of scrutiny.

"Marie!" Patty greets Mom with a tight hug. My mother's body visibly relaxes squished against the beautician's ample breasts. Patty gently takes Mom's face in her hands. "Sweetie, how are you? How is June? I heard what happened at the Rusty Bucket. Honey, that must've been terrifying."

Mom blinks several times, but she can't quite rid her eyes of the moisture gathering. "It was very scary. But we think she overheated. She's back to her normal troublemakin' self today."

My mom's smile is like wobbly scaffolding around the conviction she tries to infuse into her belief that June is going to be just fine.

Patty throws her head back and roars a laugh that is honestly too big for this small space. "Oh, darlin' she is that." She looks around my mom to me. "Hope Hall, how the hell are you?"

She releases Mom and heads for me, arms wide. There's no escaping what's coming, so I brace for impact. The hug is as aggressive as I imagined it would be, but it's also comforting. However, I only let myself rest in that comfort for a split second. I'm not so pitiful that I need a virtual stranger to soothe me.

I extricate myself from her embrace. "Hello, Patty."

"It's so good to see you, baby girl."

I ignore the endearment. I also ignore the strange warmth that the endearment elicits and focus on the fact that "baby girl" is perhaps one of the most condescending things anyone's said to me in a while. "It's good to see you too. It's been a long time."

"Honey, it's been longer than a long time." She shoves her hands into the pockets of her apron. "How's Ian? I haven't seen him..." The round, slightly panicked look in her eyes indicates she's only now remembered Ian and I aren't together anymore. "Oh, I'm..."

"Patty, I'm thinking I want to try something new with my hair today." Mom throws the poor woman a lifeline.

Patty grabs it and with a relieved breath says, "Really?" She loops her arm through my mom's and leads her toward the washbowl. "I'm all ears, sugar."

Mom looks back at me. I smile to let her know I'm okay. And I am... mostly.

The collective memory of this town is that Ian Hall and Hope James go together. But not anymore.

I wonder what their reaction will be when he comes riding into town with the new woman in his life and their baby. I already know the answer.

Joy for him.

Pity for me.

Before I can get too depressed about that, my phone rings. I check the screen and the display reads *The University of Texas*. All thoughts of Patty's endearments, probing questions, and Ian flee my brain.

"Mom." I hold my phone up with one hand and point to the street with the other. "I need to take this."

"Okay."

I answer as I'm pushing through the door, heading outside. "This is Dr. Hall."

"Dr. Hall, this is Sandra Montgomery. I'm Dr. Westmorland's assistant. He wanted me to give you a call and let you know that you are on our short list of candidates for the professorship position."

I couldn't stop the smile pulling at my lips if someone paid me. I tap down my enthusiasm and say as professionally as possible, "That's wonderful. Thank you for letting me know. What are the next steps?"

"We'll have each of the candidates in for an in-person interview within the month. Would you be able to arrange that into your schedule?"

Could I fit it into my schedule? I have no schedule. "Yes, I believe I can make that work."

"Excellent. You'll receive an email from me in the next few days." She continues, confirming my email address.

"That's correct."

"Then I have everything I need. If you have any further questions, feel free to reach out to me through my email."

"I will." We disconnect the call. I lean against the building with my phone clutched to my chest and resist the urge to pump my fist into the air. Take that, Holloway Prep. The sentiment is petty but also super satisfying.

I head back inside and see that my mom is almost done.

"Everything okay, Hope?" she asks from her position in Patty's chair.

I take a seat in the waiting area. "Everything's great, Mom."

"Can I get you something to drink, Sugar Britches?" Patty asks.

"No thanks." My eye twitches at the endearment. Sugar Britches, really? Would she call me that if I was a professor at The University of Texas? I think not.

Excitement simmers just beneath my skin. I try to control it and fail. The job isn't mine yet, but I'm one step closer to getting everything I've worked so hard for and that I want—respect, admiration, and an office with a big desk, a leather armchair in the corner, and a gold name plate on the door.

Nothing signals your life's not falling apart like a gold name plate.

"Sugar, you look fantastic! I like the change we made," Patty declares as she holds up a handheld mirror, so that Mom can see the back of her hair.

Mom turns her head this way and that, then smiles. "I love it. Thank you. You always do a great job."

It literally looks exactly as it's looked for the past thirty years. Not one thing is different, I can't tell who's gaslighting who. They seem to both believe something is different about Mom's style.

After Mom pays, I go to the door and hold it open for her. "Good to see you, Patty."

"It was great to see you too, Sugar Britches."

Once safely inside the car, I drop my plastic smile and say the words that have been fighting to be released for nearly an hour. "Oh, my gosh. In forty-five minutes, that woman single-handedly set the women's movement back sixty years."

Mom looks at me, startled. "For heaven's sake, what are you talking about?"

"She babied, sweeted, darlin'ed, sugared, sweethearted, and my personal least favorite, baby girled us to death."

The sound of her laughter is like someone took a cheese grater to my spine. "And that bothers you? I just thought she was being nice."

"You did?" I'm truly stunned.

She shrugs. "It always feels like a hug when I go to see her, like somebody really cares about me."

I put the car in drive and head out of the parking lot. "There are more respectful ways to convey care than to be so condescending."

Mom pats my hand. "I'm going to say something because I love you, Hope."

"What?"

"It's okay to just let people be nice to you, to show you affection, to love on you. It costs you nothing."

I don't reply. Because I know what my mom apparently doesn't. There's always a cost.

Love isn't ever free.

# Chapter Eleven

The May sun warms my arms and legs as I recline in a lounge chair on the dock with my sisters the next day. We've all been taking our cues from June about how much we'll talk about her upcoming MRI, so of course we're not talking about it at all. But I can tell that it's not far from my sisters' minds by the way they're following June's every move, especially Babe.

"You guys are a bunch of wussies for not getting in the water." The big floppy hat June's wearing to protect her nearly bald head and the oversized round sunglasses give her a silver screen movie star look. Unfortunately, the ugly black innertube she's floating in, that came from a tractor tire, makes it look like the movie star is vacationing at a trailer park.

Grace lowers her shades and levels June with one of her looks. "Don't think we can't see your lips quivering from the cold."

June splashes water toward us. "It's bracing. Really gets the blood flowing."

"Stop!" Babe squeals when water hits her in the face. She

tried to follow June into the tank but only got as far as sitting on the side of the dock with her feet dangling in the water.

"Sorry, Babe. I was trying to hit Grace."

She dries her face with a towel. "Well, you were way off."

"Yeah, you were way off," Grace taunts.

June sticks her tongue out at Grace.

"That's a pretty weak retort, little sister," I tease. "I honestly expect better from you."

She shrugs. "You can't be a badass all the time."

"Since when has that been your philosophy?" Joy asks from behind her own huge sunglasses.

June rests her can of soda in her lap and paddles her hands in the water to turn her tube back toward us. "I'm saving all my badassery for the Fowlers tomorrow."

I shake my head. "God help us all."

"Speaking of the Fowlers," Grace says. "I still can't believe what Marjorie Fowler did at cheer tryouts."

Babe leans back on her elbows and turns her face to the sun. "Me either. It was pretty sketchy."

June points at our third sister. "I'll tell you right now, Joy, if I were you, they'd still be trying to pull me off Marjorie."

What in the world are they talking about?

*Don't ask.*

*Don't ask.*

*Don't—* "What happened?" The question bursts from me against my will.

"Tell her, Joy." June's cheeks are flushed and she's practically vibrating with excitement.

"You know that Samantha, Marjorie's daughter, and Chloe are the same age and they're both junior varsity cheerleaders?" Joy asks.

"Mm-hmm." I try to sound only marginally interested, but in truth, June's open joy for this information is contagious.

"And Marjorie's the JV cheer coach?" Joy asks.

"I did not know that."

"At tryouts the girls hang out in the women's locker room at the school until it's their turn to try out. There's this little vestibule between the locker room and the gym with a door that leads to the outside."

I swat at a mosquito that's taken an interest in me. "Okay... so?"

"Just wait!" June shouts and laughs maniacally. She's floated away from the dock again and is paddling back toward us.

Joy grins at me. "The rumor is that Samantha didn't actually try out."

I look at my sisters, who are also grinning like idiots. "I don't understand."

Grace reaches into the cooler we brought and grabs a handful of grapes. "Everyone is saying that Marjorie got her niece, Jewel, who's a big-time cheerleader in Dallas, to try out in place of Samantha."

I look at Joy then back to Grace. "So a ringer?" I'm embarrassed at the bubbles of anticipation fizzing through my bloodstream.

"Exactly," Grace says.

"But how..."

"Samantha let Jewel in through the vestibule door, pinned the number on her shirt, and sent her to try out," Joy explains.

"It's diabolical!" June shouts. "I honestly didn't know Marjorie had it in her." There's no denying the admiration in my sister's voice.

"Wouldn't the judges have recognized that it wasn't Samantha?" I ask.

"They're all from out of town," Babe explains. "And they're gone by the time the results are announced."

"Di. A. Bolical," June howls, slapping the water with every syllable for emphasis.

I realize I've leaned forward during the telling of this story, not wanting to miss a morsel of the tale. My cheeks prickle with heat, and not from the sun, when I realize they've sucked me into this nonsense. I shake off my small-town roots and my curiosity. "You said it's only a rumor, right?"

"Hope, Samantha can't jump five inches off the ground, and the only tumbling I've ever seen her do is a cartwheel," June says, speaking to me like I'm a toddler.

"It's true, Hope. Samantha's sweet as punch, but she isn't very athletic," Babe says.

"And I've never seen the poor kid clap on beat," Grace adds. "She's got her mother's rhythm."

I turn to Joy. "But Chloe made it too, right?"

"Yes, but she did it with her own skills." She holds up her can of soda. "The cheer genes run deep in that one."

My sisters raise their drinks into the air to honor our family's cheer genes.

"Unlike Samantha," Grace jabs.

"You all do realize that you are maligning a child?" I can't hold my tongue anymore.

Grace eats another grape. "No, we're not. We're maligning her mother."

"Okay, but where's your proof?"

June throws her arms up. "Haven't you been listening? The only way Samantha got a near perfect score is if someone tried out in her place."

I shake my head. "Show me the proof."

"You're no fun to gossip with, Hope," Babe says with a grin.

"Dr. Goody-Two-Shoes is too good to gossip with us." Grace casually lobs the insult my way.

I absorb the hit but don't take the bait. "I simply don't

understand the appeal of dissecting someone else's life. I've got enough problems of my own."

Damn, I hadn't meant to say that last part.

"Speaking of, it was weird seeing Ian the other night," Babe says.

*Et tu, Babe?*

"Yeah," I say as noncommittally as possible.

June paddles closer to the dock. "Weird's one way to put it."

"I don't know why he thought we'd welcome him with open arms," Grace says.

"Right?" Joy says. "You mess with one of us, you mess with all of us."

"Hell, yeah," June yells.

"That's right," Babe agrees.

"Correct." Grace grabs another handful of grapes. "I thought he looked a little rough around the edges."

Nobody says anything, probably waiting to see how I'll react. I lower my sunglasses and stare at Grace. "Now you want to gossip about my ex-husband?"

She pops a grape into her mouth and shrugs. "Why not?"

I replace my glasses and recline back onto the lounge chair. "Why not, indeed." I wave my hand in her direction." Carry on and make it good."

The sound of my sisters' laughter rings through the air and I snuggle into it.

I won't tell them the real gossip about Marcy and the baby. Once I tell them, it's real, and I'm scared to death of that realness. So, I lock the words away and happily listen while they rip my ex a new one, as only sisters can.

# Chapter Twelve

Two days later, Mom, Grace, Joy, Babe, and I sit in our lawn chairs in our usual spot along the Bonedalia Memorial Day Parade route. Dad and June are with their float, even though Mom tried to get June to sit out the parade because of the warm temperatures.

She would've had more luck selling fire to the devil.

"I'm fine, Mom. I'm not missin' the parade. It's tradition."

And that was that. Once June makes up her mind about something, it's as good as done.

Even I have to admit that June does seem fine, which feels like a miracle given what bad shape she was in three days ago.

*Help me, Hope.*

A cold chill, completely at odds with the early May heat, ripples over my skin. I shove my lingering worry that there's something terribly wrong back where it lives and try to focus on what's going on around me. "Does anyone know what this year's theme for the float is?"

Joy shakes her head. "They haven't told us. They said that they wanted it to be a surprise."

I gather my hair into a bun on top of my head to get it off my sweaty neck. "That's not cause for worry at all."

Joy laughs. "Right?"

You can say a lot of things about my hometown, but not understanding how to celebrate Memorial Day isn't one of them. There are the usual suspects in a small-town parade. The band, the drill team, and horseback riders. The mayor and the reigning Miss Bonedalia ride in convertibles. But the big attraction is the float competition. Local businesses, social clubs, churches, and families compete for bragging rights, a trophy, and a cash prize.

"Oh, look, there's Chloe!" Babe squeals.

Chloe and the other junior varsity cheerleaders walk past, pompoms punching into the air to the beat of the song the Bonedalia High School band is playing behind them.

Grace was right. Sweet Samantha can't clap on beat. Bless her.

Babe begins chanting, "Chlo-e, Chlo-e, Chlo-e."

We all chant along in true James fashion—obnoxiously loud.

Red-faced, Chloe laughs and shakes her head. Yes, we're embarrassing, but we also love her to death, so she tolerates us.

The band stops playing and the drumline takes over as they march past us. The driving beat immediately transports me back to Friday night high school football games.

Ian was the varsity quarterback and I was the head cheerleader. I lived for those evenings on the sideline. Every time he'd throw a touchdown, he'd point to me and blow me a kiss. I would melt into a puddle every time it happened. I had it bad for that boy. His coach hated it and said he'd pull him if he didn't stop. In true Ian fashion, he ignored the coach.

He used to say, "Nothin's more important than my girl, Coach. Nothin'."

We were so naive. We thought we could have whatever we wanted. The whole dream, the house, the car, the kids.

Two out of three ain't bad.

But it is.

Ian.

Marcy.

Pregnant.

My hand goes to my mouth. I will not vomit. But I might. The reminder of Ian's future and the heat have soured the contents of my stomach.

"You okay, Hope?" Babe asks.

I suck air in through my nose then release it. "Yeah. I guess the heat's getting to me."

"Here, honey." Mom hands me a water bottle she pulled from the cooler we brought.

"Thanks." I can see the question in her eyes, but I shake my head. The Memorial Day Parade isn't the place to break the news about Ian to my family.

A tall woman with white hair twisted into a tight bun sidles up to our family. "Well, well, well, if it isn't the James gang."

Colleen Fowler.

"How are you, Colleen?" Mom asks.

Colleen looks to Heaven with her hand over her heart. "Better than I deserve."

Mom gives her a closed-mouth smile. "You're not on the float this year?" She's a better person than I am. Then again, my mom's a better person than most people.

"Not this year." Colleen turns her attention to me. "Hope, it's been a month of Sundays since I've seen you in person. I saw pictures of your big trip last summer on social media." She unfolds her lawn chair and sits next to me. "I always wanted to travel, but it's so hard with a husband and children. But not you. You jet around without a care in the world." She pats my arm. "Good for you."

I shouldn't feel this much anger for a woman I barely know, and her words shouldn't hurt so much. I have to hand it to Colleen. She managed to illuminate all of my failures with one sugar-coated insult.

Thankfully, I'm spared from answering when someone nearby shouts, "The floats!"

I look up to see the Methodist Church's float, featuring the obligatory red, white, and blue bunting, giant cowboy boots painted red, white, and blue, and kids in cowboy hats tossing candy.

"Oh, that's super cute," Mom says as she catches an individually wrapped peppermint.

The next few floats are more of the same, except aggressive candy throwing from the little league baseball float has parade-goers dodging flying butterscotch and mints.

A cheer rises from down the street at the same time the delicious smell of searing meat hits my nose. Everyone around us is craning their necks to see what's coming.

A niggle of concern settles in my chest. I'm certain that isn't June and Dad's float. I saw no evidence of food prep this morning. But if this is the Fowlers' float, then June and Dad could be in trouble. Anything with food is always hard to beat.

The float finally gets close enough for us to see who's on it. The banner reads *Stars, Stripes & BBQ—Ray John's BBQ, Bonedalia, Texas*. I breathe a sigh of relief. Although Dad and June like to win, they would be mostly okay if Ray John came in first. But they've never gotten over the few times the Fowlers have beaten them.

And June has the restraining orders to prove it.

Mom fans herself and glances down the street. "How many more floats?"

"Two," Joy says.

"So, ours and the Fowlers." Mom crosses her fingers. "Here we go."

A roar of laughter goes up as I look to the next float. The banner sparkling with red glitter reads *Stars, Stripes, and Rodeo*. Patriotic country music blares from the speakers. Then I see why everyone is laughing.

All of the adult Fowler offspring are dressed in inflatable bull costumes and are on their hands and knees bucking while Mr. Fowler sits on a sawhorse with longhorns mounted on it, waving his cowboy hat in the air.

The Fowler kids aren't the most agile or fit people in the world, so their "bucks" are a little pitiful. We're also near the end of the parade route, so they've been bucking for a while.

The two oldest boys are on their last legs. Sweat stains their inflatable suits in some unfortunate places. The youngest son's suit has deflated altogether, and poor Marjorie seems to be having the hardest time, but who can blame her? She appears to be about seven months pregnant.

Colleen stands and cheers for her family a little too enthusiastically, as if she knows this isn't their best effort but is trying to convince everyone otherwise.

"Oh, my Lord," Grace says, pointing at a sign on the side of the float that's supposed to read *Buck for Veterans* but has lost some of the glitter on the "B," and it now looks like the Fowlers are encouraging the crowd to fornicate for veterans.

"Nooo," Babe whispers.

Joy buries her head into Mom's neck, but there's no missing her shoulders shaking in laughter.

I try and fail to bite back my own amusement.

Mom is the only one acting like a grown-up, but just barely. She's biting her lip like her life depends on it.

The crowd's laughter fades and silence takes its place as the next float moves into view. The sound of a bugle pierces the air.

June rides next to Dad on the tractor, both looking somber, neither taking their eyes off the road. They pull a float with an empty rocking chair, a pair of boots, and an American flag folded on the chair, surrounded by bluebonnets, while "Taps" —that haunting, heartrending bugle call, part farewell and part remembrance—plays through the speakers and fills the air. Men remove their hats and place them over their hearts. Silent, reverent tears roll down the faces of some of the spectators around us. I'm tearing up too.

It says it all—somber and respectful, beautiful in its simplicity.

Once they've passed, I turn to see Colleen's reaction, but she's nowhere to be found.

People begin to disperse. Several give us a thumbs-up or clasp my mom's shoulder.

The five of us are silent as people clear out around us. The somber ending of the parade has hit a little too close to home after the terrifying events of Friday night and June's looming MRI tomorrow.

Babe brushes a stray tear away, and ever-stoic Grace offers a tissue without looking at her. Mom grips Joy's hand but never takes her eyes from the empty road, littered with crushed candy and confetti.

I know what they're feeling and I don't know how to help them.

I open and close my mouth several times, trying to come up with something to say to make them feel better. There isn't anything. Because we're not in a crisis. We're in the horrible in-between, where uncertainty steals your peace. So I sit quietly in this no-man's-land of *what if* and pray that if the time ever does come when *what if* turns to *the worst has happened*, I'll know what to do to help them.

Just when I think we'll never escape this moment, June comes running up to us, red-faced, sweaty, her blond hair coming loose from her ponytail, and a smile so bright it could light three counties.

She twirls and strikes a pose with the first-place banner over her head. "And that's how it's done, suckas!"

# Chapter Thirteen

The next morning, sweat runs down my temples and slides between my breasts as I finish my three-mile walk. It doesn't matter where I am, I don't miss my walk. It's been a part of my routine for as long as I can remember and has been crucial to my sanity over the last nine months.

Get up. Drink a green juice. Fifteen minutes of journaling. Meditate for fifteen minutes. Exercise for thirty minutes. Stretch. Shower.

I also drink the recommended amount of water, control my carbohydrate and sugar intake, and go to bed at the same time every night.

Some have called me obsessive—my family, Ian, and my friends—but there's nothing wrong with being disciplined. It's kept me healthy, fit, and sane over the years, especially when life has decided to play dirty.

I rest my left foot on the second step of the porch of my childhood home and bend forward to stretch my hamstring, then repeat with the right. I've extended my stay in Bonedalia for a few more days to spend a little more time with Mom and Dad.

*You also have absolutely nothing else to do.*

I ignore that unhelpful accusation.

Besides, I do have something to do. I need to make sure that June is really okay. I can't leave until I know if that was a anomaly or something more serious. I'm probably being paranoid, but I can't unhear her desperate plea for help.

After I've stretched, I grab my water bottle and sit on the porch swing. It's another warm day. I take in the fields around the house, still dotted with a few stubborn wildflowers that refuse to die.

A memory of five-year-old June covered in dirt, pink bow cockeyed on her head, offering Ian a fistful of bluebonnets, hits me out of nowhere.

*I love you, Ian.*

*Love you too, Bug.*

*Are you going to marry me?*

*I can't, Bug.*

*Why?*

*Because someday I'm gonna marry Hope.*

*Why?*

*Because I love her the most.*

June didn't speak to me for a week after that.

I was a goner that day. Completely and totally in love with that boy who loved me and didn't care who knew it. I swipe at an unwanted tear. Nobody talks enough about losing your safe place when a marriage falls apart. Ian was my safe place for so long, and then he wasn't. I think I'll feel that loss for the rest of my life.

I dry my eyes with the bottom of my shirt. Thankfully, Mom and Dad had to run an errand, and I'm here alone. I don't want to have to explain my tears. How could I? I can't explain them to myself.

Being back in Bonedalia is such a weird experience. It's as familiar as my own reflection but also feels like trying to cram my foot into a pair of shoes that are almost your size, but not quite.

Bottom line, I don't fit here anymore.

I'm not like my family. They've never wanted to be anywhere else, and I've always wanted to be anywhere else.

My phone rings and I'm grateful for the interruption. I check the screen. "Hey, Carrie. I was—"

"Hope! Get to the diner right now."

I'm moving before I can think. I grab my purse off the table just inside the front door and head to my car. "What's happened?"

"It's Grace and Joy."

"Are they hurt?" I yank open my car door and push the start button. "Were they in an accident?"

"No, they weren't in an accident, but one of them may be hurt if you don't get here quickly."

"Jimmy Jenkins." I know I'm right before she answers.

"Yep. He and Joy were having lunch when Grace and some of her coworkers came in. Words were exchanged." She gasps. "Oh, no."

"What?" I take the corner out of my parents' drive on two wheels.

"Grace threw a glass of sweet tea on Joy, and Joy retaliated with a hamburger to Grace's face."

"What in the redneck spectacle is going on?"

"Y'all, stop," Carrie tries again. But it doesn't help. I can still hear their angry words in the background.

I make it to the diner in record time. Once again, there's a throng of people around members of my family. I can hear the insults over the crowd's noise.

Carrie meets me at the door. "Hope."

The relief in her voice makes me want to laugh. I'm not sure what she thinks I can do, but I appreciate her confidence in my peace-making skills. "Thanks for calling me." I point in the direction of the hullabaloo. "I better..."

"I have to go." She checks the time on her phone. "I have an appointment."

"It's fine, Carrie. I've got this." I know for a fact that I do not have this, but fake it till you make it. "Well..." I glance over at my sisters. "I'm going in."

"Be careful. They're mean."

She's not telling me anything I don't know. "Thanks again." I shove my way through the crowd.

"You knew we were dating," Grace shouts while picking a pickle off her face.

"You're not official. I haven't seen it on social media." Joy gestures toward Jimmy, who's sitting quietly eating his fries—fries Joy paid for, I have no doubt. "If you were official, would he have accepted my invitation to lunch?"

"Yes!" several members of the crowd shout before Grace has a chance to answer.

I step between my sisters. "Okay, why don't we all calm down?" I've just inserted myself into this Jerry Springer moment. It's my worst nightmare come true. I try to cover my discomfort with an ineffective, out-of-place chuckle. "Why don't we take this outside?"

"Stay out of this, Hope." Joy sneers and points past me to Grace. "This is between her and me."

"I know this is upsetting, but"—I glance around at the spectators—"you're kind of causing a scene," I say quietly.

"Let 'em go at it, Hope. This is better than any daytime

TV," Harlan Martin, who's eighty-nine years old if he's a day, yells.

I give the man a tight smile and ask as kindly as possible, "Please mind your own business, Mr. Martin."

I'm rewarded for my politeness with a cornbread muffin to the ear. "What the hell, Harlan?" I yell at the old man.

This town.

These people, including my sisters, bring out the very worst in me, and the worst in me is just like them.

But I'm not like them.

I. Am. Not.

That thought gives me enough control to unclench my jaw and speak rationally. "Harlan, that was uncalled—" Another muffin pops me in the face.

He shoots me a snaggle-tooth sneer. "Why don't you loosen up and leave us to our fun, missy?"

This man doesn't know me. His opinion shouldn't matter, but his insult slips the grip I have on all the anger I've banked over the last nine months—hell, over my whole life. Without thinking, I grab a slice of coconut pie from the closest table and launch it toward my attacker. I miss Harlan but hit Joy when she steps in front of me to get to Grace.

Joy picks pieces of pie from her sleeve. "This is a brand-new top, Hope."

What is happening? "I'm... I'm so sorry."

She pushes me and I stumble into Grace, who falls back onto the Church of Christ pastor's table, flipping it and launching his taco salad into the air. It comes down with a sickening squish onto my head.

Somehow, I'm the only one of the three of us on the ground. Joy and Grace stare down at me, both in varying degrees of horror, like they only now realized they made a scene.

"Oh, my gosh, Hope," Joy says.

Grace extends her hand to me. "Here, let me help—"

I grab her arm and yank her down to the ground with me. She lands with an "Umph."

The next thing we know, Joy is sprawled beside us, having tripped over a dinner roll.

A sound like a donkey braying fills the air and we look up to see Jimmy standing over us, laughing hysterically. His plaid shirt with the sleeves cut off and denim shorts with frayed edges are pristine. Not one morsel of food on him. "Damn, that was funny."

I glare at him and wait for either of my sisters to say something. They don't. They just let this good-for-nothing idiot laugh at them, like he's been doing for thirty years.

"Shut up, Jimmy," I finally say.

He raises his hands into the air. "Don't yell at me. I'm not the one covered in nacho cheese." He reaches over to the table, picks up the ticket, and hands it to Joy. "Don't forget to pay the bill before you leave." Then he turns and strolls out like he hasn't a care in the world.

Still, my sisters say nothing.

Their muteness continues after the cops show up, when we're led away in handcuffs, on the ride to the police station, and when we're ushered to a cell.

I wish the condemning voice in my head was as silent, but there's no shutting it up and no denying its accuracy. Today I threw coconut pie at an eighty-nine-year-old man. I've become exactly what I've spent my whole life trying not to be. Out of control, messy, and utterly incapable of managing anything—including myself.

## Chapter Fourteen

An hour later, the door to the cell area opens. Babe and June appear. The younger rushes to the iron bars surrounding us, while June crosses her arms and leans against the door jamb.

"Are y'all alright?" Babe asks.

"What the hell? You look like a buffet blew up on you," June says and saunters toward us, shaking her head. "I'm ashamed of you three."

I swallow my embarrassment. "I know, June "

"I have a rep in this town. Did any of you consider that before you got arrested for something so petty as a food fight?"

The shame I've been feeling evaporates. "We're all well aware of your criminal past, Shifty. The Wilsons' parrot will never be the same after you stole it and took it for a joy ride."

"Hey, I liberated that bird. He was a prisoner."

Babe looks at June and rolls her eyes, then turns to us and asks, "What in all that's holy happened?"

"Hope couldn't mind her own damn business is what happened," Grace says at the same time I say, "Jimmy Jenkins."

"Don't you dare blame him," Joy says. "None of this would've happened if Grace hadn't interrupted our lunch."

I shake my head. "I can't believe you two."

Grace's gaze slices to me. If looks could kill, I'd be dead on the floor. "Here it comes. Perfect Hope with her perfect life advice, thinking she's better than all of us." She raises her finger like she's remembered something important. "Oh, excuse me, Dr. Hope Hall." She crosses her arms over her chest and looks me up and down. "But correct me if I'm wrong, aren't you unemployed, with an ex-husband who left you because"—she makes air quotes—"he couldn't take it anymore."

Babe gasps.

"Grace," Joy whispers.

"Damn, Grace," June says.

Grace looks a little shocked that she said those things out loud, but she doesn't back off. In fact, she doubles down. "What? She's always quick to point out how we should run our lives. Nobody ever calls her out."

"Wow," is all I can say, and I'm surprised I have enough air to get the word out, given the gut punch Grace just delivered.

Perfect? Is she insane? Doesn't she know I lie in bed every night recounting all the ways I've failed? One nauseating event after another rolls through my brain like a terrible documentary I can never turn off.

Babe jumps in to try to save the situation from getting out of hand. Too late. "Um, well, Sheriff Wallace said y'all could go. The diner's not pressing charges if you'll pay for the damages."

"Fine." I move to the cell door, ignoring Joy and Grace. "Tell him I'll take care of the damages. Just get me out of here."

She nods, and they leave us to tell the sheriff we've agreed.

A hand rests on my shoulder. "Hope."

I turn to look at Joy. "Yes." The word is as stiff and rigid as my back.

"I... I don't feel..."

"Don't you dare say you don't feel the same way, Joy," Grace yells from her corner of the cell. "You've literally said the same things about Dr. Perfect."

"Shut up, Grace," Joy spits out. To me, she says, "I'm sorry."

I'm prevented from answering by the return of June, Babe, and Sheriff Wallace. Though I have no idea what I would say.

We make the walk of shame to Babe's car, drive back to the diner to drop Joy and Grace at their cars, then head to my parents' house, all in complete silence. The only sound in the car is the squeak of Babe's sweaty hands as she grips the leather steering wheel cover.

"Do y'all feel the same way as Grace? Do you think I consider myself better than you all?" I finally ask.

"No," Babe says at the same time June says, "Sometimes."

June gives her a tell-the-truth look.

"Well, yeah, sometimes," she reluctantly says.

The boulder in my throat prevents me from speaking, so I nod and look out the window but can't see anything through the tears blurring my vision. I hold them back as an act of will and pride, but the insult they stem from is no less painful.

Am I in their business more than I should be? Maybe, but it's only because I love them and don't want them to make mistakes that will alter their lives. Do I give unsolicited advice? Yes, but it's advice I've found worked well for me. Do I sometimes frown on their romantic choices? Yes, but I know they deserve so much better.

"It doesn't bother us like it bothers Joy and Grace," June says. "We're younger. We've always thought you were perfect too."

"I don't think I'm perfect," I choke out.

"Maybe, but..."

"What?"

"Well, you are a little free with your advice sometimes," she says.

"But we know it's because you love us," Babe hurries to add.

Thankfully, Mom and Dad are still gone when we get back to their house. I open the car door, but before I can exit, June says, "Hope, we agree that Jimmy Jenkins is a waste of space, but it's up to Joy and Grace to figure that out. You can't save them, and you're not going to change their minds." Her alarm chimes on her phone. "Dang, I've got to go. I have my doctor's appointment later this afternoon."

I forgot she has another MRI and an appointment with the radiologist today. My system dumps a hefty amount of anxiety into the emotional swill roiling in my stomach. "Will you let me know how it goes?"

She turns to look at me. "Of course I will. We're not mad at you, Hope."

"We love you," Babe adds.

I give my youngest sister a tight-lipped smile, get out of the car, and walk into the house without looking back.

I head straight to the shower to wash away the evidence of today's fiasco, my sisters' words still assaulting my heart.

Can't they see I want what's best for them?

Don't they know how hard it is for me to see them in pain?

How can they think I look down on them?

*It causes you stress and pain when they make choices that hurt them, so it's more about you than them,* a little voice whispers.

Ignoring it, I step into the shower.

I squirt more shampoo into my hand than I'd usually use and begin scrubbing my head. I'm so sick of the high and mighty accusations. Just because I chose to leave this small, incestuous, narrow-minded town doesn't mean I hate it or think people who stay here don't have goals or that they don't care about things outside the city limits.

Okay, maybe I do.

But come on, some of the things my family worries about are ridiculous. I mean, who the hell cares if Shawna Patterson had a lingerie and sexy toy party at her house or not? Or if the city council put a giant Chia Pet longhorn on the square. Especially when you consider the larger things happening in the world, most of which they're not even aware of. Maybe that's harsh, but I'm not wrong. Case in point, the ridiculous cheer gossip from yesterday.

My muscles relax and I stand a little straighter as I rinse my head, comfortable with my righteous indignation.

*I am not like them.*

I don't have to look very far to know that's true. Look at what Grace and Joy did today and pulled me into. Fiery humiliation burns through every cell of my being.

I had a food fight.

In public.

How did I let them suck me into their insanity? I'm better than that, damn it.

I stop scrubbing my head. The floral design on the tile of the shower wall goes in and out of focus. A biting cold swirls in my gut, then radiates out over my flesh.

My bare butt hits the seat built into the shower, and the clammy surface sends another round of chills over my body.

I wipe the suds out of my eyes and push my hair away from my face. "They're right. I do think I'm better than them."

My awareness of the truth battles with my hurt feelings.

The truth wins out. I can wrap my superiority in the most

noble package that I want, but the bottom line is that I've hurt the people I love.

I mechanically finish my shower.

After I dry and put on clean clothes, I sit on the bed and try to decide what to do next. Before I know what's happening, my cheeks are wet and pitiful hiccups wrack my body. I hate crying, especially when it's because I'm feeling guilty and sorry for myself at the same time.

I'm not sure what to do next. Before my shower epiphany, I planned to go home. That's how we generally handle things. We have a blow-up, then we separate for a while, and when we come back together, we move on like nothing's happened.

Is it healthy conflict resolution? No.

Does it solve anything? Also, no.

But I think it's best if I leave and let the dust settle. I need some time to lick my wounds before I swallow my pride and apologize to my sisters for being a snobby bitch.

# Chapter Fifteen

Back in my little borrowed home, the cozy low ceilings and art deco décor settle around me the moment I walk through the door. I will forever be grateful to my friend Rachel for allowing me to retreat here and heal while she's on a year's sabbatical in Europe. I could've stayed in our house, but I had no interest in living with the ghost of marital failure.

I dump my bag in my room, make my way to the kitchen, and turn on the electric kettle. While the water heats, I check my email to see if UT has gotten back to me about the interview.

They have not.

It's probably too soon to have heard back from them, but I won't pretend that I'm not disappointed. Strangely, I'm also the tiniest bit relieved. It's probably because I don't love change, and getting this job would be a big change for me, not the least of which is that it would require me to move to Austin, nearly three hours away. I've never lived that far from my family before. Though after today, I'm not sure anyone would care if I moved to the moon.

I shake off my self-pity, take my beverage to my favorite oversized chair, and snuggle in, ignoring dirty laundry and days' worth of mail. I turn on relaxing music and sip the herbal brew.

With each moment that passes, I relax into the solitude.

I can breathe here in this peaceful space. For the last nine months, it's been my refuge, a safe space to rage, heal, and if I'm honest, hide from the failure of my marriage and the life I created and lost.

This place has given me time and safety to examine each grievance I could lay at Ian's feet, and there were many.

I've had hours and hours in this chair to try to figure out where and how it all went so wrong. Was it the miscarriages, what an emotional wreck I was from all the hormones that come with fertility treatments, the soul-crushing sense of failure that comes when those treatments don't work? Or was it the flash of disappointment in Ian's eyes when I told him I couldn't try anymore? That millisecond of emotion nearly destroyed me because I already knew my body had let us both down, and there was nothing I could do about it.

It's the only thing in my life that I've ever truly failed at.

The scar from that time remains to this day, but I can't blame infertility for the downfall of our marriage. It was much less dramatic than that—a quiet and insidious lack of care for each other that crept in over the years until we were virtually living separate lives.

Within the safety of my emotional infirmary, I've been forced to admit that our relationship had become a counterfeit version of a happy marriage that started long before Ian left. One I constructed with the force of my will and at the expense of everything I'd ever wanted. Then I held my creation up for the world to admire.

*See how handsome and successful my husband is.*

*See how he spoils me.*

Instead of having the hard conversations, I buckled down and tried to hold it all together, but with every day that didn't work, I retreated further inside my own head. Even if Ian couldn't see that something was wrong, I could, and I kept my mouth shut to keep the peace and control how our relationship looked from the outside.

A long exhale stutters from my lungs and sours the tea I drank.

I can blame Ian all I want, but the truth is I was just as culpable in the downfall of our marriage.

My phone rings, and I check the screen. It's June. I consider letting it go to voicemail. I don't want to talk about what happened earlier, but I do want to hear about her doctor's appointment this afternoon. I need something to go right today. "Hey."

"Hang on, sis," she says.

"Okay." I see all of my sisters' names pop up on the screen.

"Can y'all hear me?" June asks. She has us on speaker.

We all confirm that we can.

She takes a shaky breath and my heart drops. "The doctor said I have six to twelve weeks."

"Of radiation?" Babe asks.

"No," June answers.

"I don't understand," Babe says.

"To live," June says in a cracked voice. "I have six to twelve weeks to live."

"What?" I shout.

"No," Grace whispers.

"That's not possible," Joy cries.

"That's not funny, June." Babe's voice is like steel.

"I'm not joking, Babe. The doctor told me I have something called leptomeningeal disease, and I have six to twelve weeks to live." She's crying in earnest now. "What do I even do with that?"

No answer comes.

My brain refuses to arrange what June said into anything comprehensible. It's like she's speaking a horrible, filthy language that I have no context for. Like an alien tongue that only consists of unspeakable things happening to people you love.

The only sounds are the quiet sobs from my sisters and from Mom, Dad, and Aaron in the truck with June.

A sob works its way up my throat, but I wrestle it back to where it originated.

*Get yourself together, Hope. Your family needs you.*

I clear my throat. "Are y'all headed home?"

"Yes," my mom says. She must've taken June's phone.

"Okay. We'll be there. June? Do you hear me? We'll be there. You're not doing this alone. I promise."

"That got a little smile from her, Hope," Mom says through her tears. I never knew a sound could actually crush your soul, until this moment.

We hang up and I immediately text Grace, Joy, and Babe. Any remnants of our public embarrassment or our resentment evaporate in the face of the news we just received.

*I'll order dinner from Katie's Kitchen. Can someone pick it up?*

*Yes*. Grace texts back.

*I'll call Pastor Hal and see you at Mama's,* she adds.

A text from Joy comes through.

*Grace, I'll pick up Chloe and Max from school and drop them at my house, then see y'all at Mom and Dad's.*

After several moments, Babe texts.

*What do I do? I don't know what to do.*

Poor Babe. A tear rolls down my face before I even know I'm crying. I can hear the helplessness in her message. I shoot her a quick message back.

*Call Clay, and y'all come to Mom and Dad's. We'll figure it out together.*

I send the text and my finger hovers over the keypad. Before I can think about it too hard, I send another message.

*Also, I'm sorry about earlier. You were all right.*

Grace is the first to respond.

*None of that matters right now. See you at home.*

Typical Grace, but in this moment I'm grateful for her lack of sentimentality.

I set my phone on the table and brace myself for the crushing wave of grief or despair that will take me out, but it doesn't come.

Nothing comes.

It's like my heart is a toddler covering its ears and chanting, *Don't tell me those words. Don't tell me those words. Don't tell me those words.*

I type "leptomeningeal disease" into my phone and begin reading. I have no frame of reference for the depth of the awfulness of what I discover. My breath comes in disjointed pants.

This thing is a monster. A horrible, vicious, deadly, indiscriminate monster, and it has my sister.

With every word I read, one thing becomes crystal clear.

There's only one way that this ends.

And only one thing I know for sure.

*I'm not ready.*

*I'm not ready.*

*I'm not ready.*

# Chapter Sixteen

We're gathered in the living room of my parents' home. Each of us has some version of *what is happening* painted on our faces. We're all trying to conceal it, but like graffiti that's been uselessly painted over, there's no denying what's behind the facade.

The unthinkable has happened.

In the hours since we heard those terrible words, it's like my emotions have been trapped behind a wall of disbelief. I haven't cried in front of my family. I don't know why, exactly. Maybe it's the way June ran to me and threw her arms around my neck when I got to my parent's house, like I could somehow make it all better. It's what I get for always telling her I could do just that.

But I can't fix this.

I can't.

The wailing refrain of *six to twelve weeks to live* howls through my brain, and I wonder whose reality I'm living.

None of this feels real.

We're all shuffling around like we're a bunch of robots, like every move we make is only from muscle memory and not a voluntary action.

Go to the kitchen. Take a cup from the cabinet. Pour coffee. Add sugar. Stir. Return to the living room. Sit. Repeat.

From my seat in one of the recliners, I watch my family moving around each other, careful not to touch or make eye contact. If we do, then any minuscule illusion of normal will shatter.

June is lying on the sofa with her head in Aaron's lap.

Pain is etched into every line and hollow on his handsome face. "I called MD Anderson to see if there are any trials. There are, so I'm sure she'll get into one of them. They said they'd call back in a day or two." He strokes June's hair. "We're gonna fix this, darlin'. We're gonna fix it."

The raw, desperate hope in his voice rips at my heart. Because I know what nobody else in this room knows. Yes, the MD Anderson Cancer Center runs clinical trials for new treatments. But June's not getting into one of those, or any other trial for that matter. There's no cure for leptomeningeal disease, which, big deal, June's lived with incurable lung cancer for ten years and done fine.

But this is different. Her cancer has spread to the cerebral and spinal fluid. It's painful, brutal, and 100% deadly.

It develops in patients who've lived with cancer for a long time. The irony that because June's fought like hell to live this long, she's developed this deadly complication, isn't just shattering, it's cruel.

She will not survive this, and we will be lucky if we get the six to twelve weeks she was promised.

Even thinking those words crushes something fundamental to who I am. And knowing these things without sharing them seems indecent, but as I look at how they're all nodding in agreement with Aaron, I know they don't want the truth.

So I lock it away. It feels like the most loving thing to do right now. Is it the healthy thing to do? I have no idea. But I'll carry it for them until they're ready to face it. I can do that for them. I've done it for ten years, what's another six to twelve weeks?

A crash from the kitchen breaks the silence in the room. "Sorry! Sorry," Joy shouts. She's been in the kitchen and hasn't stopped moving since she got here, like she can outpace the reality of June's diagnosis with constant motion.

Grace sits cross-legged on the floor, staring at her hands.

And Babe... Poor Babe hasn't stopped crying since we got the phone call. She's seated on the floor in front of June, clinging to June's hand, like if she lets go, our sister will die right there on the spot. Clay's next to her, fighting back his own tears. June's been his best friend since they were kids, long before he and Babe got together.

My mom and dad are on the opposite sofa, holding hands. Mom's swollen eyes betray the bravery she's trying to portray for June. And my dad, good God, I can't look at him and the silent tears rolling down his face. I've only seen him cry once, and that was at his mother's funeral, so this unfettered display of emotion is rocking the very foundation that most of my assumptions about him are built on.

Max and Chloe each had their moment with June, then retreated to the front room. They're currently huddled together on the sofa there, watching something on Max's computer. They keep coming in to check on us, but it's clear that the weight of what's happening is too much for them to take for very long. They dip in then dip out quickly for fear of getting sucked under the squall of emotions swirling through this room.

And me? I'm trying to remain calm for June, but inside there's a bonfire of fear, uncertainty, and anger burning me alive.

June looks over and points one pink-tipped finger at me. "I'm telling you right now, if y'all let me go to my grave with chin hair, I will haunt you to your dying day."

The comment is so out of left field that we all laugh. It starts as a startled crackle of humor then quickly builds to huge guffaws that ring through the room. Once we start, we can't stop. It goes on and on. We're hysterical. But laughter seems preferable to tears.

I salute. "Order received and logged."

"I'm not kidding." She looks at Grace. "I know you always have tweezers handy. You'd better use them."

Grace raises her right hand. "I vow that your chin will be as smooth as a baby's butt."

The momentary levity gives me a few seconds to draw a clear breath, and I can feel solid ground under me again. I try to hold onto that moment and do okay, until the front door opens with a bang against the wall. I look up to see Ian striding into the room, purpose and determination in every step, and the precarious foundation that I just put my feet on crumbles.

He goes straight to June.

She pushes herself up and raises her arms as soon as he gets to her. Without hesitation, he picks her up, then sits and cradles her like a newborn.

Any lightness from the previous few minutes evaporates and we all sink back into despair, while Ian rubs little circles on June's back and coos into her ear as she sobs, like he used to when she was little and skinned her knee.

Aaron rests his elbows on his knees and drops his head into his hands. His body shakes with his own emotions. Ian takes his hand from June's back and squeezes Aaron's shoulder. The touch seems to take all of the strength from my brother-in-law, and he crumples into Ian's side.

Regardless of how I feel about Ian, I know he loves June, and I would never deny him this moment, but I don't have to watch it.

I leave the living room and head to the laundry room to move some clothes from the washer to the dryer.

Why does everyone but me get Ian's best and his care?

First Marcy.

Now June.

The resentment riding roughshod over me is shameful. I'm too fragile to fight it, so I allow myself a moment of judgment-free jealousy. Will I ever stop hurting because of this man?

*You don't want him back, Hope.*

It's not true. I want the Ian in the other room, holding my dying sister and her husband. I want that more than I can say. He's just not that person for me.

I've always hated laundry, but it's never made me cry. Now I'm weeping into a wet towel, praying the plush fabric muffles the sound.

Warm hands kneed my shoulders. I know who it is before I look, but I turn into his arms anyway. Big, huge sobs rack my body, but he holds me steady.

Somewhere in the recesses of my mind, I hear that little voice whisper, *Not safe. Not safe. Not safe.* It's only a whisper and easily ignored.

I don't know how long we stand there before I get control enough to say, "I can't."

"You can't what, Hope?" Ian asks.

"I can't fix this for her." I break down again.

"Yes, you can. You can do what you've always done. You can be with her through this. You all can."

"I don't want to," I say like a petulant child.

"I know, but you will," he says with all the confidence in the world.

His confidence in me is annoying, but it gives me the strength to pull myself together. I dry my eyes on his shirt, step back, and nod. "I will."

He smiles and drags his palms over his own wet cheeks.

*Not safe. Not safe. Not safe.*

"How did you know? Did Clay call you?"

He shakes his head. "June texted me."

I swallow down the tears that threaten to spill again. "She loves you."

"I love her, always have," he says.

"I know." I take another step away from him. We might agree on June, but that's it. The image of Marcy's baby bump is front and center in my mind. I take another step, putting more distance between us. "Thanks. I'm okay now."

His posture changes too. I can tell he liked that I needed him while I cried.

But that's done.

I draw air into my lungs, and with it comes my resolve not to get tripped up by a relationship that didn't work, to never need this man again, and to walk June down this unthinkable path.

I put the towel I cried on back into the washer. "I need to get back in there. Someone will call you if there's any change."

His shoves his hands into his front pocket. A move so familiar that it nearly brings on another wave of tears. "Thanks. Let me know if y'all need anything. I'll be here at the drop of a hat."

"For June," I say.

His sad gray eyes lock with mine. "Yeah, for June."

Something's different about him. I can't tell what it is, but I don't have the energy or desire to ferret it out. Ian isn't my business anymore. He can handle his own stuff, and I'll handle mine. And right now, all I care about is in the other room.

I move to the laundry room door. "See ya, Ian."

I leave behind a past that I no longer want and step into a future I want even less.

# Chapter Seventeen

The next morning, my sisters are back at my parents' house. The seven of us are gathered in the living room. The thought was to come up with a plan, but honestly, all we've done for the last two hours is take turns sitting next to June, shaking our heads, and repeating, "I can't believe this."

When I was a kid, I paid ten dollars I'd earned doing chores to try to catch flying dollar bills while standing in a wind tunnel. It seemed like such easy money — ten dollars for a chance to win a hundred? Who wouldn't go for that?

I entered the booth with all the confidence of someone who'd never stood in the middle of a storm and tried to make order out of chaos, while my friends stood on the other side of the glass cheering me on. They were as delusional about my abilities as I was.

I walked out ten dollars in the hole, disoriented, and embarrassed.

That's how I feel today.

Like I'm standing in the middle of the worst storm of my

life without a clue how to make sense of anything going on around me, desperately grabbing at anything that looks like it will help.

I should know what to do. That's my job. To lead in situations like this, but I'm as clueless as everyone else.

The front door opens and closes. "Yoo-hoo," a female voice calls.

One thing about my parents is that they've only just started locking their front door at night, but if anyone stops by during the day, they walk right on in.

"In here," my mom calls back.

A dark-haired woman I don't recognize walks into the living room. She looks to be about June and Babe's age. "Hey, y'all."

Babe rises from her place on the sofa and hugs the woman, confirming my suspicion that she's one of their friends. "Hey, Rhonda."

Rhonda hugs my youngest sister. "It sounds like y'all are havin' a pretty shitty day." She releases Babe and makes her way to my mom, embracing her.

"You could say that," Mom says through tears. She takes Rhonda's face in her hands. "You know all about it, don't you?"

"I do," Rhonda answers.

When she turns to hug my dad, I see a scar that runs from behind her ear to the crown of her head. The hair around the scar is shorter than the rest of her black bob.

Rhonda hugs Grace and Joy, then moves to the sofa and sits next to June. My sister crumples into the woman's ample chest, weeping as her friend holds her. Her sobs are contagious and set off another round of bawling by the rest of my family.

That's how it's been since we got the news yesterday. We're locked on a roller coaster of emotions and can't get off. We're all exhausted, especially June, and because of that, none of us would get off this horrible ride even if we could. If she's on it, then so are we.

After several minutes, June sits up, tears still clinging to her lashes. "Rhonda, have you met my big sister? Hope, this is Rhonda Norman. She went to school with Babe and me."

The name means nothing to me. But then again, since June and Babe are so much younger than I am, I don't really know many of their friends.

"Nice to meet you, Rhonda."

Rhonda smiles. "You too." She turns back to June. "So, tell me what the doctor said." It's a command, not a question. She's not trying to get in our business. She's on a mission.

June relays what the radiologist said.

Rhonda bites her lip and nods. "That's what they told me too."

"When was that?" I ask.

"A year ago."

I sit up straighter. "You had the same thing June does?"

She shakes her head. "No, but the prognosis was the same."

"Then, how..."

Rhonda shrugs. "I didn't listen to 'em. My aunt heard about this doctor who deals specifically with really difficult brain cancers, the kind that everyone else has given up on."

"And he helped you?" It's a stupid question since the woman is sitting here in front of us.

She holds her arms wide. "I'm cancer-free."

An electric charge zings from the middle of my chest out to my extremities. "How?"

"He's good at what he does."

"Where is he?" My dad moves to the edge of his seat.

She smiles like she has a secret. "In Dallas."

"Oh, Rhonda. Do you think he treats this kind of cancer?" The hope in my mom's voice is heartbreaking.

"He does."

"Really?" June asks. "My doctor says there isn't a treatment."

Rhonda's nodding before June stops speaking. "It's a new treatment." She bites her lip and scrunches her nose. "I hope it's okay, but I called my nurse at his office and told her about you and asked if they deal with this kind of cancer."

"Of course it's okay," June says.

Rhonda looks relieved, like it just occurred to her that what she did might be considered meddling. "According to my nurse, he's the only one in this part of the country doing this treatment." She reaches into her purse and pulls out a card. "Give them a call. He's busy, but hopefully you can get in to see him. He won't bullshit you. If he can't help, he'll tell you. But if he says he can, he means it."

Babe bursts into tears. "Thank you, Rhonda."

"Oh, sweet girl, thank you," Mom says and runs her palms over her face to clear the tears.

Rhonda grins but is clearly uncomfortable with the praise. "No problem at all." She hugs June and stands. "Welp, I'd better get going. June, our church has put you on our prayer chain."

June nods and adjusts her position with a wince. "That's so kind. Thank you. But listen, if you know anyone who'd say that heifer deserves it, please don't tell them."

Rhonda's big, joyful, infectious laugh fills the room. We all laugh too, but ours is a little too loud, a little too long, and riding that razor's edge of mania. Our emotions are swinging bigger and higher than an elephant on a trapeze.

Rhonda pulls her purse onto her shoulder. "Girl, you're crazy."

Mom stands to escort our guest to the door. "She is that, for sure."

No one says anything for a long moment. Each of us is lost in what we just heard. I grab hold of this information with both hands. I have a project. The relief of having something productive to do is intoxicating. My phone is in my hand, and I'm searching the internet before I can draw another breath.

June raises her hand. "Babe, help me up."

"Where are you going?" Grace asks.

"To the bathroom."

"I'll go with you," I say at the same time as Joy, Grace, and Babe.

"Oh, good Lord. I'm capable of going to the toilet by myself. I'm not dead yet." There's a beat of silence, then she asks, "Too soon?"

"Yes," Mom says as she walks back into the room.

"Fair." June takes a wobbly step. "Ugh, I've been sitting too long."

Six anxious pairs of eyes follow her out of the room. We all hold our breath until we hear the bathroom door close.

Babe's still looking down the hall. "Does she seem—"

"Unsteady?" Joy asks.

"Yeah," Babe answers.

"Yes," I say.

My dad gets up to grab the TV remote. "Y'all are just lookin' for things. She seems fine to me."

He's probably right. But it still annoys me that he's dismissing our concerns.

Mom must sense my annoyance because she asks me, "So what do you think about what Rhonda said?"

Before I can answer, a crash comes from the bathroom. We all nearly break our necks squeezing down the hallway to the toilet. I'm the first to get there. I swing the door open. The wrought iron shelving unit that's usually next to the toilet is on the floor, and June is sprawled next to it, eyes closed and her pants down around her ankles.

"June!" Mom screams.

I rush into the room and drop to the ground beside her. "Junie. Can you hear me?"

I hear Dad barking orders. "Joy, call 911. Grace, call Aaron."

They obey and stay in the hall.

I take my sister's hand. "Wake up, Junie."

June's eyes flutter and open. "My head. Hurts."

"It's alright." I push her hair from her pale face. My hand isn't shaking, odd given the hellish horror rocking the rest of my body. "Joy's calling 911. The ambulance will be here any minute."

That rouses her from the post-faint haze. She tries to sit but can't. "Help."

"We're getting help, June," Babe says from our sister's other side.

June grabs Babe's shirt and pulls her down so she can look her in the eye. "No. Help me get my pants up. I can't have Rick Stokes see me with my pants around my ankles. I haven't waxed in forever." Her words sound like Jello looks but are no less ferocious.

"June, it's fine," Grace says. She and Joy have joined us in the bathroom. "We'll cover you with a towel."

"No!" June tries to shout but it's a pitiful effort. "His first time seeing me naked cannot be with a full bush and pee running down my legs." Her pain-glazed eyes find mine. "Please, Hope."

I can't ignore her plea. "Alright. Grace, Joy, can y'all help?"

Babe moves the shelving unit then joins us, and the four of us gather around her and work to get her pants up. It's hard because she can't help at all, we're operating with limited space, and any movement causes her pain. We're also working against the clock. Bonedalia's a small town. It's not going to take the ambulance long to get here.

At the sound of sirens in the distance, June whimpers. "Please, hurry."

"We're trying. Are you sure we can't cover you with a towel?" Joy asks.

"No!" She's crying now. "Please."

Babe slaps Joy's hand away from June's jeans. "I've got it."

You've heard stories of mothers getting a burst of adrenaline and lifting cars off their children. Well, that's what happens with Babe. Where we were all fumbling, Babe grabs June's pants with both hands, then lifts and pulls. In a matter of seconds, her jeans are up far enough to be considered modest.

"Look at The Baby..." June says, but her voice fades out on the last word.

"I think she fainted again," Grace says.

Relief floods through me at the sound of Rick Stokes's voice in the hallway. He starts to move into the room and stops.

"I don't think we can all be in here. Do you ladies mind waiting in the hall?"

"Um..." Babe says.

"I'll take care of her. I promise." His gentle, compassionate voice is a balm to my fractured heart.

"Let's go," I command, and my sisters obey.

Once we're out of the way, Rick goes to my sister, who's come to again. He kneels down next to her. "We've got to stop meeting like this, June Bug."

She tries to smile, but winces in pain. She blinks like she's having trouble focusing.

Rick wraps the blood pressure cuff around her arm. "Can you tell me what hurts?"

"Head and neck." If words had a form, June's would be smoke.

Rick and his partner exchange medical jargon and get a history of what happened from Joy.

A high-pitched wail from the living room has me moving before I can form another thought. I skid to a stop when I see my mom and dad locked in a desperate embrace. My mom's body shakes as she cries into my dad's chest, while those damn silent tears streak my dad's cheeks.

I have to look away. Their pain is too much, and I'm not sure I can absorb it and stay upright. I turn to go back to the bathroom but am met with Rick and the other EMT steering June on the gurney down the hall. I'm forced to step into the living room to get out of their way.

My parents look up at the crowd following me, and I barely recognize the two people standing before me. They look frail, as if they can't walk another mile while carrying this burden.

"Are we going back to Reece Medical Center?" Rick asks.

"Yes," Grace says.

"Alright, we'll see you there."

"Dad," June says and holds her hand out to him.

He clasps her hand in both of his. "Yeah?"

"I'm a little scared."

He uses his shoulder to dry the tears from one cheek. "Me too, Junie, but we're gonna do this together. Okay?"

"Okay." Her limp hand slips from his as she's wheeled past him to the front door.

I'm fighting for air. My lungs refuse to expand far enough to draw a deep breath. How am I supposed to survive this for six to twelve more weeks? How are any of us going to survive? As bad as I ever imagined this would be, it's worse. So much worse.

Joy makes her way to us, a weird look on her face.

"What's wrong?" I ask. I don't think I can take one more thing.

She swallows but doesn't seem to be able to get the words out.

"What is it?" Grace demands.

Joy bites her lip like she's trying not to smile. "Evidently, June didn't have a chance to flush before she fainted."

We all look at her like she has three heads. What the hell does that have to do with anything? They've just wheeled our terminally ill sister out of our house on a gurney. I open my mouth to tell her just that, then it hits me. "So, Rick Stokes didn't see June's unshaved hoo-ha, but he did see her..."

"'Fraid so."

"Oh, that's shitty," Grace says, biting back a smile.

"Literally." Joy's laughing now.

"Oh, no." Mom chokes back a laugh.

A wheezing sound draws my attention. Dad is resting both hands on the back of a kitchen chair, his body vibrating with uncontrolled laughter.

Deep, painful belly laughs spill from us all. I'd feel bad if I didn't know with absolute certainty that June would be rolling on the floor laughing at any of us in the same situation. We all know it's true. It's probably why we can't seem to get control of ourselves.

The elephant on the trapeze takes another giant swing through the room.

Babe gains her composure first and points her finger at each of us. "First, we're all going to hell. And second, we have to swear never to tell her. If she knew, the humiliation would kill her long before the cancer does." When no one answers, she yells, "Swear."

We raise our right hands and nod.

Then we load into the car to follow the ambulance and face what comes next… together.

# Chapter Eighteen

The ER waiting room at Reece Medical Center is like the love child of a petri dish and a combat zone—not a place you want to hang out in. Our family is cowering in a corner, trying not to breathe the diseased air around us.

Babe, in particular, is having a hard time. To say my youngest sister is a germaphobe would be the understatement of the century. She wraps the blanket she brought from home tighter around her. Not one inch of her skin is exposed from the neck down. "I don't know how y'all are letting any part of your skin touch those chairs."

Grace gives her a flat look. "Not all of us are neurotic, Babe."

She squares her shoulders. "You're not going to shame me into dropping this blanket. Come tell me how dumb you think I am when you get what that guy has." She juts her chin in the direction of a man with weepy, open sores on his legs.

"Babe," Mom scolds.

My youngest sister shrugs and pulls the blanket up to cover her mouth and nose.

Joy looks up from her phone and says to Grace, "Chloe just texted. She and Max made it to my house."

Grace pulls her phone out, then holds it up. "Of course, I don't have a message." She shakes her head. "Welcome to being a boy mom. So there wasn't a problem with Max riding the bus with her?"

"Apparently not. She says they're good. I told them to order a pizza and have it delivered."

"Thanks. Venmo me what I owe you."

I watch the exchange in fascination.

"What?" Grace asks.

I shrug. "Nothing."

Grace rolls her eyes. "We can be civil."

Joy slips her phone into her purse. "Yeah, we're not heathens."

I don't remind them of their food fight at the diner, but it's on the tip of my tongue. "I didn't say a word."

The doors to the patient rooms open and Aaron comes out. It's hard to read his expression. But the way the skin is drawn tight over his handsome face and the stiffness of his gait tell me that things aren't good.

"She told me to eat something and wants you four to come back with her." His voice is flat, like he's used up all his words and has none left. He turns to my parents and in the same crushed tone says, "Y'all too."

Mom stands and goes to Aaron. "We'll give her a bit of time with her sisters, then we'll go back." She reaches for his hand. "Don't worry. We'll take care of her, until you get back."

In that moment, I know how much this man loves my sister and us. This is a sacrificial gift. There's no place he'd rather be than with June, but he knows the five of us need to be together right now and he's giving us that time.

Mom must understand that too because she says, "Y'all go on back and be with your sister. We'll be along in a bit."

Clay rises and slaps him on the shoulder. "Come on, I'm starving too. I'll buy you a crappy sandwich in the cafeteria."

I squeeze his arm. "We'll take care of her." Then I follow my sisters through the doors to where the patient rooms are located.

We wind our way through the labyrinth until we find June.

They've put her in an actual room and not a space cordoned off by curtains. I'm not sure what we expected, but June sitting up, drinking juice, and laughing with the nurse is not it.

"Sue, these are my sisters," she says to the nurse.

Sue, who looks like she's seen some things, asks, "Are you as crazy as this woman?"

"Not even close," I say and move to June's bedside. "You look like you're feeling better."

"They gave me the good stuff again." She whispers and blinks both eyes, but it's intended to be a wink.

I laugh. "I can see that."

"Can we get some?" Joy drops down into one of the two chairs in the room.

I know what she means. Anything to take the edge off this situation would be welcome.

"What'd the doctor say?" Grace asks.

June takes a slug of her juice and smacks her lips. "I haven't seen one yet."

"Someone should be in shortly," Sue says from the other side of the room. She finishes typing and stands. "I'll go check and see where they're at."

"Thank you, Sue," I say.

"What the hell, Babe?" June blinks up at our youngest sister then laughs as only someone high on pain meds can.

Babe gingerly sits in the other chair, still wrapped in her blanket. "I'm not taking any chances."

Grace rolls her eyes. "Don't even try to talk sense into her. She's not droppin' that blanket for anyone or anything."

Babe sticks her tongue out at Grace.

"Real mature," Grace says.

Babe snuggles into the chair. "Mature and germ-free."

June pushes herself up in the bed. "I've been thinking, and you know what would be fun? If we all went on a cruise next summer."

The change in subject is so jarring that it takes me a minute to catch up. "A cruise?"

"Yeah. We could go on spring break and sail out of Galveston." She takes a sip of her drink. "Maybe we could all go. Do you think Carrie would join us, Hope?"

"I... I don't know." I try not to let my astonishment at her request into my voice.

"I hope she can." She looks at our other sisters, whose faces reflect the same confusion I feel. "What about y'all? Could y'all take time off work for a cruise?"

Ever practical, Grace is the first to speak. "Spring break's nine months away."

"I know." There's an edge of a plea in June's tone. She's begging us to join her in the warm pool of delusion, desperate for it, if the look in her eyes is any indication.

I stand there in heartbroken silence, swallowing the urge to bawl at June's attempt to plan for a future she doesn't have.

Babe is the first to wade into the waters of delusion to join June. "What a great idea. And spring break's a great time to go." Babe gives Joy and Grace an *answer now and make it good,* look.

Joy and Grace give similar replies but with less enthusiasm. Babe's censorious expression clearly indicates that they did not sell their response effectively.

June doesn't seem to notice their lack of fervor. She falls back onto the pillow and grins. "Yay. It'll be so much fun. Babe, you and I need to renew our gym memberships to try to find our bikini bods. Oh, and spray tans. We'll need those too. As pale and fluffy as I am, I'll look like the Dough Boy at sea if I don't do something." Her laughter is wobbly, like a bubble that hasn't quite decided if it wants to be a bubble or not.

A knock at the door interrupts any further discussion of cruises. A young woman in a white coat walks in. She sticks one of her hands under the hand sanitizer dispenser, then rubs them both together. "Hi, June. I'm Dr. Anderson."

"Hello," June says with a little less enthusiasm than she did when we walked in.

I look at her. "Are you alright?"

She smiles, but the jovial glint in her eyes has been replaced by a shadow of confusion. Her hand goes to her temple, and she rubs little circles. "I'm... My head's starting to hurt again."

"Can I ask you some questions, June?" Dr. Anderson asks, seemingly oblivious to the fact that June looks like she's wilting into the pillow.

June blinks twice like she's trying to focus. "Sure."

The sight of the color leaching from my sister's face is alarming. Her muddled expression makes it clear that she's not all with us, and this has nothing to do with the drug-induced high she was riding a few moments ago. This is the disease slowly taking possession of her. It's horrifying to watch. How did she turn so fast?

"So what brings you in today?" the doctor asks, still rubbing her hands together.

"Headache." June doesn't elaborate.

"Okay." Dr. Anderson takes the electronic tablet out from under her arm and removes the stylus from its holder. Tap, tap, tap. "And when did the symptoms start?"

"Earlier today." June's words are taking on that watery consistency that's become all too familiar.

Tap, tap, tap. "And do you have a history of headaches?"

"Um..." It's clear she's having trouble finding words to answer. "I've been having them a lot lately."

I look over at my sisters and the three of them look the same way I'm feeling. What kind of questions are these?

TAP. TAP. TAP.

The sound scratches against my very last nerve.

"Mmm, so you can't tell me when they started? And you're here today for what? Medication?" There's an accusatory edge to the question that I do not like.

"I... um..."

I step between the doctor and June's bed. "The headaches started a few weeks before she got her terminal diagnosis. She has stage four cancer that's spread to her brain. That's why she's having headaches."

She gives me a patronizing closed-mouth smile. "It's protocol to get a full history—"

"You have a full history. She was here a few days ago. All her records are here. I also know for a fact that the EMTs gave you her medical history when they brought her in. I don't see the reason for these triage questions." I try to control my anger. It doesn't really work. "I know you're following protocol, but we're way past"—I make quotation marks with my fingers—"when did your symptoms start?"

"My sister's right," Joy says and steps up beside me. "This is a waste of time. And you're damn right, she wants medication."

She motions toward the bed, where June is now lying motionless, grimacing in pain. "You give her whatever will help her."

"Look at her," Grace says. "She just went from laughing to being barely coherent. If you're not the doctor who can help her, go find the one who can."

Dr. Anderson looks taken aback but recovers quickly. "I understand." She takes a penlight out of her pocket and takes a step toward June, but Joy and I are in her way. "May I?" she asks.

Joy and I move out of her way.

"June, I'm going to look at your eyes. This might be bright, but I'll be quick," she says gently.

June nods and it's clear even that slight movement is incredibly painful.

After several moments examining June, the doctor orders more pain meds to see if they can give her some relief, then leaves the room.

The four of us gather around June's bed, guarding what's most precious to us. Grace and I each take one of June's hands. I extend my other hand to Joy, who grabs it and holds tight. Grace holds her other hand out to Babe, who's still wrapped in her blanket. There's only the slightest hesitation, then the blanket hits the floor and Babe threads her fingers through Grace's. It's as natural and expected as our next breath.

We're silent as we hold vigil for our sister.

June's lids flutter open and her glazed gaze finds us, then she closes her eyes again. "Thank y'all for being here."

"Always," I push past my constricted vocal cords.

June smiles, still with her eyes closed. "And y'all don't let Babe burn herself when she sets that blanket on fire."

# Chapter Nineteen

The next morning, I push through the door of the sleek high-rise building in downtown Dallas where The Starling Realtor Group is located, carrying my bag, coffee, and a mild case of irritation. I should be at the hospital with June, but instead, I'm here closing on the house that I owned with Ian.

It shouldn't be this hard to separate one life from another. Our divorce has been final for months, and today we cut the final tether connecting me to this man.

He's scrolling his phone and waiting by the bank of gold elevators. My stomach does the flippy thing it's done since I was fifteen years old. Granted, it's more of a toddler's forward roll now, as opposed to the full-on Olympic level front flip with a twist it was back then.

But it's still there.

It's unwanted.

Now I'm more than a little irritated.

He looks up as I approach and slides his phone into his blazer pocket. "Good morning."

I bank my annoyance and answer as pleasantly as possible. "Morning."

"We could've rescheduled this, Hope," he says as he pushes the button to call the elevator. "Especially with June still being in the hospital. How is she?"

Once we finally saw the attending doctor last night, he thought it would be a good idea for June to stay in the hospital for a few days to see if the palliative care team could get her pain under control. "Last I heard, she was bossing Grace around."

His deep, rich chuckle takes up every ounce of oxygen in the elevator. "That sounds about right." I see him run his fingers through his hair in the mirrored door. "Are you sure you want to do this, Hope?"

"For the millionth time, Ian, this is what I want. I don't have any use for the house. Frankly, I don't understand why you're so against it." I want this over and settled. The house is the last thing connecting me to my old life.

He smooths his tie. "I just think it's a good investment for you."

Lie.

This house stands as a monument to his success and all he did for me.

What he never seemed to understand, was all I did for him. It was my salary that kept us afloat while he built his business. The late nights I endured alone. The dismissal of my feelings. The loneliness of the last ten years. I bent myself into whatever shape I thought he wanted me to be, and I did it all with every ounce of perfection in my body.

*If you were so perfect, then why did he leave? There had to have been something else you could've done.*

The thought has worn a groove in my psyche, a scratch that

catches every time it plays. And it's been playing my whole damn life.

I want to defend myself against it. But of course, if I had done more, maybe...

"Hope?"

"Um..." It takes me a moment to drag myself out of the spiral. I pull on the mask that hides my insecurities, even from him. Especially from him. "If you think it's such a good investment, then you should've bought me out." It's on the tip of my tongue to ask, won't he and Marcy need the house for their growing family, but I don't. I can feel him scowl at me. Good. Pacifying Ian Hall and trying to figure out what he needs aren't my jobs anymore.

"Do you have somewhere picked out to buy? I can help—"

"I'm not going to buy a house."

"What? Hope, you know renting is throwing your money away."

What I do is none of his business anymore. "You know what, Ian, I don't know what I'm going to do. Remember, I own an RV now, maybe I'll live there." That shuts him up. For a minute, anyway.

"You cannot be serious, Hope. What the hell do you know about driving a big-ass rig like an RV? I assumed you only wanted ours out of spite, not because you were going to actually try to drive it somewhere."

He's right about wanting the RV to spite him. One of the many toys he had was a thirty-five-foot RV with all the bells and whistles. He bought it a few months before he left, and for some reason, he seemed particularly fond of it, so I took it—my first act of defiance.

I pull my purse higher on my shoulder. "I guess you don't remember that I've driven an RV before?"

"What? When?"

I give a sad chuckle and shake my head. "My sisters, Mom, and I rented an RV a couple of years ago and road tripped to Tennessee."

The elevator comes to a stop, the doors slide open, and I step out, expecting him to follow. But I turn to see him still inside the lift, holding the doors open with both hands.

Two lines form between his brows, and I can see his mind working, like he's flipping through an old Rolodex, trying to retrieve the memory.

That confused look on his face is why we're here. "Don't tax yourself, Ian. It doesn't matter." I check the time. "We should go. We're going to be late." I make my way down the hall. When the elevator alarm goes off, I glance back and see him still standing in the same position. "Are you coming?"

"Huh?" He blinks at me. "Um, yeah."

I don't recognize the expression on his face. If I were forced to put a name to it, I'd say it was regret. But it's way past time for regret. We're in the *moving on with our lives* phase of this divorce. He should know that more than me. He's got a whole new life growing with Marcy and her baby.

The thought opens another cut in my soul. Sorrow begins to well up from the wound, but I force it back. If I don't stop it, then I'll bleed misery all over this pristine office building.

Not what I want, especially on the day of my final separation from him.

The realtor's office is all straight lines and recessed lighting, orderly in its minimalism. It smells of vanilla, and classical music plays quietly over the speakers. It's the kind of space that I would normally admire. But something about it is unexpectedly offensive. Too ordered. Too controlled. Like it's mocking the chaos of what my life has become.

"Ian. Hope. Good to see you," our realtor, Ben Hanscom, says. "Come this way." He leads us to a room with a conference table. "Can I get you anything to drink?"

Ian takes a seat on one side of the table and scoots the chair next to him out for me. "Not for me."

I ignore his gesture and sit opposite him. "Not for me either."

Ben sits at the head of the table. "Alright. I guess you're ready to get this done."

I pick up one of the pens in the middle of the table. "I am." I glance at Ian for confirmation, but he's staring at the tabletop. "Are you ready, Ian?"

When his eyes meet mine, there's that same look I saw while he was in the elevator. "Um..." He takes a pen and turns his attention to our realtor. "Yeah."

Ben opens the folder containing our documents. The next few minutes are a blur of explanations, legalese, initials, and signatures.

Ben slides a document my direction. "Initial here."

I move the form in front of me. There's something heartbreakingly appropriate about the little yellow arrow pointing to the blank line on the page. Like it's saying, *See, this is what the life you thought you'd have amounted to. A big fat nothing.*

An uninvited memory of the day we closed on the house rudely barges into my mind. Ian carrying me across the threshold of our beautiful home we worked so hard for. Me, holding an open magnum of champagne by the neck, each of us taking slugs from the bottle. The texture of the image is so visceral that I can nearly feel the tickle of popping bubbles in the back of my throat. We were a little drunk, a lot happy, and so hopeful for the future. Two stupid people who thought they'd made it—that the hard times were behind them.

Idiots.

That last thought gives me the resolve to place my pen on the blank line. It shakes a little as I sign, but I don't try to hide it. I think I've earned it. Every swipe of the pen pries my fingers from the life I built and tried so hard to hang onto.

"And here," Ben says.

I release the memory of the two of us christening the house by making love in every room.

Ben uselessly points at another yellow arrow. "Last time."

I block out the image of thousands of sparkling twinkle lights illuminating the house our first Christmas there, and Ian's delight in how happy it made me.

"And finally, sign here."

I close the door on the place that was our forever home, where we were supposed to grow old together.

Once I sign my name to the last page and slide it across the table for Ian's signature, the question of *What was this all for?* settles over me. It seems louder and stronger than when we signed the divorce papers.

Twenty-five years, reduced to a few signatures and a notary stamp.

*There must have been something else I could've done.*

I sidestep that thought and gather the broken pieces of my life and shove them into something that looks like acceptance. Ian and I had some good years, followed by some bad ones, and then he walked away. I should probably thank him for leaving because I would've probably stayed in that misery forever.

Now I'm free. The tie has truly been severed.

"That's it." Ben holds the stack of papers and taps them against the tabletop to straighten them. "It was a pleasure working with the two of you."

We say our goodbyes to Ben and leave without celebration or ceremony.

The elevator ride is silent.

Once we step outside, I suck in a lungful of humid Texas air, then release it.

I pull my phone from my bag and see a missed call from Grace and a text. My heart stutters then kicks into overdrive. I quickly open my phone and read.

*There's no emergency.*

Relief jolts my heart back into a normal rhythm. Thank God.

*June's hungry for a sandwich from Morgan's. Can you pick one up and bring it to the hospital?*

I can't stop the smile that stretches my lips. After the insanity of the last few days, I've never been so happy to run a mundane errand in my life.

"Everything alright?" Ian asks.

Without thinking, I answer, "June wants a sandwich from Morgan's."

"That's got to be a good sign." He sounds like the rest of us, grasping at anything that gives us hope that maybe she's not as sick as the doctors say she is.

I don't answer and slip my phone back into my purse. "I'd better get going." There's an awkward beat of silence. What do you say in situations like this?

*See ya?*

*Later?*

*I'm sorry I couldn't be whatever it is you wanted me to be.*

I settle on, "Take care, Ian."

He slips his hands into the front pockets of his slacks. "You too."

I open my car door, but he calls my name. I turn to see the same confused, almost regretful look I saw in the elevator. "Yes?"

"I wanted to tell you..." He turns his head and surveys the parking lot.

I watch the slide of his Adam's apple as dread fills my chest. Oh, crap. He's about to drop the Marcy-and-baby bomb. Sweat slicks on my upper lip, and my knees stage a mutiny. I white-knuckle the top of the door in order to stay upright. He can't possibly be doing this here. Now?

He slips his sunglasses off and stares at them in his hand. "I need to tell you—"

"Ian, I have to go." There's a lot I can't control right now, but I can control whether I stay for this confession or not. I will not.

He takes a step toward the car. "But—"

I hold up my phone. "Sorry. You know how June gets when she's hangry." I quickly slide into my car, close the door, and lock it. My fingers tremble as I push the start button.

He was going to tell me about Marcy.

About the baby.

About everything I couldn't give him.

I try to swallow past the choking sorrow and grief stuck in my throat. My tears shove hard against the back of my eyes. I hold them off until I pull out of the parking lot, then I can't contain them any longer. I give them free rein to fall, in honor of the good years we had, the sweet memories we shared, and the life we built before it fell apart. Then to mourn the new life he's building without me. I think I'm owed this breakdown.

*There must have been something else you could've done.*

I'm out of tears by the time I get to Morgan's. I press the heels of my hands against my eyes as a few more hiccupping breaths escape.

My phone dings once more. It's Grace again.

*June wants to know where the hell you are. Her words, not mine.*

A stuttered laugh pushes any lingering sorrow away. I can't

think about Ian. I can't think about Marcy, or babies, or any of it.

June needs me. That's all that matters.

I can get this sandwich.

I can show up for June.

That's all I can handle right now.

# Chapter Twenty

"Say that again. I'm sure I didn't hear you correctly," Carrie says through the car's speakers.

My grip tightens on the steering wheel. "I'm moving home for a while."

"Has hell frozen over?"

"You're hilarious."

Carrie laughs. "Correct me if I'm wrong, but have you or have you not said that you would never live in Bonedalia again?"

I ignore the cage door slamming feeling when I cross into the city limits and say, "It's not like I'm moving here to live, live, but when I woke up this morning, I knew that I needed to be in Bonedalia to take care of June and my family."

Carrie doesn't say anything and for a moment I think I might have dropped her call. I check the screen and see that we're still connected. "Carrie?"

"Yeah, I'm here. It's just..."

"What's the matter?"

"Who's going to take care of you, Hope?"

"I'm fine. I don't—"

"Don't give me that bull crap that you don't need anyone to take care of you. We all need help, especially with what you all are facing. Promise me you'll call me if things get to be too much."

The seriousness in her tone stops my automatic appeasement. This is my best friend, and she'll know if I'm lying. She also knows that asking for help is nearly impossible for me. "I promise."

"I mean it, Hope. You can't do this by yourself."

Everything in me screams that I don't want to do this at all, but I don't dare let the words loose for fear that I might turn this car around and drive until I'm as far as I can get from this nightmare. "I said I promise, Carrie. I'll call you."

"Have you been able to get June an earlier appointment with the doctor Rhonda told y'all about?"

I turn into Mom and Dad's driveway and the queasiness that's become my unwelcome companion intensifies, whether because I'm really moving home or because of Carrie's question. June has an appointment with Dr. Yovan, but not for four weeks. According to my research, in four weeks it'll be too late. The disease will be too advanced. So I've called every single day, begging for a cancelation.

So far, they haven't had one, but I'm not giving up.

I can't.

"No. But I'll keep trying."

"How is she today?" I don't miss the hitch in her voice. She loves my sister nearly as much as me.

I slide my car in next to Dad's truck. "She's coming home from the hospital today. Thankfully, the palliative care team was able to get her pain under control and keep it that way."

"So she's better?"

"I think at this point, better is relative, but she was more like herself yesterday—funny, demanding, and uncomfortably inappropriate. You know, normal June."

Carrie laughs. "I suspect that even cancer can't make June comfortably appropriate."

"True. I'm here, so I'll call you later," I say and turn my car off.

"I know you will because you promised, remember?"

"Yes, Mom... and thank you."

"I love you, sister-friend."

"Love you too."

I hang up, then rest my forehead on the steering wheel. "You got this, Hope." Lord, I want to believe that more than I've wanted to believe anything in my life. I'm just not sure I do *got* this. And if the last nine months are any indication, then I most definitely do not *got* this. But got it or not, here we are.

The cool wind whips at my hair when I exit the car and retrieve my bags from the trunk. The temperature has done that thing it does in May, when it can't decide if it's ready to usher summer in or not.

Mom steps out onto the porch wiping her hands on a cup towel. "Hope. You're here." She glances down at the two large suitcases I'm rolling behind me. "And it looks like you came to stay a while."

"I did. I hope that's alright. I probably should've checked with y'all first."

Mom loops her arm through mine. "Of course it's fine. You know you're always welcome."

"Thanks, Mom." I nod to my suitcases. "I'm going to take these upstairs. I'll be down in a minute."

"Do you need any help?"

"No. I'm good."

"Okay. Come down when you're ready."

I make my way up the stairs to my childhood room. The

soft powder-blue walls are a vast improvement over the hot pink they were when I was a kid. There's a reason teenagers aren't interior designers.

I loved those pink walls, though. Ian and I spent a whole weekend painting them. I can't help but smile when I remember getting busted for doing a little more than painting.

"Boy, are those your pink handprints on my daughter's backside?"

All things considered, Dad had shown a huge amount of restraint, especially when Ian's admission came with a cocky grin. Nobody in my world ever went toe-to-toe with my dad. It was a foolish move, but that's the moment I fell in love with him.

I check my phone to see if Dr. Yovan's office has got back to me with a new appointment for June. Nothing. I already talked to them earlier, but I'm tempted to call again. And again. Whatever it takes to give my sister a chance.

The roar of Aaron's diesel truck coming up the drive draws my attention. I glance out the window and see June smiling in the passenger seat. My heart lightens at the sight of that smile. I watch as Aaron opens her door and helps her out of the truck.

Unpacking and future employment forgotten, I make my way down to join my family in welcoming June home. But once I'm downstairs, I don't find them gathered in joyful reunion. Instead, there are frantic voices coming from outside.

I run to the door and see June on the ground with everyone encircling her. Before my next thought, I'm sprinting to my sister..

"What happened?" I ask when I get to Babe's side.

"I don't... I don't know. She was fine, then she collapsed."

"Did she faint? Maybe she just stood up too fast," I say, but even I don't believe it.

"I didn't faint," June says. "The ground started moving, and I couldn't stay upright."

It's an inevitable and terrible confirmation. Loss of balance and the ability to be ambulatory are among the first signs that the disease is progressing. I know this because I've spent the last week reading everything I can find—medical journals, case studies, and patient forums. I've made myself an expert. As if my knowledge can protect us against this insidious disease.

"You ready to stand up now, baby?" Aaron asks June.

She raises her hand. "Yeah, but I think you're going to have to hold onto me and help me walk."

He winks at her. "I got you."

We all give them room as he helps June to her feet and then into the house. Once they're safely inside, my mom breaks. My dad puts his arm around her shaking shoulders. He's no less upset, but his pain is soundless and leaving salty tracks down his face.

My dad isn't an emotional powerhouse. In many ways, he's emotionally illiterate. But since we got the news that June's cancer was terminal, he's lost any ability to hide or control his sorrow.

"I thought she was better. Didn't you say she was better, Babe?" Joy asks.

"She was better. We walked around the hospital yesterday. She was totally fine." She looks at me. "I don't understand."

I struggle with the words that I know will destroy their hope, but must be said. "I did some research on leptomeningeal disease and... well... loss of balance is one of the signs that the disease is progressing."

Mom grabs Dad's arm. "No." The word is a plea, a prayer, an accusation

I fold my arms around my stomach. "I debated whether I

should tell y'all, but I think it's important for us to be prepared, especially because neither June nor Aaron wants to know this."

"Shit," Grace says and storms off, then marches back to the group. "Shit. Shit. Shit."

I understand her anger. I'm mad too. It's still unclear who I'm mad at. Her doctor? Cancer? God? The whole damn world?

I glance over at Dad. His face is unreadable, but his hunched shoulders say it all. He knows as well as me, that this isn't good.

Joy's standing with her fingers interlocked on her head like she just sprinted a quarter mile and is trying to fill her lungs with enough air to continue.

"Maybe she tripped over a rock." Babe's dainty jaw is set in a mulish expression.

I lower my gaze and move the gravel around with my toe. "You heard her, Babe. She said the ground started moving."

Babe crosses her arms over her chest, and her chin juts up. "God can still heal her."

"Amen," Mom says.

"He can," I say, mostly because it's what's expected. "But until that happens, we should make sure someone's with her, to help her get around. I took the liberty of making a schedule."

"Of course you did," Grace says.

I give my second sister a level look. I'm not scared of her anger, but I don't like it. "Feel free to make any adjustments you think are necessary, but I'm in a unique position right now. I can be here around the clock, so nobody has to miss work."

Joy steps up next to me. "That sounds good, Hope." Then she gives Grace a look. "The only thing that matters is June right now."

Grace bites her lip and looks out over the yard.

"Y'all stop talking about me and get in here. I'm hungry," June calls from inside the house.

"She must not be that bad off. She's as demanding as always." Joy chuckles.

My mom takes Babe and Grace's hands and heads toward the front door. Dad follows in their wake. "Let's go feed her before she gets hangry."

Joy bumps my shoulder. "You did the right thing."

"Did I? I feel like I just kicked a litter of puppies."

"We needed to know. But I'm with Babe. I believe God is going to heal her," she says, then heads for the house.

I follow, wishing I were still a true believer. But too much has happened over the last nine months for me to be certain of anything anymore.

Before I get to the front door, my phone rings. I check the screen, and it's Dr. Yovan's office. "Hello."

"Ms. Hall, this is Rodrigo, Dr. Yovan's physician's assistant. Sara from our front desk says you've been trying to get your sister in to see the doctor, but I also see that she has an appointment in four weeks."

"She does, but Rodrigo, you and I both know that will be too late. We need to get her in as soon as possible."

"Alright, hang on."

Desperation and anxiety have me pacing the length of the porch.

"Ms. Hall," Rodrigo says.

"Yes," I yell. I moderate my tone. "Yes, I'm here."

"If your sister can be here at nine a.m., right when we first open, Dr. Yovan will see her."

My legs refuse to hold me, and I collapse into the nearest chair, nearly missing the seat and ending up sprawled on the porch. "We'll be there." Suddenly, emotion is fighting its way up my throat and pressing on the back of my eyes. "I don't know how to thank you."

"It's no problem. We understand."

His compassion is my undoing. Tears burst from me in big, deep sobs. "I'm sorry. I'm just so relieved."

"It's fine, Ms. Hall. We'll see you in the morning."

"Thank you." I disconnect the call, and tears that have been dammed behind my careful control stream down my face.

I did it. I did it. I did it. I finally fixed something.

The relief uncoils my muscles and sets off another round of tears.

"Hope?" June calls from inside the house. "What are you doing out there?"

I wipe my face and blow out a breath. "Coming." I take another moment to get myself under control, then I head inside to give my family the good news.

Hopefully, I've bought us a little more time.

# Chapter Twenty-One

At six thirty the next morning, I find my dad standing over June as she sleeps. She and Aaron stayed the night at my parents' house, since we need to leave so early for her doctor's appointment.

Dad's back is to me, but I can see his hand hovering above her, like he wants to stroke her head. After several frozen heartbeats, he lowers his arm to his side, never touching her. But he stays where he is, watching her sleep.

Torrents of pity expand through my chest until I'm taking small gasping breaths, when he wipes his face with the sleeve of his shirt. The urge to go to him pulls at me, but I don't. The moment is too precious and sacred to interrupt.

I force my gaze away and head downstairs.

I pass Aaron on the staircase. "Did y'all get any sleep?"

His puffy eyes are my answer, but he says, "Not much. She finally fell asleep around four this morning."

Yesterday afternoon, June's pain broke through the medication that had been working so well while she was in the hospital. We were helpless to do anything to ease her agony.

She's deteriorating quickly.

And today, we find out if Dr. Yovan can help her. If he can't help us, then June's fight is over.

Everything is riding on this appointment. We all feel it, especially Aaron.

My arms are around his shoulders before I have time to consider whether it will be welcome. "I'm so sorry, Aaron."

His whole body relaxes into mine, and I have to lock my knees to take his weight. He doesn't answer, but I can feel him nod. Aaron and I aren't usually so huggy, but fighting for the life of the same person will bond you to someone quickly.

After a few moments, awkwardness butts into the moment, and I release him.

He hooks his thumb toward the top of the stairs. "I'm gonna go..."

"Okay. I need coffee," I say, like what just happened didn't happen.

When I go into the kitchen, Babe and Mom are at the table. "Good morning," I say and hope it will be.

Mom's smile is weak but warm. "Morning, honey."

Babe only lifts her mug in response.

I grab a coffee cup from the cabinet and fill it to the brim. "Are you going with us, Babe?"

"Yes."

I turn and lean my backside against the counter and blow into my coffee. "Are you sure? It could get a little intense." I worry about my youngest sister's fragile feelings.

"I'm sure." The resolve in her voice and expression tells me what I can do with my concern.

I hold my arms up in surrender, careful not to spill my coffee. "Okay, badass."

That teases a grin from her, and for a moment, the tightness in my chest uncoils.

Dad and Aaron join Mom and Babe at the table.

"Can I get you a cup, Dad?" I ask.

He shakes his head. "Naw. I've already had a few."

"Okay." I check my phone. "What time—"

"Help. Somebody help me," June calls from somewhere in the house.

"Where is she?" I ask, but the four of them are already running out of the room. I set down my cup and follow.

We all head to the downstairs bathroom and burst through the door to find June sitting on the toilet with her pants around her ankles and fury in her eyes.

"What the hell, y'all? You left me in here with no toilet paper. Was this some test to see if I'm really as incapable of taking care of myself as I appear to be?"

Aaron moves to her. "I'm sorry, baby."

"You can't just leave me sitting on the toilet." She's still mad, but her words have lost their fire. It's like four sentences used up every ounce of strength she had.

Babe goes to the cabinet under the sink, grabs a roll of toilet paper, and hands it to June. "Yes. And you failed. Do you need me to wipe your butt too?"

I've never heard Babe speak to June like that.

Silence hangs over the moment like a wrecking ball suspended by a frayed wire. The drip from the leaky faucet is the only sound in the bathroom.

June snorts. "No, smartass, I can handle it. Now y'all get out of here. This is weird." But as we file out, she says "Babe."

"Yeah?"

"You better be glad I'm not at my fighting weight, or I'd kick your skinny ass."

Babe laughs, but it's tinged with sadness. "You're real threatening sitting there with your pants around your ankles. Now, hurry up. We've got places to be."

Once in the hall, Babe's tears begin to fall. I take her into my arms.

"It's so hard to see her so helpless," she sobs into my neck.

"It is."

"I don't think I can do this, Hope."

I rub her back. "Me either."

For years, I've wondered how we would survive watching June die. And now that we're standing on the precipice of that place where the black curtain of grief, fear, and uncertainty hides what's beyond, I still don't have the answer.

The toilet flushes, and Aaron pushes past into the bathroom to help June.

I take Babe by the shoulders and look her in the eye. "We may not be able to win this battle, but we can still give cancer a hell of a fight. For June."

She takes a couple of stuttering breaths, then repeats. "For June."

I don't know if fighting is enough. I don't know if showing up is enough. I don't know if love is enough.

But it's all we have.

Aaron and June appear in the hallway. She's so weak he's having to support most of her weight. "We should head out," Aaron says.

I take a breath. Time to find out if Dr. Yovan can help us.

We arrive at Dr. Yovan's office at eight forty-five a.m. The waiting room is sterile and quiet. Too quiet. There's nothing to distract us from our terrifying, racing thoughts.

By the time we got here, June couldn't walk. We had to use a wheelchair to get her from the car to the office. The rate of her decline is shocking, making it impossible to find steady emotional footing.

I've made myself an expert in this terrible disease to protect us. Knowledge has always been what's strengthened me.

Education has been what I've wrapped myself in to guard against all my feelings of inadequacy. But there is no safe place in any of this. We're in enemy territory, and our enemy is playing a game for which there are no rules.

Ten years ago, Ian and I drove the Road to Hana on our anniversary trip in Maui. At one point we were trying to drive up a very large hill in the little convertible we'd rented. The road was loose gravel, and the car was no match for that hill. We'd move forward three feet and think we were making progress, then the gravel would shift and we'd slide back five feet. It was impossible to get any traction. And to make matters worse, there was a huge drop-off on the left side of the hill, with no guardrail.

That's how I feel now. Every time I think I have a handle on what to do next, or what will help June or my family, the ground shifts and we slide back past where we started, with nothing to grab onto. It's exhausting in its futility. But we can't stop. We can't go back. We have to keep moving forward.

The door to the patient rooms opens. A young woman in light blue scrubs calls June's name. We all stand.

"Just June and one other person," the nurse says.

Aaron goes without question. The rest of us sit back down.

Mom reaches for my hand. "He's going to help her. I know he is."

I want to believe her. But my research tells me the odds aren't good.

Twenty minutes pass.

Thirty.

Forty-five.

Finally, the door opens again. Aaron's face is unreadable. "He says you can all come back."

We all crowd into the small patient room. June is resting on the exam table, looking even weaker than she did when Aaron wheeled her back here.

Dr. Yovan doesn't waste time. "I believe I can help you, June."

Seven words can change everything.

Mom gasps and grabs Aaron's arm. Good thing too, because he looks like he might fall to the floor. Dad grabs the back of a chair to steady himself. Babe leans against the wall and buries her face in her hands.

I stand frozen. I prepared myself for the worst, and now that the opposite is happening, I have no idea what to do. Finally, I ask, "What happens next?"

"Because chemo doesn't cross the blood-brain barrier," Dr. Yovan says, "we'll need to implant a well in your head that delivers the chemo directly to the cerebral fluid and spinal fluid."

A well? In her head?

"Is that what you want?" he asks.

My mom and Aaron immediately say, "Yes."

Dr. Yovan ignores my mother and brother-in-law and keeps his gaze on June. "Is that what you want, June?"

"Will I feel better?" Her voice is barely above a whisper. "Will the pain be better?"

"If the treatment works, yes. Your symptoms should improve. But you should know this isn't a cure. It can give you more time with your family, but I can't cure you."

June rotates her head toward Aaron, and it's clear that move takes every ounce of her strength..

Aaron nods, and the plea in his eyes is a blade to my gut.

"Yes," she whispers.

"Very well," Dr. Yovan says. "I'll have my PA explain the next steps. When he's done, I want you to go directly to the ER.

We'll admit you through there and perform the surgery in the morning."

"So soon?" Mom asks.

"Yes. I don't believe we have any time to waste." He makes a few notes on his electronic pad. When he's done, he squeezes June's shoulder. "We'll take good care of you, June."

When the door closes behind him, Aaron, Mom, and Dad rush to June's side. Babe slides down the wall that's been holding her up for the last few minutes. Her butt hits the ground, and tears spill from her eyes.

I stand there, unable to move.

He can help her. He can actually help her.

But he also said he can't cure her. This buys time, that's all. Borrowed time.

I pull out my phone and text Joy, Grace, and Carrie. My finger hovers over Ian's number. I hit it and send him the same text. Not because I want to, but I know it's what June would want.

The next couple of hours are a blur of medical histories, admissions, pain maintenance, and the slightest bit of hope.

Mom, Dad, and I go to the hospital cafeteria while the admissions process is going on.

"This is good news, don't you think?" Mom asks. It's clear she's riding the thin line between hysteria and despair.

I unwrap my sandwich. "Yes. But you did hear him say he couldn't cure her, right?"

"He can't, but God can. This gives us more time for that to happen," Mom says, like it's a foregone conclusion.

I sneak a glance at my dad to see what his response to this is, only to be met with another one of those silent tears rolling down his cheek.

Words that I've been holding back since I saw him standing

over June this morning escape my lips before I can think better of it. "Dad, I saw you this morning in June's room."

He looks up, and there's no hiding the flush of red spreading up his neck and over his cheeks.

"If you want to stroke her head, then stroke her head. If you want to hug her, then hug her. Hell, if you want to crawl into bed with her and hold her, do it. We don't know how long we have. We should all take every opportunity to show her how much we love her." All this is said to the sandwich in my hand. Somehow, it feels less invasive.

His weathered, tan, sun-spotted hand comes into my vision and he places his hand over mine. "I think that's good advice, Hope."

I raise my gaze to his and see relief there. It's a small stitch in the wound that is our relationship.

After lunch, we make our way back to the ER waiting room, where we see Babe and Aaron. Why isn't one of them with June?

"Hey, what's up?" I ask.

"I had to go outside to get service to call Clay," Babe says.

"June's hungry. So I'm going to get her some food," Aaron says.

"Did the doctors say she could eat?" June is not known as a rule follower, so I want to make sure this food run is a sanctioned activity.

Aaron looks confused. "She said they did."

I exchange a look with Babe. "I'll be right back." I push through the doors to the patient area and head for June's room.

There's a lot of activity. Nurses and security personnel are hustling around like they've lost something.

I slip into June's room and pull back the curtain.

June is sitting up, laughing with a man seated next to her bed.

A naked man.

"Hey, Hope," June says, like there isn't a nude stranger with a People magazine strategically placed over his lap. "Have you met my good friend, Garrett?" The sentence comes out as one boneless word. She's clearly been given the good drugs again.

"Um, no. I haven't had the pleasure."

June swings her arm in my direction. "Garrett, this my number one sister, Hope." Her speech pattern has the consistency of a wet noodle.

Garrett starts to stand. "Keep your seat, Garrett." I look to June. "So, what's up?"

"Garrett's hiding from the staff," she explains. "They're being totally unweas... unweasnon..." She stops and forms her lips carefully around each syllable. "Un-rea-son-able, by trying to make him take medication he doesn't need."

Garrett turns his pale hazel eyes to me. "I'm not unstable."

He's sitting naked in my dying sister's hospital room, his bits covered by Brad Pitt's face, insisting there's not a thing in the world wrong with him.

June leans toward him. "Here's an idea. What if you went back to your room, took the medicine, and showed them there was nothing wrong with you to begin with? Whaddya think?" She tries to pat his shoulder, but misses. Thank God, the man is filthy.

Garrett nibbles a grubby thumbnail. "Beat 'em at their own game." He winks at June. "I like it."

June does that owl blink thing she did the last time she was in the hospital and high as a kite.

Our visitor rubs his scraggly beard and chuckles. "I can't wait to see that battle-axe of a nurse when I prove her wrong."

June rests her head back onto the pillow and smiles, but it's tinged with discomfort. The meds must be wearing off. "It'll be hard, but don't rub it in. Remember, she's just tryin' to do her job."

He wags his finger at June, like she's said the wisest thing he's ever heard. "Nobody likes a braggart."

"Exactly," she whispers.

I'm in awe of my sister in this moment. Her ability to just be in an out-of-control situation is humbling.

I wish I were more like her. My brain has been working nonstop since I walked in here, trying to figure out how I can get this man out of here. Unlike June, who isn't the least bit bothered by the insanity of this situation.

Garrett takes her hand and I immediately want to slap it away and bathe her in hand sanitizer. She must see my intention because she shakes her head ever so slightly at me.

"Before I go, Ms. June, can I pray for you?"

She closes her eyes and sighs. "I would love that, Garrett."

He holds his hand out to me, but I deliberately fold both of mine beneath my chin. The universal sign for prayer. He nods approvingly and says, "Let's pray."

We all bow our heads.

"Lord," Garrett begins. "I pray for my sister June here. I call down your angels to surround her and comfort her." He's silent for a moment, and I think he's done, then he yells, "Oh, Lord! You're the mighty healer and a good, good father. We beg for healing for my friend June. We know you have all the power in the universe, so this cancer is nothing for you to defeat. Heal my sister, Lord. Heal her in the most fantastic way possible, so that there can be no doubt as to who healed her. And if you choose to heal her by giving her a new body in Heaven, carry her there in your loving arms and give her and her family all the comfort Heaven has to offer. In your sweet, sweet name, Amen."

The last word of the most powerful, lucid prayer I've ever

heard lingers in the air like tolling from a bell tower. June and I share a tear-filled look.

Where did that come from?

Garrett stands, and the magazine falls to the ground. He steps closer to June and places his hand on her head. "God bless you, Ms. June."

My sister takes his dirty hand and brings it to her cheek. "Thank you, Garrett."

"Well, I guess I'd better go show these yahoos that they're a bunch of idiots. Nice to meet you, Hope."

"It was very nice to meet you, Garrett. Would you like a blanket?"

His bushy eyebrows scrunch together like two caterpillars kissing. "Why?"

I shake my head. "No reason."

He moves to the door and leaves without another word.

Our parents come in as he's leaving. My mom looks over her shoulder. "What's going on?" As if finding a naked man in her fourth daughter's hospital room is odd, but not completely unexpected.

June presses the blanket to her wet eyes and laughs. "I think we were just visited by a naked angel." She looks to me for confirmation.

"Pretty much."

# Chapter Twenty-Two

The surgery that was supposed to happen this morning ended up being delayed until late this afternoon, due to an emergency with one of Dr. Yovan's other patients. We're all gathered in the surgical waiting room. Over the last few hours, we've paced, bickered, shared memes, and chewed our nails to the quick.

Thankfully, they had June so medicated that she didn't notice the change in schedule. But the rest of us have been twitchy as a bunch of hens peckin' at corn. The Jameses are a lot of things but peaceful and patient aren't two of them.

So, when we hear footsteps coming down the hall, we all jump to attention, only to be disappointed when Ian swings into the room with a to-go carafe of coffee in one hand and a brown paper bag with Sandy's Sandwiches printed on it in the other.

"Ian!" Clay yells.

Well, almost all of us were disappointed. Of course, Ian's fan club president is glad to see him.

"Hey, y'all. I thought you might need some sustenance."

He holds up the cardboard carafe. "And hospital coffee is notoriously bad." He sets everything on the small side table underneath the television mounted on the wall.

Clay falls on the sandwiches like he hasn't eaten in a week. "Thanks, Ian," he says through a mouthful of food.

Ian chuckles and slaps him on the shoulder. "No problem, bud." Then he turns to my mom. "Can I get you a cup of coffee, Marie?"

"Yes, please." Mom motions toward the spread. "This is very thoughtful of you, Ian. Thank you."

"You're welcome, Marie." He dispenses the coffee into a paper cup, then asks, "Anyone else?"

Everyone, except me, accepts his offer. He sets about fixing their coffees. Once he's handed out the drinks, he turns to me. "Hope, what about you?"

A snarky answer about how he probably doesn't know how I like my coffee lurks just behind my lips, but I bite it back and say, "Yes, thank you."

I move to the door of the waiting room and glance toward the surgery center. I've got bigger problems than the fact that my ex-husband is here with food and drinks for my family.

"Coming right up."

I'm surprised at how happy my answer seems to make him. Whatever. My gaze goes back to the double doors at the end of the hall.

"Here you go." He hands me the paper cup. "One sweetener and sweet cream."

Apparently, he does know how I like my coffee. I sip my drink and resist the urge to moan. He's right. I tried the hospital coffee earlier and feared I'd been poisoned.

"Thank you."

"I wish y'all'd quit thanking me. Do you want a sandwich?"

"I'll get it."

At the food table, I grab a turkey and Swiss on wheat. I remove the tomatoes, because who wants a soggy sandwich, and watch my family. The pent-up anxiety that had us all in a chokehold moments before is gone while they all eat and drink. Strange how something so simple can change the room's temperature. Ian did that. Gratitude expands in my chest and refuses to remain contained.

I search the room for Ian to thank him, but don't see him. "Did Ian leave?" I ask Clay. If anyone knows where Ian is, it's his biggest fan.

"He went out in the hallway to make a call," he says around a mouthful of ham and cheese.

I nod and leave the room to find my ex-husband, who is on a call.

"Yeah, thanks, Bob. Be sure to tell Marcy that I'm sorry I can't make it."

At the sound of Marcy's name, my legs stop working. I want to retreat back into the waiting room, but I cannot move. I'm frozen in place by masochistic curiosity.

*Marcy. Baby. Ian.*

He looks up and sees me. "Listen, Bob, I've got to go. Tell her I said congratulations." He slides his phone into his pocket. "Sorry. Marcy Williams is getting married tonight. Bob and I were going to ride together. I needed to let him know I can't make it. I'd like to stay until Bug gets out of surgery, if that's okay?"

I nod. I can't answer because something short-circuits in my brain. Are those English words he's speaking? They don't make sense. Finally, I manage, "She is?"

He chuckles and rubs the back of his neck "Yeah. I'm happy for her, but I'm also losing one of my best salespeople. She's pregnant and is going to stay home with the baby for a while."

I'm mute. I have no outward reaction to this information. But internally... I don't have words for what's happening. If I had to give it a name? Relieved. And then, right behind it, more than a little embarrassed.

The reality I've been living in since I saw Marcy from my bathroom stall hiding place hasn't been real. I created it, nurtured it, then tortured myself with it because it fit some screwed-up narrative about my life.

*How could I be so wrong about something so important? What else have I been wrong about?*

Ian must take my silence for disinterest because he asks, "Are there any chicken salad sandwiches left?"

All I can muster is another nod, and frankly, I'm surprised I can even do that.

"I'd better grab one before Clay eats 'em all." He moves past me into the waiting room.

"Okay," I say after he's already gone.

Marcy's pregnant with someone else's baby.

Ian's not going to be a father. I'm shocked to find that there's a small part of me that's sad for him.

I pull out my phone and shoot a quick text to Carrie.

*The baby's not Ian's.*

My phone rings immediately, and I answer. "Hey."

"How do you know?" Carrie asks.

"I just overheard him giving his regrets for not attending her wedding today." I peek back into the room to make sure Ian is still by the food. "I doubt she'd be getting married to someone else if the baby was his."

"Right." I can hear the relief in Carrie's voice. "So he's there, at the hospital?"

I lean my shoulder against the wall. "Yes. He brought food."

"That was nice of him." She says it like someone holding their hand out to a stray they're not sure they can trust.

"It was." That's all I'm willing to give, regardless of how grateful I am for the distraction. That probably makes me petty but right now, I don't care.

"Any word?" Carrie asks.

I return to my family. "Not yet. I'll let you know."

"I'll be waiting. Tell everyone I love them."

I disconnect the call and say, "That was Carrie. She sends her love."

"She's the best," Joy says. "Did you know she's volunteered to be on call for Max and Chloe while we're all out of pocket?"

I take a cookie from the food table. "I didn't know, but I'm not surprised."

We continue our milling, pacing, and hand wringing. After what seems like an eternity, Dr. Yovan appears in the doorway.

"How is she?" Mom asks.

"June came through the surgery like a champ. The well was inserted successfully. We'll monitor her for a few hours, then she will be discharged. I'll see her in my office tomorrow for her first dose of chemo."

Mom jumps up and wraps her arms around him. "Oh, thank you, Jesus."

"Dr. Yovan," he says.

The crying woman wrapped around him looks up, confused. "Pardon?"

"Doc's got jokes." Clay laughs.

The tips of the stoic physician's ears redden. "I'm sorry. A little doctor humor."

Mom steps back and dabs at her nose with a tissue. "Then you'll fit in perfectly with this bunch."

"When can we see her?" Aaron asks.

"In about an hour. The nurse will come and get you."

Dad stands and extends his hand to Dr. Yovan. "Thank you for taking care of our girl."

The doctor takes his hand. "My pleasure."

"Um, before you go," I say. "How long until we know if the medication is working?"

He takes off the cap he's wearing and slips it into the back pocket of his scrubs. "Every time we treat her, we'll withdraw a bit of cerebral fluid, then we'll administer the chemo. We evaluate the markers from that bit of fluid. If her numbers improve, then we know it's working. There should also be an improvement in symptoms."

I nod, too relieved to speak. The thought that June will get some relief from the horrible pain makes my muscles go slack.

"But I do want to reiterate, this is not a cure. It is a treatment that can give her more time, maybe as much as twelve months, but this disease will ultimately take her life." He looks at my mother, then Aaron. "I'm sorry to be blunt, but I've found that having realistic expectations is the best path forward in these circumstances." He nods. "I'll see you tomorrow."

My gaze travels to June's husband, who's sitting with his elbows on his knees, hands clasped together and head bowed. I want to go to him, but can't. I hate that he's sitting there alone. But my feet will simply not move. His pain is an inferno that will burn me alive if I get too close. Relief floods through me when Ian moves to his side and places his big hand on Aaron's shoulder.

Ian and I lock eyes, and his clearly say, *Deal with your own pain. I've got this.*

The silence in the room is suffocating. It's like Dr. Yovan took all the oxygen with him when he left.

I search for something encouraging to say, anything to save us from asphyxiating, but I can't think of a thing that will help.

Just when I think the anguish will consume each of us,

Clay says, "He's got jokes, but his bedside manner is fuckin' awful."

The collective gasps aren't from the shock of the F bomb, but from finding a pocket of air, where we can draw a clean breath.

"True that," Joy agrees. "I bet he's fun at parties."

"Can you imagine him in bed?" Grace says.

"Grace Katherine," Mom scolds. But her reproach is lost when she snort laughs.

Grace clears her throat. "Thank you for sex. It was satisfactory. Perhaps we could partake once more?" It's a respectable impression of the doctor.

Laughter beats back the hopelessness, if only for a moment.

That elephant on the trapeze is getting a workout.

I look at Clay, smile, and nod.

He winks. Who would've thought that Clay would be the one to save us all from drowning in the despair that was quickly filling the room?

And just like that, we're back, united with the common goal of walking June along this unbearable path—as a family.

# Chapter Twenty-Three

The black and blue bruise forming on the right side of June's forehead is impressive, but the swollen bump just above it, where they placed the well, is the real star of the show. She's a badass, always has been. But lying there with her eyes closed, battered and bruised, she looks fragile as spun sugar in a heavy breeze. It's disorienting.

Mom goes to her and gently caresses the injured areas.

Her eyes flutter open. "Hi, Mom."

"Hi, Junie." One of Mom's tears drops onto my sister's face.

"Mom, you're leaking," she says.

Mom thumbs the tear from Junes' cheek. "I am. Sorry about that. The doctor said the surgery was successful."

"Good," June breathes.

Aaron kisses the uninjured side of her forehead. "Hey, baby."

The sweet smile on my sister's face is heartrending. "Hey, you." She tries to raise her hand but can't quite make it all the way to his face. "I'm weak as a newborn colt."

We're all standing around her bed. All nine of us are touching her, silently lending her our strength.

The nurse comes in to turn off a beeping machine. "How are you doing, June?"

"Tired," is all she can muster.

"That's a combination of anesthesia and pain meds. You probably will be for a while." She looks at us. "You all should get some rest too. She's most likely going to sleep until morning."

"You all go. I'll stay with her," Babe volunteers.

"No, I'll stay," Aaron says.

Babe points to the small love seat in the room. "There's no way you can sleep on that," she says to our six-foot-three-inch brother-in-law. "Go home, take care of your animals, and get some sleep, then you'll be rested to take care of her when she comes home tomorrow."

He eyes the two-person couch that folds out into a bed. "Alright, but you'll call me if anything happens."

Babe raises her right hand. "Promise."

"Babe, are you sure you're up for this?" Grace asks, voicing what we're all thinking.

Babe is a very capable woman, but she doesn't always realize her capabilities. That's probably our fault. All her life, we've all taken care of her.

Her chin juts out like a pissed-off toddler. "I can handle it, Grace."

"Nobody's saying you can't handle it. I'm only wondering if you're up for it," Grace tries again.

"Yes, I'm up for it. Besides, they said she'd sleep most of the night. There shouldn't be that much to handle."

"And that settles it," Mom, ever the peacemaker, says. "We'll get some sleep and get ready for June to come home tomorrow."

We say our goodbyes and leave. The sudden transition from the cold hospital to the warm outside air shocks gooseflesh over my skin. I wrap my arms around myself. A warm jacket is placed on my shoulders and I turn to see Ian standing behind me. I step away from him and the coat. "I'm fine."

"You looked cold."

"Just chilled. I'll be fine as soon as I get into my car."

He doesn't press the issue, only drapes his jacket over his arm. "How are you holding up? I know it's a lot."

It's a living nightmare and more than I ever imagined I could bear, but I don't say that. "It is a lot."

He slips his hands into the front pockets of his jeans. "The doctor didn't make this treatment sound like a miracle cure."

I bite the inside of my lip and look up at the moon. When I look back at Ian, he's looking at the moon too. He's uncharacteristically patient. Usually, he wants information quickly and succinctly, so he can fix whatever problem is in front of him.

"The leptomeningeal disease is terminal. You heard Dr. Yovan say there's no cure. But if he can give her more time, even if it's only the year he mentioned, it will be worth it." I lower my eyes and shrug. "It's better than six to twelve weeks."

"I'm so damn sorry, Hope." His voice breaks on my name.

My head comes up, and I see the raw pain in his eyes. No quick fix. No dismissal. Just honest, unadulterated agony for me, for him, for the whole horrible situation. "Me too."

His gaze goes to the moon again. "I want to wrap my arms around you and try to take some of the pain away." He looks back at me, judging my reaction to what he said.

I take a step back because somewhere deep inside, I want the same thing. But he's not safe. He left me in every way possible. So, I don't respond to his declaration. "Thank you for the coffee and sandwiches. They really made a difference."

"I'm glad it helped."

His feelings aren't mine to carry. I'm exhausted from holding my family's emotions, not to mention my own.

I motion to my car. "I'm going to go."

He nods. "Night, Hope."

"Good night, Ian." I don't look back on my way to my car, or when I reverse out of my parking spot, or when I pull out of the lot. There's no use. There's nothing for me there.

# Chapter Twenty-Four

The ringing of my phone jars me from fitful sleep. I reluctantly claw my way to consciousness and answer without looking at the screen. "Hello."

"Hope!" Babe's frantic voice drills into my ear.

"What's wrong, Babe?"

"It's June. They think she's had a stroke."

"What?" I check the time. It's three a.m. and I'm now fully awake. "Tell me what happened." Her labored breathing blows through the phone. "Babe, listen to me."

"Yeah." Her voice is small and fragile.

"Take a deep breath."

"Okay."

"Now another." I hear her follow my instructions and switch my phone to hands-free mode so I can get dressed. "Alright, now tell me what happened."

"Um... Well... It's been a bad night. She's been in a lot of pain and kind of agitated. I've never seen her like this. She kept calling the nurse in, and when she wasn't doing that, she wanted me to be right beside her, which of course I didn't mind, but it wasn't like her, you know?"

I slip my shirt over my head. "Mm-hmm."

"Anyway, I thought we'd finally gotten her comfortable, so I went back to the love seat, but she called me over again. I asked her what she needed, thinking it was her pillow or to cover her feet, or to call the nurse, but she had trouble telling me what was wrong. Then, while she was talking, she started slurring her words and dropping her head to the side." She takes a shaky breath. "It was so scary, Hope."

"It sounds terrifying."

"I called the nurse, and before I knew it, there were six people in the room. They turned on all the lights and kicked me out into the hall. I was bawlin' and had no idea what to do. I've never felt so helpless."

"You did good, Babe. You got her help. That was your job, and you did good." My lack of proper grammar isn't important right now. My sister's feelings are.

More sniffles come through the line. "Thanks."

"Where is she now?"

"They took her for a CAT scan. They said it could be a stroke, Hope. A. Stroke. How is this happening?"

"I don't know, Babe. It's awful." I slip my feet into my sneakers and tie them. "Did you call Aaron?"

"Yes."

"Anyone else?"

"Grace, Joy, and Clay."

"But not Mom and Dad?"

"No. I couldn't tell them." She begins to cry again.

"That's okay. They're right down the hall. I'll tell them, then we'll head that way. Do you want me to stay on the phone with you?"

A few more stuttered breaths. "It's alright. I'm back in her room now. I'll be fine until someone gets here."

I know it will take at least forty-five minutes for any of us to get there. "Call Ian. He can be there faster than any of us."

"Are you sure?"

"Yes." And I find that I mean it. "I don't want you to be by yourself. We'll be there as fast as we can, but in the meantime, you have to be her advocate, Babe."

"Okay." She doesn't sound at all confident.

"Listen to me, Babe. If you're concerned about anything, get the nurse back into that room. If you don't understand something they say, ask them to explain it as many times as you need to understand. If they're doing something you don't like, tell them. You are her voice. She can't advocate for herself. She needs you to stand in the gap for her. I know you can do that for her."

The crying on the other end of the line abruptly ends. "I can. I will." She no longer sounds like my younger, more vulnerable sister.

"Good. Don't take any shit."

"If they try"—she sniffs back any remaining tears—"they'll find they've messed with the wrong person." The badassery in her voice is so surprising and unexpected that it makes me smile.

"You got this, killer." I chuckle. "There's no one I would trust more with June's well-being than you. We'll be there as fast as we can. Love you."

"I love you."

We disconnect the call. I rest my elbow on my knee and drop my head into my hand. I should've stayed. Maybe if I'd been there—

*You couldn't have stopped this*, the voice in my head says.

It's right. I know it, but that only eases the guilt slightly.

I take several deep breaths to beat back my own panic and make my way to my parents' room. I know why Babe didn't want to call them. They were so hopeful after her surgery.

Now I'm the one who gets to crush those hopes.

I crack the door open and knock. "Mom. Dad."

Mom bolts upright. "Huh? What? Who is it?"

I move to her side of the bed and flip on the bedside light. "It's me, Mom."

She grabs her glasses and slips them on. "Is it June?"

"Is what June?" Dad says and sits up.

"Yes. Babe just called. She's had..." I don't want to say the word *stroke* until we're sure that's what happened. "An episode."

Dad's already out of bed and moving to get his clothes on. "What kind of episode?" His voice cracks. He clears his throat. "Is she..." He can't finish the question.

"They're not sure what happened." I hand Mom her robe. "She's getting a scan now, but Babe said we should come."

Mom, who's standing by the bed as if she's not sure what her next move should be, says, "But they said everything went well."

"That doesn't matter now, Marie. Get your clothes on. We gotta go," my dad barks.

Usually, I'd be offended on my mom's behalf at his abrupt order, but in this instance, I appreciate his urgency, and it works.

Mom jumps into action and is dressed in a few minutes.

"Where the hell are my boots?" Dad yells.

"They're by the back door, Russ." Even though I can see the panic rising in Mom's eyes, her voice has the same soft tone she uses with my dad when he's about to lose his cool. "Why don't you go start the truck, and we'll be down in a minute."

Without a word of acknowledgment, he walks out the door.

Mom grabs a light jacket from her closet. "Ready?"

"I'm worried about Dad," I say honestly.

She stops on her way out the door and looks at me. "You are?"

"Well, yeah." I'm a little offended by the surprise in her voice. "I mean, let's face it, he's not really equipped to handle this."

"None of us are, Hope." Tears make every word as thick as tree sap. "Not one of us, but that doesn't mean we aren't going to keep goin'. Remember what I used to say when y'all were kids?"

I grin in spite of everything going on around me. "We're the Jameses, and we don't give up."

"Y'all need to come on," my dad yells from downstairs.

"On our way," Mom calls back and heads for the stairs. She turns to me. "You comin'?"

"Yes."

She holds her hand out to me, and I take it. "Let's go and not give up."

# Chapter Twenty-Five

June didn't have a stroke, thank God. But she did have a seizure, which has earned her a continued stay in the hospital.

Her coordination has also been affected. She can't walk without assistance. No one can say for sure if it's from the surgery, the seizure, or the leptomeningeal disease. Either way, she can't be left alone. Not that we would. Remember, we travel in a pack.

We set up a schedule. Between the four sisters, my parents, and Aaron, someone is always with her. At June's insistence, Aaron is still working his normal job, which includes traveling. It's another way for June to shield him from the reality of her disease. And I realize now, she's been doing that throughout her entire cancer journey.

No criticism—it's how they've handled a horrible situation. I have no idea how I would've navigated ten years of stage four cancer. But I do think it's allowed him a measure of separation from some of the realities of her illness, and the present situation is no different.

"She seems agitated to me," Mom whispers to me while the nurse is doing her hourly assessment. "Like, she just can't get comfortable."

"Babe said that's how she was last night, too." I watch June rub her eye, then close one, then the other, for the tenth time in the last hour.

"June, do you have something in your eye?" I ask from my position on the sofa. We've been moved to a better room with a full sofa and a recliner since they decided to extend her stay.

She flops her hand down on the bed. "I don't know. It's like I have fuzz or something in this one."

"Let me take a look," her nurse, Katie, says. She examines June's right eye. "Hmm." She pulls out a penlight. "June, I'm going to shine a light in your eyes, okay?"

"Can I stop you?"

Katie laughs. "Probably not."

"Then do your worst."

Katie is as sweet as pie. Unfortunately, June is acting like she hates pie, which indicates how off she must feel.

Katie takes a few moments to shine the light into both eyes, then clicks it off and returns it to her pocket. "Done. That wasn't too bad, was it?"

"It was fine, but why couldn't I see it as well in my right eye?"

That sentence is like a cattle prod to the nervous system for the three of us on the sofa.

"What do you mean you couldn't see it as well out of your right eye?" I ask.

"It's like it's muted. Like she put tissue paper over it or something."

Our heads swivel to Katie, who looks concerned. "June, your right pupil is a little larger than the left."

"What does that mean?" Dad asks.

Katie writes a few things down on a piece of paper she pulls from her pocket, then types something into the computer. "I'm not sure. I'm going to call the doctor and see what he wants to do."

I move to June's side, and sure enough, her right pupil is bigger than the left. "Is it from the surgery?"

"I don't know." She slides the computer's keyboard back under the monitor. "Let's see what the doctor says."

After she leaves, the three of us not in the hospital bed share concerned looks, but June seems oddly unaffected.

"Mom?"

Our mother moves to June's other side. "Yes, baby."

"Will you hold my hand?" Maybe June's more affected than she appears.

A sweet smile stretches my mother's face. "I sure will."

The door to the room flies open, and a beautiful, petite, brown-skinned woman enters the room in a cloud of Jungle Gardenia perfume. On anyone else, it would be too much, but on Aaron's mother, Betty Ann, it's just right. She rushes to my sister. "Oh, sweet girl."

I move so she can have my place next to June.

A broad smile splits June's pale, bruised face. "Hi, Betty Ann. I thought you were in North Carolina."

"I was, but Aaron called during the night, and I took the first flight home."

June frowns. "You didn't have to do that. I know your mom needs you there."

"Don't you worry about that. My sister flew in to help with Mom so that I could be here. They both send their love." She lightly caresses June's face. "How is my girl?"

June closes her eyes and leans into Betty Ann's touch. "Not too good."

I'm caught off guard by a couple of things. One, I didn't know June and Betty Ann had such a close relationship. Two, that June admitted she isn't doing well. It's so unlike her to admit she's feeling bad. It rattles me.

And in that moment, I realize that Aaron's not the only one June has been protecting. It's been all of us.

Mom is equally affected, if the tears slipping from her eyes are any indication.

I get Betty Ann a chair. She sits on June's other side and takes her hand. I focus on the two of them. I can't look at my mother or I'll lose it too.

And I have to keep it together.

My family is depending on me.

June is depending on me.

I won't let them all down.

"Oh, honey, your hands are so dry," Betty Ann says. She bends over and digs into the tote bag she brought, retrieving a tube of lotion. "Do you mind if I put some lotion on you?"

The patient still has her eyes closed, but she says, "That would be nice."

Betty Ann begins by moisturizing June's hands, which soon turns into a massage. A ghost of a smile settles on my sister's face, and a deep moan rises from her throat. The tension in her features relaxes, and within minutes, she's asleep.

"That's the first time she's slept since right after her surgery," Mom says.

Betty Ann never takes her attention from her work. "Who doesn't like a good hand massage?" She looks at Mom. "Switch with me, Marie?"

The two switch places, and Betty Ann continues her ministrations. The gentleness and care she brings to her task cause a knot of tears to form in my throat.

So many people love my sister.

If love were a cure, then June would be healed.

Love isn't a cure, but it does make this whole situation a lot more bearable and, at the same time, so much more unbearable.

It's a hellish paradox that I wouldn't wish on my worst enemy.

# Chapter Twenty-Six

"Joy, if you offer me that damn chocolate pudding again, I'm gonna shove it down your throat."

Joy laughs. "You and what army, Junie?"

Two weeks later, and we're still in the hospital. June's had four treatments, and according to Dr. Yovan, her numbers are improving. Unfortunately, her physical condition is not and, in some ways, is worse. She's now mostly blind in her right eye and began losing sight in her left a couple of days ago. She also has virtually no appetite.

A smile spreads over June's face. "You got me there. I couldn't even whip Babe's ass in this condition."

"Hey!" The Baby says from the recliner. "I'm a pacifist. Besides, you always fought anyone who crossed the line with me before I had a chance. Poor Scooby Reynolds. He's never been the same since you took him to the ground in ninth grade for standing me up at the homecoming dance."

June chuckles weakly. "Good times."

I change out the cold cloth on June's head. "You do realize

that you're the only one of us who has actually been in a physical altercation, right?"

"Yeah." The pride in her tone makes me laugh.

"You're incorrigible."

June holds up her hand. "Somebody hold my hand." It's a request she's been making more often in the last few days.

Grace moves to her side and takes hold of her baby-pink-tipped fingers. A few days ago, June's friends had someone come to the hospital to do her nails. That small kindness made my sister so happy.

"I got you." As soon as Grace takes June's hand, she visibly relaxes.

All four of us are here this evening. I'll stay the night, but Grace, Joy, and Babe didn't want to leave when everyone else left earlier.

Over the last ten years, I've occasionally let my mind wander to the place where the cancer came for June and wondered how my family would survive it. And now that we're here, it's like we were born for this. Like our job, since before we were formed, was to walk her to the end of her life.

Joy moves the tray of food that June's barely touched to the counter by the door. "It's getting late. We should probably go so you can get some sleep, June."

Babe checks her phone. "Yeah, we should probably go."

The three of them begin to gather their bags and purses. I look over at June and she has a panicked look on her face. "What's wrong, June? Are you okay?"

"No."

Purses and bags forgotten, we're all at her side in an instant.

"What is it?" The concern in Babe's voice is a living, breathing thing.

June searches for Babe's hand. "I don't want y'all to leave. Can you stay?"

"Sure, we can stay a little while longer," Grace says.

June shakes her head. "No. Can you stay the night?"

"Yes," Babe says without hesitation.

Grace, Joy, and I look at each other, then at the accommodations, knowing we'll all be sleeping sitting up, if we sleep at all.

Joy shrugs. "Absolutely. I haven't seen my chiropractor in a while. It'll be good to see her again."

Grace laughs. "Yeah, we'll stay."

"Thank you." The two words come out on a tiny sob. "Oh, wait, what about Max and Chloe?"

"Chloe's at Carrie's. I'll text and see if she can spend the night. I'm sure it won't be a problem," Joy says.

"And Max is already spending the night at a friend's," Grace adds. "But I do need to make a call." Grace exits the room without looking at any of us, but we all, including Joy, know she's calling Jimmy.

I hold my breath and wait for Joy to explode, but she barely reacts. Instead she says, "Babe, if we're gonna have a slumber party, we need snacks. Let's go hit the vending machines."

June's nurse Katie comes in as they're leaving. She's become our favorite over the last couple of weeks. She gets June in a way some of the other nurses don't. "June, it's time for your meds."

I catch Katie's eye. "I'm glad you're here." I don't want to voice my concern in front of June, but begging my sisters to stay the night is definitely out of character for her.

Katie immediately picks up on what I'm concerned about. "What's going on?"

With her head against the pillow, June slowly turns toward Katie. "I don't know. I just feel weird."

This is bad. Really bad. June tries very hard to be the model patient. She hates to call the nurses in or bother them, so for her to admit this to Katie, and in front of me, means something is definitely not right.

Katie begins her routine exam. "Weird, like how? Are you in more pain?" Her tone is casual, but I can see that her examination is not.

"My head does hurt, but..."

"Yes?" Katie asks while checking the IV bag.

"I feel like I might be dying."

Katie scans the medication she brought in on a little tray with the scanner on the computer. "Oh. Tell me more about that," she asks, like she's asking about a recipe.

"I don't know. I kind of feel like I'm not connected to my body. And... I don't think I can see out of my left eye."

"Mmm-hmm."

I appreciate that Katie's trying not to alarm any of us, but a little urgency might be in order. All I want to do is run from the room screaming, My sister thinks she's dying. Somebody, help!

Once she's injected June's medication into the IV line, Katie checks her eyes with the penlight again. "June, can you see the light?"

"No."

"Not on either side?"

"No."

Katie closes out her session on the computer. "Okay. Let me call the doctor. I'll be back in a minute."

I've nearly bitten through my cheek, and my palms have nail marks. I'm fighting for control like never before. I can't break down right now. But the cruelty of this disease is almost more than I can take. Hasn't my sister suffered enough? Now it takes her eyesight.

"Hope!" The urgency in June's voice jolts me out of my anger.

I take her hand. "I'm here."

"Don't leave me alone."

"I wouldn't. I won't."

June fumbles around for my shirt. She grabs it and pulls me to her. "DNR, Hope."

"What?"

"D.N.R." She says the three letters succinctly and carefully, like she knows she's dropping a bomb and hates it, but it has to be done.

"You want a DNR?"

"Yes," she gasps.

"You know what that means, right?"

She nods. "I don't want to be kept alive on some machine. Tell Aaron."

"Honey, you know I'd do just about anything for you, but I think that's something you have to tell him." I hate denying her anything, but I can't fulfill her request.

"Call him." The plea is soft but no less commanding.

"Okay." I dial the number and put it on speaker.

He answers on the first ring. "Hope? Is everything alright?"

"It's me, Aaron," June says.

"Oh, hey, darlin'." His voice immediately changes from alarmed to the honey-rich tone he uses with June.

"Aaron, I want a DNR." There's no preamble, only the heartbreaking announcement.

There's silence on the phone.

"Are you still there, Aaron?" she asks.

"I'm here."

"I can't see anymore," she blurts out on a sob.

"You can't see at all?" he presses.

"No." Another sob.

"It's just happened, Aaron," I add. "Katie was checking her eyes, and June told her she couldn't see the light."

"I don't want to be kept alive on some machine, Aaron. I'm sorry. I know this is hard, but I just can't. Promise me."

"I… I promise." A heavy sigh comes through the line. "I hate it, but I understand. I know you're tired." The tears in my brother-in-law's voice make me want to cover my ears. It seems indecent that I'm here to witness this kind of open, raw pain from him.

"I'm going to tell the doc…" June's voice trails off.

"June, baby?" The alarm in Aaron's voice matches my own.

I take my sister's face in my hands. "June? Junie?"

There's nothing in her eyes. Nothing.

"What's happening, Hope?" Aaron shouts through the phone.

I slap the call button for the nurse. "I don't know."

"Can I help you?" comes the disembodied voice through the speaker.

"We need some help in here. Something's happened."

"Okay, we'll be right there."

"Please hurry."

# Chapter Twenty-Seven

Katie's in the room before I can consider who I should call first. "What's happening?"

I back up to give her room to examine June. "I don't know. She was talking to her husband, then she slurred her words, and now she's simply not with us."

"Hope?" Aaron again.

I forgot he was still on the call. "Aaron, I don't know what's happened. She's not responsive." I squeeze my forehead with my free hand. "Do you want to stay on the line?"

"No. I'm headed that way."

"Alright. I'll call you when I know more." I disconnect the phone, as five people in purple scrubs rush into the room.

"Ma'am, you'll need to wait outside," a woman with "Trauma Team" written on her top says.

"I... can I stay?"

"No."

Katie ushers me to the door. "I promise I'll let you know what's happening as soon as we know."

I nod. It's all I can do. The numbness begins at the top of

my head and spreads throughout my entire body. I have no conscious memory of moving into the hall, but somehow that's where I end up. I lean on the wall to help keep me upright.

The trauma team is rushing in and out of the room. I barely notice them. I keep trying to figure out what happened. One minute she was fine, and the next she was just... gone.

"Hope?" Babe is rushing toward me, with Joy and Grace behind her. "What's happened? Did she have another seizure?"

I look at Babe. "How...?"

"This is the same team that rushed in when she had the seizure after her surgery."

"I don't know. She was talking to Aaron on the phone and telling him she wanted a DNR, then she faded away." I push my hair out of my face. "They haven't—"

"A DNR?" Babe asks.

"Yes, she told me she wanted a DNR." I close my eyes to get my thoughts in order. "She wanted me to tell Aaron, but I told her she had to tell him."

"And you didn't try to talk her out of it?" It's an accusation, not a question.

"Um, no."

"Why?" Babe's pretty face looks like it's made of granite.

"Why, what, Babe?"

She slams her hands onto her hips. "Why didn't you tell her that was a ridiculous thing to ask for?"

The fury radiating off my youngest sister is disorienting. That kind of anger is usually reserved for Grace. She's rarely, if ever, directed it at me. "One, because it's her decision. And two, given where we are, I don't think it's a bad idea."

She throws her hands into the air. "How can you say that? She's going to get better. You've heard the doctor. Her markers are improving every time she gets a treatment."

I ignore her anger and quiet my voice. "Babe. Honey,

that's what we all want, but I think we should prepare for all eventualities. Honestly, it would be irresponsible of June not to ask for a DNR. She doesn't want us to be put in a situation where we're having to make difficult decisions on her behalf." I carefully reach for her. In case she decides to take a swing at me. When she doesn't, I draw her into a hug. "It's loving of her to do this for us, and loving of us to accept it's what she wants."

I look to Joy and Grace to back me up, but they're silent. Their shared look tells me they agree with Babe.

Babe's body rocks with sobs. "I hate this. And I kind of hate you right now."

I rub circles on her back. "I do too." I let her insult roll off of me. She's in pain. Besides, I kind of hate myself for not taking better care of June. How did this happen on my watch?

"But you're not falling apart like me. I can't do this. I just can't." That declaration brings on a new round of body-wracking weeping.

Grace and Joy step up then and begin to comfort Babe.

"Come on, Babe. Let's take a walk," Joy says.

Babe steps away from me and heads down the hall with our sister.

I stare after them, dumbfounded. How can she think I'm not falling apart? My whole world has been rattled off its axis. "How can she say that?"

Grace has turned her attention back to June's room. "A DNR is really final."

"Not that." I'm shocked at the fire in my response.

Grace must be, too, because she jerks her attention back to me. "What are you talking about, then?"

"How can she think I'm not falling apart? I'm devastated."

Grace crosses her thin arms over her stomach and glances to June's room again, then back to me. "Really?"

"Yes, really." I'm practically shouting. "Do you think that too? Does everyone think that I'm this cold, heartless bitch?"

"We don't think you're a cold, heartless bitch."

"But?"

"But you do seem to be approaching this more like a project to manage rather than a family member dying," she says matter-of-factly. Not like it's the nastiest indictment on my character she's ever made.

The blow lands, and I stumble back a step. "What?"

"I don't think any of us have seen you cry. You move through this like you're immune to the wreckage the rest of us are dealin' with." She shrugs. "It's not a bad thing, necessarily, Hope. We need you to handle things, but it's a little insultin' when you expect the rest of us to operate at the same level that you're functionin' at."

I stare at her. The obscenity of the insult makes it hard to form words. Our least affectionate sister is lecturing me on my lack of emotion.

"I. Am. Destroyed." The words barely make it through my gritted teeth. "Destroyed." I point to the chaos in June's room. "I can't do anything to stop this." I swipe at a tear that escapes from my eye. "I can't help her. I'm helpless to save her." The tears are flowing freely now and I don't care. "I can't stop this tragedy from obliterating Mom and Dad, or you guys... or Aaron."

Warm arms wrap around me. Babe and Joy. I didn't even hear them approach.

"You don't have to protect us, Hope," Joy says.

"I'm sorry, Hope," Babe whispers and holds her hand out to Grace, inviting her to join the group hug.

Grace reluctantly accepts it and moves into our space, but I can see she's as stiff as a board.

After several long moments of tears and hugs, Grace steps

out of the circle. "Okay, that's enough." She smooths her hair away from her face. "Y'all know I can only take so much mushy stuff."

Katie comes out of June's room. Her blond hair has come loose from her messy bun. "They're taking her to get an MRI." She glances over her shoulder. "Have you called the rest of your family?"

"No," Joy says.

She squeezes Joy's arm. "You should do that." Then she walks away.

The trauma team emerges from the room and wheels June down the hall without a word.

# Chapter Twenty-Eight

I'm still staring at the doors they wheeled June through when Ian steps into my line of sight. "I'll call your parents."

"How...?"

"Aaron called me." He turns his attention to Babe. "Does Clay know?"

For a second, Babe looks like she's never met a Clay, then she shakes her head. "No, but I'll call him." She pulls her phone from her pocket and moves down the hall.

"Thank you." It's all I've got. After what's just happened with June and the run-in with my sisters, I have absolutely nothing left and can't deal with him. So I remove myself from the situation, moving blindly down the hall until I find a door that takes me to an outside patio.

I grab the railing to stay upright. I suck as much air as I can into my lungs, release it, then do it again. Grace's accusations have flayed me wide open. I'm not sure how much more I can take. I am hanging on by the thinnest of threads.

I try again, but it's not working. Nothing's working. Not here, not in my life, not any-fucking-where.

"Hope?"

Oh, good God, the man cannot take a hint.

"What, Ian?" The words come out on shards of ice.

He doesn't seem affected by my tone because he stands beside me at the railing. "I called your parents. They're on their way."

I nod, not trusting myself to speak. I shove down the words that are clawing up my throat. Clamp my lips shut, so I don't spew the vitriol begging to be loosed. The last thing this night needs is me unloading on him.

No, you know what. Screw it.

I square up on him like a boxer headed into the ring. "Why the ever-lovin' hell are you here, Ian?"

"Aaron—"

"I know Aaron called you, but why are you here?"

"I thought you might need the support. I wanted to be here for you."

I laugh, like a full-on belly laugh. Not even the confused look on his face can make me stop. He doesn't say anything, only shifts his gaze from me to the skyline. After several minutes, I wind down.

I dry my eyes with the sleeve of my shirt. "Why are you suddenly interested in supporting me? Or"—I make air quotes—"being here for me, when you haven't been here for me in years." I take a step toward him, my chin raised. "You weren't there for me when you left me at the hospital and had Steve from the parts department at the dealership pick me up after my hysterectomy. You weren't there for me when my job, the thing I loved most, became unbearable. And you were a no-show for every couple's therapy appointment."

The shock on his face is comical. I've never stood up to him like this. I was either sweet and compliant or avoidant. Either way, my behavior made his life easier and mine harder.

I cock my head. "You know, I owe you a great big thank you."

The muscle in his jaw knots and it takes him a second to ask, "Really, for what?"

"For freeing me from a miserable existence that I accepted as normal life."

We stare at each other, twenty-five years of unfinished business crackling between us.

His Adam's apple bobs and he crosses his arms. His go-to move for when he's about to mansplain or gaslight me. But I'm ready for him tonight. He will not win this time. I wait for his retort, loaded for bear.

But he says nothing.

His white teeth bite into his bottom lip, and he examines the skyline. He unfolds his arms and grips the balcony railing so tightly that his knuckles blanch. When he turns his head to me, his eyes are dull and there's a resignation there. "I'll go." He turns to leave, then stops and, without looking back, asks, "Will you let me know when it's time to say goodbye to June?"

I nod my agreement, then realize he can't see me. "Yes."

"I'd like the chance to do that."

"I'll text you."

"Thank you."

The door closes on a whisper. He's leaving.

I win.

The metal balcony railing under my hands is as cold as the victory. There are no winners. We're all losers because June's still dying.

# Chapter Twenty-Nine

We're all back in June's room an hour later. Well, all of us but Ian. I have no idea where he went after he left me. Nor do I care.

June's surprisingly lucid for a woman who just had a seizure that warranted the trauma team. "Thank y'all for being here."

Mom's sitting on the side of the bed, holding her hand. "Where else would we be?"

"I was going to talk to everyone tomorrow, but since you're here now, I wanted to let you know that I'm going to ask the doctor about signing a DNR."

My dad makes a sobbing sound that he tries to mask with a cough.

June smiles sadly in his direction. "You're the best dad."

He presses his lips and nods, though she can't see him.

She brings Mom's hand to her lips. "Don't cry, Mama. I'm going to be okay. One way or the other."

Mom leans over and kisses June's head, then murmurs against her bruised skin, "I know you are."

"Aaron, the best day of my life was the day I met you," June continues.

He turns his head, but not before a tear falls to the front of his shirt. "Same goes, darlin'." The endearment sounds like it traveled over broken glass.

"Clay?"

He raises his hand. "Here."

"Have I ever told you how happy I was when you got your head out of your butt and married my sister?"

Clay laughs. "Not exactly in those words."

A drowsy smile pulls at June's lips. "Well, now I have."

"Love you, June Bug," Clay says around a throat full of emotion.

June blows a kiss in his direction.

"Grace, thank you for letting me live with you during the wild years, and for not telling Mom most of the crap I got up to."

Mom looks from June to Grace. "There's more I don't know?"

Grace grins. "Sooo much more."

Mom covers her ears. "I don't want to know."

"No, you don't," Grace says.

"Zip it, Grace," June slurs.

"Zipping it."

"Joy, thanks for being my first friend, and for defending me until I could defend myself."

Tears roll down Joy's face. She opens her mouth to speak, closes it, and opens it again, but nothing comes out. So she nods.

"She's nodding, Junie," I say.

"It's okay, Joy. I know you love me."

"Another nod," I narrate.

"Hope, you've always been the one to make things better. The person I've always aspired to be like."

Her compliment is as surprising as it is lovely. I snuggle it to my chest and know that it will live there for the rest of my life. The irony that I've always wished I were more like June isn't lost on me. The rawness of the night lands squarely on me along with her sweet words, and I can't control my emotions. With my face soaking wet, I manage, "Love you, Junie."

She holds her other hand up. "Babe?"

Babe takes the hand Mom's not holding. "I'm here."

"If this takes me out"—June licks her dry lips—"you'd better make sure I look good in that coffin. If you don't, I will not give you a day's peace for the rest of your life."

Babe, who's crying in earnest, sputters out a laugh. "I will make sure you look gorgeous."

"I don't know if we can get all the way to gorgeous. I'll be dead, for heaven's sake, but don't let me look like Carolyn Baker. Man, they did her dirty."

The Baby wipes her wet face. "They did. I swear I'll do better."

"You better." She turns her attention to the rest of us. "I'm not givin' up, I'm still fightin' this, but I don't want y'all to have to make a hard decision because I didn't make a plan." She yawns. "What time is it?"

"A little past midnight," Clay says.

"Oh, my gosh. Y'all need to get home."

Mom straightens Junie's blankets. "We can stay."

June stills Mom's hands. "No. Go home. Hope will stay with me." She turns her gaze in the direction where I assume she thinks I'm standing. "Right, Hope?"

"Yes."

She jerks her head to where I'm actually standing. "Damn it. Stop moving around. You were over there earlier."

I grin. "I like to keep you on your toes."

"Well, stop it. It's not nice to tease the blind, dying girl."

We all laugh. I'm not sure how, but we're all so exhausted and emotionally wrung out that we've lost our filter.

"I'll stay," Aaron jumps in to say.

"No. You go home and take care of the animals. Hope will be here and will let you know if anything happens."

"I don't need to. Ian has been taking care of them while I've been out of pocket."

What? I can't possibly have heard him correctly. "Every day?"

Aaron looks over at me like he forgot I was there. "Yeah. It's helped that I haven't had to worry about them."

"He's driven to Bonedalia every day to take care of your animals?" I'm sure I look like a stressed out, exhausted owl, slow blinking while this information tries to find a place to rest in my brain.

"That's really great of Ian," June says. "But you'll sleep better in your own bed. Plus, you have work tomorrow."

He doesn't look happy, but he says, "Okay."

"Do you still want us all to stay, June?" Grace asks.

Her eyes close. "No. I'm too tired to have any fun."

"Then I'll cancel the strippers," Joy says.

Mom covers her ears again. "I don't want to know."

Clay stands and pulls Babe to her feet. "Let's go, Babe."

She pats June's foot. "I'll see you in the morning, sister."

"Not if I see you first," June says.

Clay snorts. "Blind girl humor."

"Too much?" June asks.

Dad leans over and smacks his lips on June's head. "Yes. But we would expect nothing else from you, troublemaker."

June raises her hands to search for Dad's face. She places her palms on his cheeks. "I learned it from you, old man."

He laughs. "I guess you did."

We all move to the hall to give June and Aaron a moment alone. Before the door closes behind me, I look back and see Aaron sitting on the edge of the bed, his forehead to June's. They're not speaking, just resting in each other's presence.

He wouldn't send a lackey from work to give her a ride home from a hysterectomy. That's for damn sure.

I close the door and see my family walking toward the elevators, Grace lagging behind them.

She turns to me. "We good?"

I nod. "We're good."

"Okay." She heads to the elevators.

"I love you, too, Grace," I say.

She raises her hand and waves without turning around.

That's the thing about family. You can want to strangle them, but in the end, you love them. We all get to decide what we focus on. The strangling part or the love part. At this moment, I can see that love led me to want to do bodily harm to my sister.

She really did do me a favor.

Our interaction shook something loose in me and gave me the courage or the crazy to say to Ian all the things I've needed to say for a long time.

In a way, she finally freed me to let him and that relationship go.

The door behind me opens, and Aaron walks out.

"I wish she'd let me stay."

"I know." I wrap my sweater around me. I wonder if he knows that she's trying to protect him.

The sad grin he gives the closed door makes me think he does. "You know how she is."

"I do."

His strong arms go around me. "Take care of her, Hope."

I hug him back. "With my life."

## Chapter Thirty

I slide my hand under the sanitizer dispenser outside June's room and rub my palms together. Two weeks ago the sharp smell burned my nose. Now it barely registers. The anxiety that always meets me at this threshold ticks up. I shove it down, adjust my laptop bag on my shoulder, and push the door handle with my elbow.

The scene playing out before me does nothing to even out my pulse. June is lying in the bed shaking her head back and forth, whimpering and repeating, "I can't. I can't. I can't."

Joy and Nurse Katie are standing on either side of a contraption that's not quite a wheelchair, but has been used to transport my sister to and from the bathroom or to help her practice standing, then sitting.

"Come on, Junie. I know you can do it," Joy coaxes.

"I can't, Joy." June uses what strength she has to yell at our sister.

Over the last few days, they've been trying to get June up and moving, and that along with the physical therapy she's been going to every day have exhausted her and frankly made her mean as a snake. That's not an indictment, simply the reality of where we're at.

"But June, you have to try—"

"I said I can't!"

I understand the urgency in Joy's tone. The doctors are saying June has to be ambulatory before they can release her. Also, we're all desperate for any indication she's getting better. And moments like this crush those hopes spectacularly.

Time to step in. "Never fear, big sister's here."

The relief in Joy's face is telling, and I don't like the story it's conveying.

"Hope, tell them..." June whines.

I drop my belongings on the sofa and move to her side and take her hand. "Tell them what, June?"

"Tell them I don't want to try." Her eyes are glassy, like they get when her pain is intense.

I place my hand on her forehead. "Are you in pain?"

"Yes," is her whispered reply.

I look to Katie. "Can she have something for the pain?"

"I gave her something a few minutes ago." She slides her badge over the pad next to the computer to log in. After a few minutes of typing she says, "June, why don't we give those pain meds time to work, then we'll try this again?"

June sucks her lips between her teeth and nods.

"Okay. That's a plan."

I love Katie. She knows exactly how to deal with my sister.

While we've been talking, Joy has gathered her things to leave. "Now that Hope's here, June, I'm gonna go."

June stays silent, with her eyes closed.

"Anything I should know before you go?" I ask Joy as we walk to the door.

She shakes her head. I can see how defeated she is. Caring for someone so horribly ill isn't for sissies, that's for sure. I wrap my arms around her and whisper in her ear, "You didn't do anything wrong."

Her exhausted body relaxes into mine. "It's just hard."

"I know."

"I know y'all are talkin' about me." The mulish expression on June's face would be funny if we weren't so worried about her.

"I'm telling Hope about our night," Joy explains with an admirable amount of kindness, given the abuse she's just taken from June.

The patient sniffs and turns her face from us.

Joy gives June one more worried look, then faces me. "They did have to up her pain medication overnight."

I wrap the light sweater that's become my uniform in this cold room tighter around me. "Okay." I don't say that can't be good, but I can tell Joy and I are in agreement on the development.

"I'm leaving, June. I'll see you tomorrow night," Joy says.

June doesn't answer.

Joy's sad eyes find mine, and I just shake my head.

Just before Joy gets to the door, June says, "I'm sorry, Joy. Thank you for being here." The hitch in her voice is enough to crack even the coldest person's heart wide open.

Joy moves to the bed, leans over, and kisses June's head. "There's no place I'd rather be. But you better give Hope the same hell you gave me, or I will be offended."

June loses the fight with a smile. "I'll give it my best shot."

"You better," Joy says, then leaves.

After she's gone, I take my position sitting next to June's bed. "Do you need anything?"

"No. I'm just glad you're here."

I take her frail hand. "Just like Joy, there's no place I'd rather be."

June swipes at a tear with her free hand. "I'm such a bitch."

"You're in pain. There's a difference."

"Do you think she forgives me?" The frailty of her voice is at such odds with who June is to me... to all of us.

"I'm confident that she forgives you." I gently slide my fingertips over her forehead several times. "Promise me you won't worry about this anymore."

She doesn't answer, but within minutes her furrowed brow smooths out and her breathing becomes less labored. Sleep for June is precious and usually medically induced these days due to her pain.

As I watch her sleep, I replay the scene I walked in on. June's not usually so uncooperative or unwilling to try to do what the doctors have said will help her get stronger. I know she understands how important it is that she try to get out of bed.

I'm worried, of course. But there's something else, and I'm very afraid it's irritation and anger. If she stops fighting, then who will lead the charge? She's been our leader in this battle against cancer. Who does she think will fight if she stops? I mean, what are we all supposed to do? Just accept defeat? Which is her death.

Hot static fills my chest, and it confirms that I am indeed mad at my dying sister for not fighting hard enough. The longer I sit with it, that's exactly how I'm feeling, and I have no idea what to do with these feelings.

Even thinking it makes me ill. What kind of sister am I?

One who knows we can't possibly survive her death.

*I'm not ready.*

*I'm not ready.*

*I'm not ready.*

Just when I think I may drown from the guilt of my revelation, my phone buzzes with a text. I retrieve it from my purse and see that it's Carrie.

*Hey, how are things today?*

I quickly text back.

*Not great.*

Her response is immediate.

*Oh, no. What's happened?*

I consider lying and giving the pat excuse of June's pain. It's a perfectly reasonable response and wouldn't invite any uncomfortable questions. But I can't lie to Carrie.

*I'm angry June isn't fighting harder.*

Carrie's response doesn't come as quickly this time. My shame rises with every second the three dots dance on the screen.

*That must be hard to admit. You want to tell me what you mean, or did you just want to get it off your chest?*

Did I? Maybe it is enough that I typed it out loud. But the gnawing in my stomach tells me it's not.

*For ten years she's fought like a wildcat. She's been the poster child for doing battle with this disease. And now... I don't know. It's like she's not giving the fight what she has in the past. We've always taken our cues from her, and now it feels like we've lost our leader.*

This time Carrie doesn't make me wait.

*It sounds like you're more scared than angry.*

She's right. We're all scared to death. This is a June we've never seen before.

Another text from Carrie.

*Also, I've never known June to back down from a fight, even when she should.*

That makes me smile. She's not wrong.

The three dots are on the screen again.

*I think if she could fight the way she has in the past, she would. But maybe she's fighting a different battle now, one that involves her own mortality. And that's a much more personal struggle.*

As I watch the rise and fall of June's chest, the truth settles over me. June's no longer fighting for her life, she's fighting to die well.

*Thanks for always knowing what I need to hear, whether I want to hear it or not.*

Heart emojis come up on the screen, followed by,

*No problem. I love you and your family. Please let me know what I can do to help.*

*Love you too.*

I slip my phone into my sweater pocket. I've spent ten years trying to keep June alive. How in the hell do I flip the switch to help her die well? Can I even do that, when my mind repels any version of life without her?

"Hope, help me," she murmurs.

"What can I do, Junie?"

She blinks, her eyes unable to focus. "What?"

"You asked me to help you."

"I did?"

I pull her blanket up to her chin. "You did. Were you dreaming?"

"I must've been."

"Well, I'm your girl, for whatever you need."

She lifts her hand and I take it. "I know you are." In an instant she's asleep again.

I heave out a breath, and with it the death grip I have on the version of the future that I think I can live with. I'll do anything this incredible person needs me to do.

# Chapter Thirty-One

Over the next couple of weeks, June continues to receive her treatments, but her condition doesn't improve. She's still having seizures and some disorientation, her mobility decreases, and her eyesight doesn't get any better. The problem is that she can't leave the hospital until she gets stronger, and that isn't happening. However, she doesn't get worse either. The perpetual limbo is grueling for her. It's hard to watch and harder for her to live.

We all take turns staying with her during the week. Thankfully, my schedule's wide open, and Babe, being a teacher, is out on summer break, so she and I usually take the day shifts with our parents, and Joy and Grace alternate staying with her at night after they get off work. Aaron comes to see her every night, and he has the weekend shifts. He's tried to take days off work to be with June during the week, but she always gets upset. She doesn't want him living this every day. What she doesn't realize is that he's living this regardless of where he is.

It's taking a toll on all of us, but leaving her alone isn't an option.

Babe and I have started staggering our shifts so we can have some time to take care of things or simply have a small moment of self-care. This morning is that day for me. I haven't had my nails done in weeks, so I treat myself to a quick nail appointment.

The message notifications begin chiming the minute I get back to my car and turn my phone on.

Six from Babe.

Four from both Grace and Joy.

Three from Mom.

I open my text thread with Babe first.

Hope, call me.

The following four messages from her are the same.

CALL ME.

The last?

WHERE THE HELL ARE YOU?

I immediately press the button to call my youngest sister.

"Hope," Babe's frantic voice comes through the phone.

"I'm here. Sorry, I had my phone turned off. I was getting a —You know what, it doesn't matter. What's happening?"

"June can't breathe. She started complaining about her chest feeling tight, then the next thing I know, she's gasping for air."

"What's wrong?"

"They don't know. They've taken her for an MRI."

I put the car in reverse and back out of the parking spot. "Okay, I'll be there in ten minutes." My phone beeps with another call. "It's Mom. I'll see you soon." I disconnect from Babe and answer Mom's call. "I'm sorry, my phone was off."

"So you heard?" she asks.

"Yes. I just spoke with Babe. I'm on my way to the hospital."

My mom sniffs several times, and I know she's crying.

"Good. Your dad's in a doctor's appointment, so we can't head that way until he finishes."

"Okay. Drive carefully. Love you, Mom."

"You too, sweetie. Call me when you know anything."

"I will." I disconnect the call and realize that every ounce of calm I gained over the last hour is completely gone.

I barge into June's room at a near run, expecting to see the rest of my family, but only Babe is here. June lies motionless in the bed with an oxygen mask covering her mouth and nose. Babe stands in the corner of the room with her arms wrapped around her waist, staring at June, tear tracks on her face.

I look to Babe, then June, then back to Babe. "What's happening?"

My youngest sister shakes her head and motions toward the bed.

"What?" I ask.

"Hope," June says.

I rush to her and take her outstretched hand. "Hey, Junie. Are you making trouble again?"

June doesn't smile."I'm tired, Hope."

I rub my hand over her head. "That's okay. You rest."

"No!" The exclamation seems to take everything out of her.

"Alright," I coo. "Tell big sister what you want, and I'll make it happen."

A tear develops at the corner of her left eye and hangs there like she's willing it away. But the tear is stronger than my sister's will and rolls down her temple into her ear.

I take the end of the sheet and wipe it away. "You're killing me, Junie. What can I do?"

She struggles to take her next breath. "I'm tired, Hope. So, so tired."

I hear Babe sniffle in the corner. I almost forgot she was

there. Then it hits me. Now this whole somber scene makes sense.

June's tired of fighting.

Babe blows her nose. "June, you have to keep fighting. You're not a quitter."

"Hope." The plea in June's voice is a vise I couldn't escape even if I wanted to.

And I know what I have to do. I kiss her fingers still wrapped around mine. "Listen to me, June. The minute you see Jesus, do not hesitate. Run. To. Him. Do you hear me?"

There's a sharp intake of air from the corner. I ignore Babe. She's not my problem at the moment. She's not dying.

June closes her eyes, and a sob comes from behind the oxygen mask. "I will."

My fingers wrap tighter around June's. "As fast as you can, June." I kiss the back of her hand. "We'll be okay. I promise."

"No. We won't," Babe says and leaves the room.

I sit on the side of the bed and stroke June's head. "She doesn't mean it. She's just sad."

June nods, and another tear slides down her temple.

I dry her ear again. "You don't have to fight one minute longer than you think you can. None of us are going to blame you for choosing your own way." I kiss her fingers once more. "Let's see what the doctor says before you make any decisions."

Another nod.

"This is your battle, June. I will fight with you as long as you want to fight. We all will. But the minute you decide you're done, then I will hold your hand into the next life."

June's only response is to exhale and close her eyes. Soon her muscles relax, and her breathing becomes easier and steadier.

Minutes click by, then I look toward the door.

Time to face the music.

I find Babe in the hall with Clay and the rest of my family.

"Babe..." I begin, but my sister turns and walks away, Clay in tow.

"How is she?" Mom asks, a little more stiffly than usual.

"She's asleep."

"She has pneumonia?" Grace asks.

"Pneumonia?" I realize I never found out why June was having trouble breathing.

"Apparently," Joy says and looks down the hall toward Babe and Clay.

I follow her gaze. "She's mad at me." It's not a question. I know she's mad. They probably all are. But I only said what needed to be said. It's not fair for us to ask June to continue this fight just because we can't bear to lose her. It's selfish.

Mom grips my arm. "No, honey. She's sad. We all are."

I nod. Because, despite what my family thinks, I'm sad too. Rocked to my absolute core. Why can't they see that?

"How did this happen?" Mom asks.

"I don't know, Mom." I'm talking to her, but my attention is at the end of the hall, where Aaron is talking to Babe and Clay. He looks over his shoulder, and the raw agony etched into his face pins me to the spot. I resist the urge to run when he begins to stride toward me.

My heart lurches with every step he takes. "Aaron... I... I'm sorry." I don't really know what I'm apologizing for. I don't regret what I said to June and would do it again, but the man looks like he just lost the only friend he ever had.

His big arms go around me in an embrace so fierce that my bones crack. "Thank you for saying what none of us could," he whispers in my ear.

The pressure against the back of my eyes builds until I can no longer keep the tears from falling. My throat is so full of emotion that I can't reply.

He releases me and takes several stuttering breaths.

I rub his arm. "Do you want some time alone with her?"

His gaze goes to June's door, and every line on his face is made up of dread. A fortifying breath, like he's about to go into battle, then he shakes his head.

"Okay. We'll all go in." I take his hand. "Let's go see our girl."

# Chapter Thirty-Two

We're all in June's room the next day, when Dr. Yovan comes in. He's his usual unflappable, steady self. "Sounds like you've had an eventful day yesterday, June."

June smiles weakly. She's receiving antibiotics and is now breathing without the oxygen mask. "I'm always a party."

He chuckles and squeezes her shoulder. "How are you feeling now?"

"Better, but I'm tired."

He crosses his arms over his chest and nods. "According to your current numbers, the therapy is working. There is a reduction in leptomeningeal disease, as we've discussed. With those numbers, we should see you living for at least six more months."

"But..."

"But what?" he asks.

"Why am I not better?" It comes out as a whine, and who can blame her? She's done everything they've said to do, endured a grueling surgery and recovery, only to be worse off now than before.

He never takes his gaze from her. "I'm not sure, June. We would expect to see improvement of symptoms, not an escalation."

She doesn't speak for a moment. "Do you think they will get better?"

"No." The finality of the word holds the room hostage.

The only sounds are a few gasps from my mom and sisters, who are sitting on the sofa to my right.

The doctor touches June's shoulder again. "I am sorry."

"But we can continue the treatment?" Mom asks.

Dr. Yovan looks over at the occupants of the sofa like he just realized they were sitting there. "Yes. But as I said, her condition will not improve from this point."

"We don't know that. God can do anything." Mom's declaration sounds more like petulance than faith.

Dr. Yovan doesn't respond to Mom. It's clear from the look on his face that he's had this very discussion before with families. "June. What do you want to do?"

"I want to stop."

Various versions of no come from my family.

June ignores the chorus and asks the doctor, "What's next?"

"You would go into hospice care."

"Can I do that at home?"

"Yes."

June relieved smile is heartbreaking. "Then that's what I want to do. How long?"

"I'd say about a month," Dr. Yovan says.

The muffled sobs coming from my family fill the room with love and anguish.

All my tears are dammed behind a wall of disbelief. Even

after everything we've all been through this last month, I still find myself asking, how did we get here?

It's the last place in the world I want to be, but I made June a promise, so I clear my throat. "If this is what June wants, then that's what we'll do." I look at the doctor. "Does the social worker have resources for us? We've never done this before." My voice breaks at the end of the sentence, so maybe I'm not as numb as I think I am. I swallow my sorrow. This is too important to miss any information.

Dr. Yovan slips his hands into the pockets of his white lab coat. "Yes. I'll tell the nurse to send her in."

I dip my chin, not trusting that the shaky breath in my lungs can even form words.

"What will it be like?" June asks.

Dr. Yovan turns his attention back to my sister. "Hospice means there will be no life-saving intervention. However, they will give you medication to make you comfortable."

June's shaking her head before he finishes. "No. That's not what I mean. What will" —she swallows—"dying be like?"

Babe buries her head in Clay's neck. Grace grabs Joy's hand, and Dad pulls my mom into him. Only Aaron has no outward reaction. He stands with his arms to his sides, stone still in the corner of the room, like if he doesn't make any sudden movements, the reality of losing his whole world won't find him.

I squeeze my eyes shut, as if the thin flesh of my eyelids could possibly protect me from the question or the answer.

The doctor takes June's hand. "You will go to sleep and not wake up. It will be peaceful."

"It won't be painful?"

"The dying won't be, no."

Every muscle in June's body relaxes. She closes her eyes,

and a single tear runs down her cheek. "Then that's what I want."

Still holding her hand, Dr. Yovan says, "Alright. I'll tell the nurse to send in the social worker. We'll get your discharge paperwork together and get you home." He takes a beat and looks around the room. "It's been a pleasure meeting you, June. You and your family have touched us all."

June smiles. "They are pretty great."

He smiles back at her. "I'll talk to the nurses."

There are some muttered thanks from my family as he leaves the room.

"Aaron?" June says.

He moves to her side like there's an elastic cord between them and she just yanked on it. He takes her hand and sits on the side of the bed. "I'm here."

"I'm sorry—"

"You don't have to—"

"I just can't—"

"I know."

Crying from the sofa catches her attention. "I'm sorry, y'all."

"Oh, June, don't you dare apologize," Mom says. "Of course we want you to keep fighting, but we also can't stand to see you in this much pain, and if that's not going to get better, then... we understand."

I've never seen a more courageous act of love in my whole life. What that must cost her... more than I've ever paid for anything in my life.

"Hope?"

I squeeze her foot. "I'm here."

"Will you let Ian know?"

It's the last thing I want to do, but I don't hesitate. "Of course."

"Thank you."

We're all silent. Each of us lost in our own helpless thoughts.

"Excuse me," I finally say and leave the room to call Ian.

The strength in my legs only lasts until I get to the hall, then I slump against the wall. I'm living in a horrible movie, and I can't affect the plot. I desperately want the film to end, but I also know that the ending is worse than where I am now. So I'll play my part as best I can, for June.

# Chapter Thirty-Three

The next few hours are a blur of activity. After the social worker arrived and explained what would happen next, we all got moving.

June decided she wanted to be at Mom and Dad's house. Aaron wanted us to find a hospice facility, but June refused. She said she wanted to be with her family. Once that was settled, she asked for the strongest pain meds they had, and she's been asleep ever since.

Joy, Grace, and Dad left to get the house ready for the hospital bed. Babe and Clay went to pick up a wheelchair that a friend of theirs is lending us. And June sent Aaron home to get some things for her, but I think she just wanted to give him a task. Plus, it's June doing what June does, what she's always done with Aaron, putting a buffer between the cancer and him. Unfortunately, I think we're way past that point now, but it's not my business, so I stay out of it.

Mom and I are listening to the nurse's instructions when there's a knock at the door.

"Come in," Mom says.

The EMTs who will transport June to my parents' house enter with a stretcher. "Hello, I'm Eric," a stocky guy with sandy blond hair says at a normal volume, then notices June sleeping and lowers his voice. "This is Marty. We're here to pick up June Phillips."

I wave my hand. "No need to whisper. She's dead to the world." I bite my lip and look at Mom. "Too soon?"

Mom spits her coffee out and chuckles. "Maybe a little."

I nod. "Yeah, it didn't feel right to me either."

She pats my hand. "June would've thought it was hilarious, so..."

Eric and the nurse laugh, but Marty looks decidedly uncomfortable. Eric and the nurse are our people.

"Since Ms. June's kind of out of it, I need the next of kin to sign her DNR." Eric holds out a clipboard.

I point to Mom. "That would be her, but June already signed a DNR here at the hospital."

"That's for the hospital," Marty says. "This is a universal DNR."

Eric hands the clipboard to my mom. She looks at it like it's a snake, then turns her watery gaze to me. "I can't." She passes the clipboard to me. "Will you..."

I take it and look at Eric. "I'm her sister. Is that alright?"

"It's fine."

I read over the document quickly and sign it, like doing so fast will negate the fact that my name will be on my sister's DO NOT RESUSCITATE document forever.

This is what June wants.

I hand it back to Eric with a shaky hand. The man's kind, knowing smile is nearly my undoing, but I rein it in and remember my promise to June.

After several long minutes, they're finally ready to move June from her hospital bed to the gurney. She does rouse then.

Any movement at all is so painful for her. It's heartbreaking and terrifying. And we know it will only get worse over the next few weeks.

Once she's secured on the gurney, Mom and I gather our things and follow them from the hospital. Katie and the other nurses, most of whom have taken care of June during her stay, are lined up by the nurses' station to say goodbye, to honor June. I lose the battle with my emotions when I see that they're all weeping.

Mom and I hug each one of them. These women have not only taken such loving care of my sister but also of our family, and we will never be able to express our gratitude to them.

The ride home is silent. What's there to say?

Mom finally breaks the silence. "Do you think she's scared?"

"I think she was until the doctor told her it would be peaceful."

"Are you scared?" My mom no longer sounds like my mother, my caretaker, my rock. The question is one a child would ask before she boards the scariest rollercoaster she's ever seen.

"Terrified."

The sound my mother makes sounds like dry bones clacking together. "Me too. How do you watch your child die?"

I put my blinker on to exit to Bonedalia and fight for my next breath. "I don't know, Mom. I honestly don't." I take her hand. "We're not there yet. Right now, we only have to get her home and comfortable. I'm convinced we can do that."

She exhales loudly and grips my hand tighter. "Yes. We can do that."

I release her hand so I can turn into our driveway. "From this point forward, we just do the next thing, whatever that is. I think that's how we get through this."

When we arrive home, Dad, Grace, and Joy have rearranged things, and the delivery company has already set up the hospital bed in the living room. June, being June, didn't want to be relegated to a bedroom. She wanted to be out in the middle of things.

Once the EMTs get her situated and leave, we all stand looking at each other.

What now?

June must sense our uncertainty because she says, "Why's it so quiet?"

My mom goes to her. "No reason, Junie. Do you need anything?"

"I need to pee."

"Oh, here!" Clay exclaims and barrels toward the hospital bed with the borrowed wheelchair like he's part of a pit crew at the Daytona 500.

"Are you sure you're okay to do this, Junie?" Mom asks.

"As long as somebody comes with me."

"I'll go," my sisters and I say in unison.

June chuckles. "I haven't had anyone be this excited to go to the bathroom with me since I took a bottle of vodka to school in my backpack in ninth grade."

Mom covers her ears. "I don't want to know."

The four of us wheel June to the bathroom.

"I'm gonna need help," she says, with no apology or embarrassment.

I love that she knows she can ask us for anything, from taking care of her most intimate personal needs to watching her die, and we'll be there, no questions asked.

I stand in front of her. "Alright. I'll help you stand and turn you. Grace, you and Joy get her pants. Babe, you spot us and make sure she doesn't fall."

They all nod, not seeming to mind that I'm bossing them

around. We all take our positions, and I lean down to June. "Okay, Junie, put your arms around my neck." She obeys, and I wrap my arms around her. "We'll stand on three."

She nods.

"One. Two."

Her arms tighten around my neck. "Don't drop me," she whispers desperately, and it breaks my heart.

"Never," I promise.. "Three."

We stand, and a whimper of pain rises from her throat.

"I've got you." I tighten my grip. "Now let's turn. Three little steps. You can do it."

"Okay."

We get her positioned in front of the toilet. Joy and Grace get her pants down, then I lower her to the seat.

"There you go, princess," Grace says.

"Thank you. But I can't do my business with you watching me. Turn around," she orders.

We do as we're told.

When June is done, she clears her throat and asks, "Which of you is on wiping duty?"

I see the same expression on my sisters' faces that I have on mine in the mirror in front of us. A mixture of surprise and a little horror, but all tempered by our willingness to do whatever June needs.

Before one of us can volunteer, June cracks up. "Y'all are too easy. I can still wipe my own ass." She handles the chore and flushes the toilet. "But you bitches better not hesitate when the time comes for you to do the deed. I'd do it for you."

"You would not," Grace says. "You've specifically said multiple times that you would not do that for me."

June shakes her head. "That was theoretical. Kind of like when I said I'd never kiss Corey Shackelford, but then when I was bored and three drinks in at Roadies one night, I changed my mind."

"So what you're saying is that you'd have to be drunk to wipe my ass?" Grace asks.

June chuckles. "It can't be any worse than kissing Corey Shackelford."

"True that," Babe mutters as she hands June an antibacterial cloth to clean her hands.

"You didn't," June says.

Babe shrugs. "I too was bored and three drinks in at Roadies one night."

"Remind me to never go to Roadies for drinks," I say.

Babe moves the wheelchair into position. "What are you talking about? You, Grace, and Joy all had your first kiss with Charlie Rogers. Tell me that's not weird."

"Didn't you say you thought Charlie was trying to kill you when he kissed you, Hope?" June laughs.

"I swear he was," I say. "We were on a hayride, and I was already having trouble breathing from all the hay. As soon as the trailer started moving, he covered our heads with a blanket, trapping all the allergens with us. Then, when he kissed me"—I cover my mouth and nose with my hand—"he covered every orifice needed for life with his thin lips. I couldn't wait until it ended so I could draw a clean breath. Unfortunately, that didn't happen due to his nacho Doritos breath."

They're all laughing now.

I cross my arms. "You laugh, but I was fightin' for my life."

"As I recall, you didn't date him very long after that," Grace says.

"No. He went back to school on Monday and told everyone what happened. I kicked him to the curb faster than you can say halitosis. You don't kiss and tell."

Grace leans against the bathroom counter. "The only good thing about having Charlie as your first kiss was—"

"It could only get better from there," Joy finishes. Our laughter reverberates off the bathroom walls, and the sound makes me so happy.

I move in front of June. "You ready to do this again?"

"Ready."

"Put your arms around my neck."

Once she's back in the wheelchair, we head for the living room.

Without turning around or looking at any of us, June says, "Thank you. I know how lucky I am to have y'all."

"That's real nice, June," Grace says. "But I'm still not wiping your ass."

June raises her middle finger, and we crack up all over again.

Cancer may steal my sister's life, but it will never take her spirit.

# Chapter Thirty-Four

The sight when I return to the living room stops me dead in my tracks. Ian is in the kitchen, wearing an apron, as friends and church members bring food into the house like it's their job.

Ian's voice is louder than the commotion. "Virgie, you can put that salad in the fridge in the other room." He points in the direction of the laundry room. "It's right through there. Thanks."

"Ian, we've got drinks too," Mike Powell, the youth pastor, says from the front door.

My ex-husband wipes his hands on his apron. "I set up a couple of coolers on the back porch. There's ice in the deep freezer. Do you mind icing them down?"

"You got it," Mike answers and heads to the back porch, followed by Max and Chloe, who are both loaded down with canned drinks

Where did all these people come from? How long were we in the bathroom?

I move to Mom, take her arm, and pull her into the hallway. "What's going on?"

The shell-shocked look on her face is almost comical. "I'm not sure. Ian pulled up in an RV with all these people following behind him." She looks back at the kitchen. "I tried to help, but he wouldn't let me."

"Did he coordinate all this food?"

"I think so."

"Why?"

Before she can answer, the pastor of my parents' church walks into the living room.

"Excuse me, honey," Mom says. "I need to greet Pastor Hal." With every step she takes toward the man, her strength seems to melt away, so that by the time she reaches him, it's like her bones are nonexistent. She crumples into his big, burly arms. It physically hurts to look at her.

I turn my focus back to the kitchen, where Ian is the center of attention. Just the way he likes it. It irritates me, but if this takes some of the stress off us, then I'm willing to ignore him and let him have the spotlight. Then I remember Mom said he came in an RV. "Oh, hell no." I march into the kitchen and grab his arm.

"Oh, hi, Hope." He looks over my head. "Maryann, you can put the paper products in the pantry, over there."

I drag him into the dining room away from everyone else. "What are you doing?"

He doesn't answer but looks directly into my eyes like he's trying to dissect my soul. "How are you?"

"What?" I shake my head. "I asked you a question."

"I'm here to help." He places his hands on my upper arms. "How are you?"

I step out of his grasp. "I'm horrible, Ian. How the hell do you think I am?"

He seems unaffected by my anger. "I'm so damn sorry, Hope."

The genuine pain in his eyes siphons some of the anger out of me and makes me feel a little bad for my attack. I modulate my voice. "I know you are." I grab the elastic off my wrist and pile my hair on top of my head in a messy bun. "Why are you here in the RV? My RV, I might add. How did you even get it?"

"I still have a set of keys." He says it like he's batting away a fly. "Besides, I need somewhere to stay."

I ignore the fact that he kept a set of keys to my RV and address the more urgent issue. "Stay where?"

"Here." The casualness of his response gets my anger up again.

I shake my head like doing so will rattle the words into some semblance of sense. "Why?"

"It's too far to drive from Dallas every day."

"Every day?" I swear I feel like I'm in some bad comedy skit. "What about work?"

"I can do most of it remotely, but what's the point of owning your own business if you can't take personal time?"

Oh, now I know this is a joke. I used to say the same thing to him when I tried to convince him to go on vacations or take a couple's weekend away, and he always said he couldn't be away from work.

The pain his response causes is no longer worth my time, so I ask, "Why can't you stay with your mother?" I have no idea why I'm engaging in this ridiculous discussion, but here we are.

He shakes his head. "Too far away. I need to be close so I can get y'all's meals together, run errands, or keep Russ off the roof." He chuckles, and the sound is like a pebble in my shoe.

I cross my arms over my chest. "Ian, I don't understand."

One side of his mouth kicks up in a sad sort of smile. "I

know. And I don't blame you, but will you let me take care of your family, Hope?"

I can't form words. I have no frame of reference for this.

He does a double take at something behind me. "No. That doesn't go there." He takes my shoulders in his hands and kisses my forehead. "I gotta handle this." He moves past me, yelling, "We're putting desserts in the front room on the buffet, Virgie."

His lips leave a mark. Not literally, but I know they've been there, and that only adds to my irritation. My eyes track his retreat.

"Hope?"

I turn to see Carrie. There's no thought to my next move. I run to her, and she catches me as I collapse into her. My body shudders as the events of the day spill out of me. When I'm cried out, I pull back and see that her face is wet with tears too.

I place my palms on her cheeks. "Thank you for coming."

She sniffs. "Where else would I be?" She looks through the dining room door to the chaos happening in the rest of the downstairs. "People have really shown up for y'all."

I nod, then see Ian through the door. "You saw Ian?"

"I did. He called to see if Jack and I could come help."

I cross my arms to cover the soft spot that his actions want to worm into. "He stole my RV." It's a stupid thing to say, but I don't know how to handle this version of Ian.

"He what?"

"Never mind. But he says he's staying to 'take care of us.' Can you believe that?" I take several deep breaths. "Ian hasn't taken care of anyone but himself in a very long time. I doubt he even knows how to anymore."

Carrie and I watch him carry my mom a bottle of water without being asked. "He seems pretty committed to this though."

"It'll only be a matter of a day or so before he gets bored and leaves. He's not capable of anything else, Carrie."

"I don't know, Hope. You know how he is." She hugs me again. "I better go help before he yells at me for slacking."

The air is moving freely in and out of my chest now. It's all going to be okay. I do know how he is.

He'll get bored.

He'll lose interest.

Then he'll be gone.

# Chapter Thirty-Five

He is still here.

It's been a week, and Ian's still coordinating meals and food drop-offs, and in some cases cooking for us. Not very Ian-like at all. Or at least not the Ian of late. Oh, and the RV is still parked in front of my parents' house.

If I think about it too much, it messes with my head, so I don't think about it. It's been easy to ignore him with all the activity around the house. Who knew dying was such a busy business?

The steady stream of friends and family makes the days both so, so sweet and brutal beyond belief. Their stories and memories are a welcome distraction. But the inevitable farewells are a haunting confirmation that June is really dying, and this is really happening. The finality of it all keeps my family trapped in a horrible fever dream that plays on a continuous loop.

So a quiet afternoon like today is a nice reprieve. Mom, Dad, Aaron, Babe, and I are here today, like almost every day.

Grace, Joy, and Clay are at work during the day but are all here in the evenings and on weekends.

Oh, and Ian. Can't forget him. At the moment, he's in the kitchen organizing the food that Joy's friends have dropped off for us.

"Ian!" June calls.

He hustles to her bedside. "I'm here, Bug."

She holds her hand up to him. "Sit with me."

He takes her hand and sits in a chair next to her bed. "You got it."

Her face turns to him, though she can't see him. "I need a favor."

"Anything." He holds up a finger. "Well, anything except toilet papering the Fowlers' house."

June's been trying to recruit us to TP the Fowlers' house since she realized that our family won't be able to compete in the City of Bonedalia's Labor Day Games. Honestly, she's taken that news worse than she took going into hospice care.

June makes a face. "You're all a bunch of wienies."

Ian barks a laugh. "Wienies that want to stay out of jail."

"I don't know why everybody in this family is so scared of jail. It's not that bad, and you meet some really interesting people. Right, Hope?"

Ian jerks his head toward me but says to June, "How would she know?"

I ignore him and concentrate on the crossword puzzle I've been trying to complete.

"She did a couple of hours in county a few weeks ago with Grace and Joy."

"Snitches get stitches, June," I say, still not looking at the pair.

She grins. "Man, jail has made you mean, Hope."

I finally move my gaze from my crossword to Ian. "Grace and Joy got into a fight at the diner, and I made the mistake of trying to break it up."

"Was anybody hurt?" he asks.

"Just my pride." I'm still not over that afternoon, so I'm done with this conversation. "What did you want to ask Ian, Junie?"

Ian turns his attention back to her. "Yeah, what do you need, Bug?"

"Will you be a pallbearer?"

The question is as casual as asking for a piece of gum, but as soon as it's out of her mouth, silence falls over the room.

"Ian?" she asks.

There's not an ounce of color in his face. I've rarely, if ever, seen him so rattled.

"I..." He clears his throat, and it takes him several more swallows to get the words past whatever emotions are choking him. "It'd be... It'd be an honor, Bug." When he lifts her fingers to his lips, a tear drops onto their joined hands.

The sunlight from the window glistens on June's wet cheeks. "Are you crying too?"

"Yeah." He huffs like it's the only way to get air out of his lungs. "I am, Bug."

"I didn't mean to make you cry."

"I know, darlin'. This is hard stuff."

She brings their joined hands to her chest, then adds her other hand. "It is. Thank you for being here."

"Always." He stands and kisses her forehead. "When the time comes, I'll be there for you. Thank you for asking me."

Her frail hand goes to his cheek. "I figured you've carried me out of a lot of situations, may as well do it one last time."

His nod is jerky. "Sounds good. I... um... I need to take care of something in the kitchen."

"Okay."

He bypasses the kitchen and heads out the front door.

June rubs her hands over her wet cheeks.. "Now that's how you respond to an invitation to be someone's pallbearer. If anyone gives me less than that when I ask them, they're getting moved to B team, and we're finding a sub."

"You're the boss, Junie," Mom says, taking Ian's spot on the chair.

"That's right, I am," June confirms. "Hope?"

"I'm here," I say from my seat on the sofa.

She waves her hand in the direction of the front door. "Will you go check on him?"

"He probably just needs a minute, June. That was a big ask," I say.

"Please."

"Sure." It's a good thing she can't see my face because I know it's giving me away right now.

I find Ian on the porch steps, legs splayed, elbows on knees, and his head in his hands.

"Mind if I sit?"

He shakes his head but doesn't look at me.

My position next to him is close enough to convey that I care, but far enough away to signal that this is only a platonic inquiry. "Are you okay?"

He snorts, still not looking at me. "What is it you said? I'm horrible. How the hell do you think I am?"

I pull my knees to my chest and wrap my arms around them. "Yeah."

A couple of swallows play around the bird bath in my parents' front yard. I'm jealous of how oblivious and simple their lives are. Was I ever that carefree? Watching them dip their heads in the water, then shake it from their feathers, the answer comes easily. No. Even as a child I had a death grip on life, trying to shape it into something I could control.

Ian's eyes are red, and moisture coats his lashes when he turns to me. It's clear from his expression that he's not the same man he was before June's question. I understand. Standing that close to love and death rearranges your DNA. Nobody gets out of these moments unchanged.

"How are you doing this?"

My shoulders rise and fall. "I just am."

"But you're doing it with such grace. You all are." He motions toward the front door. "I was a blubbering idiot in there."

A laugh escapes, tinged with sadness. "You were not a blubbering idiot. Your response was perfect. In fact, she's now measuring everyone else's response to that question based on your reaction. She said that if she receives less than what you gave, the person would be moved to B team and she would get a substitute."

He chuckles. "She would say that."

"Yes, she would."

The rattle of the cicadas in the trees is the only sound as we sit lost in our own thoughts and grief. Conversation isn't necessary or expected.

After a while, I say, "I think in these situations, the best thing you can do is to make decisions based on what you will and won't regret when your person's gone. That's what I'm doing anyway." I push a stray hair out of my face. "So many choices are taken from you when you're fighting a disease that can't be beaten. But the choice we still have is how we'll spend these last days. I choose to be here." My knees pop when I stand. "It appears that's your choice too. Thank you for being here, Ian." Surprisingly, the words don't taste like sand on my tongue. "It means a lot to June and my family." In for a penny... "And it means a lot to me, too."

He doesn't answer but nods, then drops his head back into his hands.

As I push through the front door, I remember what I said to Mom on the way home from the hospital. From this point forward, we just do the next thing. Who knew the next thing on my to-do list would be to thank Ian Hall for anything?

# Chapter Thirty-Six

Over the next few days, an attorney visits the house to assist Aaron and June in drafting a will, a difficult but necessary task. June finishes securing her pallbearers. Luckily, only one friend, who said they needed to think about it, gets kicked off the first string and moved to the B team.

My sisters, Max, Mom, and I help June plan her funeral service down to the last detail, from what she'll wear—a green dress, socks, and absolutely no bra—to who will speak and how long it should last.

No one objects to anything she wants. If she wanted to be escorted in and out of the service with a dozen elephants in polka dot tutus, one of us would try to make it happen. That's how "Picture Me Rollin'" by Tupac is chosen as the final song to be played as her casket is wheeled out of the church.

"That's going to raise some eyebrows," Joy says.

"I think it's sick," Max, who's taking his turn holding June's hand, says.

"Yeah, it's sick, Joy," June says and shrugs her thin shoulders. "People who don't like it can deal with it. It's my funeral. What are they going to do? Complain to me about it?"

"Even in death, you're a troublemaker," Grace says with affection I've rarely heard from her.

A horn honks outside at the same time Max's phone dings with a text. He looks at it and says, "I gotta go. I've got baseball practice."

He stands, but June doesn't let go of his hand. "Remember Max, you play like you practice."

One side of his mouth kicks up in a cocky grin. "I know, Aunt June. You've been telling me that since I was little."

"Because it's true. Now give me a kiss and get out of here."

He makes a loud smooching noise when he kisses her forehead. "See ya."

"Wouldn't want to be ya," June calls after him.

We all hear him laugh as he exits the house.

"He's a good kid, Grace. You did good," June says.

Grace takes Max's place in the chair. "He's alright."

I look over the list we've just made. "Well, I think that's it. Anything else, June?"

"I don't think so." The sentence comes out *Idonthinso*. The doctor increased June's morphine yesterday after a terrible night, and it's left her woozy when she's awake. "Hope!" she yells.

My stomach clenches. I'm in charge of her medication, and it's my name she screams when she's in agony. It kills me every time. But she just took her morphine and can't have more for several more hours.

"I'm here, June," I say from next to the bed.

She startles and jerks her head toward me. "Don't sneak up on me like that."

"I didn't. I was—it doesn't matter. What do you need?"

"We have to make sure Mom has her Viagra."

The five of us look at each other. "What did you say, June?" Grace asks.

"Mom needs her Viagra. I don't want us to forget to get it for her. She shouldn't be without it."

I cup her cheek with my hand. "I'll make sure she has it."

"What is she talking about?" Grace mouths.

I point to the TV, where there's a Viagra commercial playing. She's done this a few times. She hears something on the television and incorporates it into our conversation.

Joy picks up the remote and turns down the TV. "Oh, that's funny."

"What's funny?" June asks.

Babe swallows a laugh. "Nothing."

June frowns. "Whatever. I'm gonna to rest now."

"June, your bedding is all twisted up." I try to pull her blanket out, but it won't budge. "Let us straighten it."

"Do we have to?" she whines.

I understand her reluctance. It's excruciating anytime we move her. Changing her absorbent underwear is torture for her and for us because we're the cause of her misery. "We'll be quick and gentle. Then you'll rest better."

"Fine." She huffs out a resigned breath. "You might as well change the underwear while you're at it."

The four of us take up positions around the bed.

"Alright, on three. One, two, roll," Babe says.

Babe and I roll her to one side by holding her upper body and legs.

June cries out in pain, then whimpers while we hold her on her side so Grace and Joy can straighten the bedding and handle the underwear change. It's awful for all of us.

"I'm here, Junie." Mom is bent over the head of the bed, crooning into June's ear. "They're almost done."

"Oh, shit," June exclaims. "Who has my legs?"

"I do," I answer.

"Damn, Hope, you have man hands!"

I immediately loosen my grip. "Am I holding you too tight?"

"Yes, with your man hands." June groans.

"I'm sorry. I guess I got carried away trying to go fast."

"Done," Grace says.

We roll her onto her back. "There, is that better?" I ask.

She only nods, eyes closed, breathing through the pain.

Joy tucks the blanket around her. "Okay, June. You sleep now."

"I can't. All I can think about are Hope's man hands."

"I don't have man hands, June."

"Yes, you do. And now I'm worried about Ian," she says.

"Why?" I ask.

"If you used those man hands on his tallywacker, then he can't be okay."

"June!" Mom gasps, then ruins her reprimand by laughing.

"Now that you mention it," Grace says, "I think he's walking better since the divorce."

June raises both hands and flexes her fingers like she's grabbing for something. "I'm Hope Hall, and I have man hands. No tallywacker is safe around me."

They're all cracking up. Grace has actually fallen onto the bed laughing.

I snort. "I never heard any complaints from him."

"Yeah, because he was afraid of your man hands."

"Shut up, June," I say, and this time I kind of mean it. At first it was funny, but now it's just insulting.

"What's all this racket?" Ian says as he comes in from outside.

"Hope possibly crippling you with her man hands," June howls.

Ian blinks and looks from me to my sisters. "What's she talking about?"

Heat crawls over my skin like fire ants headed to a summer picnic. "Nothing. She's just talkin'."

"Ian, come here," June says.

He crosses the room to her. "Whatcha need, Bug?"

She holds up her hand and he takes it. "How's your tallywacker?"

"Excuse me?" He searches around the room for someone who isn't hysterically laughing to tell him what's going on. Unfortunately, there isn't anyone. Even I've lost control.

"Hope was changing my bed and used her man hands on me. And now I'm worried that when she used them on your tallywacker, she might've done permanent damage."

"Umm..." Ian glances around again. When he finds no help from any of us, he says, "I'm fine, Bug. You don't have to worry about me."

"Oh, thank God! But I still don't think you should be using that thing. You just got divorced from my sister."

He shoves his free hand through his hair. "Can we stop talking about my dick and how and when I use it?" He clamps his mouth shut and looks at Mom. "Sorry, Marie."

I didn't know there was a color redder than crimson, but apparently there is, if Ian's stained cheeks are any indication.

Mom wipes her eyes and waves him off. "It's alright. I completely agree with you."

June finally releases Ian's hand and pulls the covers up to her chin. "If y'all aren't going to let the dying girl have any fun, then I'm going to sleep." She closes her eyes, and within seconds she's out.

Ian and I purposely avoid making eye contact.

He motions toward the kitchen. "I'm gonna..."

"I think that's best," I say, still not looking at him.

His retreat is quick, which makes my sisters laugh again.

Except June. She's sleeping like she hasn't a care in the world. How like her to pull the pin on a grenade, then step back and watch the fallout.

Troublemaker, indeed.

# Chapter Thirty-Seven

That night, I'm in the kitchen getting June's bedtime meds ready. "June, will you take your full dose of morphine, now that everyone's gone home?"

"Yes."

It's one word, but it tells me everything. June has been in incredible pain today, mostly because she refuses to be medicated as much as she could be. She desperately wants to be present to the point that she's suffering because of it.

Ian is in the kitchen with me, but I'm too distracted with the medication to pay much attention to him.

On the way to take June her medicine, I catch a glimpse of myself in a mirror Mom has hanging on the wall in the living room. I look rough—like really rough. I don't know the last time I washed my hair.

I must make a noise because June asks, "What?"

"I just saw my reflection in the mirror. It ain't good. My hair is one big grease pit."

June's smile is laced with pain. She rubs her fuzzy head. "Yeah, I don't have that problem."

"Sorry." Shame blooms through me. "That was insensitive. Of course there are more important things than my hair."

"Hope, I was kidding." The stupid is implied.

I try to tuck my shame back into the little pocket purse it lives in and hold her medication up to her mouth. She can no longer swallow pills, so everything is administered through a syringe. "Alright, trouble, open up." I squirt the liquid into her mouth.

Her face screws up. "Damn. That's bad."

"Want some water?"

"Please."

I hold the straw to her mouth. She takes a bird's drink, then pushes my hand away.

"You sure you don't want any more, Junie?" Mom asks.

She shakes her head.

That's another thing. She stopped eating a while ago, but now she's begun refusing water too. Her refusing liquids has upset my family. The hospice nurse has told us that this is normal as a person moves toward the end of their life. It's another confirmation that there is only one way this ends.

"Coffee's made, Bug," Ian says as he comes to her bedside. "All Hope has to do is warm it up."

"Thanks, Ian."

We think it's because of her blindness, but whenever she wakes up, she thinks it's morning and therefore wants her coffee. It's the only thing she'll actually finish. Every night, before Ian goes to his RV, he brews up a cup or two for her. It's very sweet.

I'd be lying if I didn't acknowledge that his constant presence is a comfort. I don't really know what to do with that information, so I ignore it. Easy to do with everything going on with June.

He bends to kiss her head. "Good night, Bug."

"Night."

Ian turns to me. "I'm just outside if you need anything." He says this every night.

I nod, which I also do every night.

June reaches her hand out. "Mom?"

Mom moves to her side. "I'm here, June."

"I love you, Mom."

"I loved you first, Junie."

"Mom."

"Yes, honey."

"I think it's time."

"Time for what?"

"I think it's time. Tonight. I think I'm dying tonight."

Ian stops beside me, and I unconsciously grab his arm and ask, "Why do you think that, June?"

"I don't know. I just think it is. Can you call Aaron and tell him to come back?" Aaron has been sleeping at their house during the week to care for their animals, and staying at Mom and Dad's on the weekends.

Ian has his phone in his hand before she finishes the question. "I'm on it, Bug." To me, he says, "I'll call everyone else too."

I nod and grab my phone to call Stephanie, the hospice nurse.

She picks up on the third ring. "This is Stephanie."

"Stephanie, it's Hope Hall. June just told us she thinks tonight is the night."

"Really? Her vitals were all fine when I was there a few hours ago."

I move to the kitchen. "I know. Do you mind coming and evaluating her?"

"Not at all. That's my job. I'll be there in a bit. I'm finishing up with another patient, and she lives about thirty minutes away."

"Thanks, Stephanie." I disconnect the call and go back into the living room.

"Hope, will you put on some praise music?" June asks.

"Sure," I manage around the tears working their way up my throat.

She holds her other hand up. "Dad?"

In all the commotion, I've forgotten about him. He's on the opposite side of the room from June's bed. Instead of going to her when she calls him, he takes several steps back until his back is flat against the wall. If I thought his silent tears were heartbreaking, the dry-eyed panic keeping him rooted to the spot might be the absolute end of me.

"Dad?" June asks again.

I have no idea what to do. Should I help him? He and I don't really have that kind of relationship.

He cuts his gaze to me, and there's a plea there, but I'm not sure what he's asking for.

Get me out of here.

Make it stop.

Help me!

For the first time in a long time, I choose to assume the best of my dad. Without a word, I go to him. I loop my arm through his.

One step.

Then two.

On the third step, he slips away from me and practically runs to June. "I'm here, baby girl." He grabs her outstretched hand, as if by the force of his grip, he can keep her here with us.

"I think it's time, Dad."

He opens and closes his mouth several times, then swallows hard. "I heard. How do you feel about that?"

"It's okay." She the heel of her hand over her wet lashes. "I'm ready."

He lowers his head to their joined hands. "You know, I think you've been the best dad, right?"

A nod seems to be all he can manage.

"Will you do something for me?" she asks.

He dips his face to his shoulder to dry his cheek. "Anything."

"Whip the Fowlers' ass at Halloween."

He and Mom burst out laughing, then he kisses her fingers and says, "You got it."

"I love you, Daddy."

"I love you, Junie. Always."

The short, panting breaths that have replaced my normal breathing hurt almost as much as watching this beautiful horror show in front of me. How did we get here? It's the question that's run on repeat, since that terrible afternoon when we got her terminal diagnosis.

June smiles and releases Dad's hand. He immediately goes to Mom and wraps his arm around her shoulder, and she melts into his side.

Caring for someone who's dying is like living inside a kaleidoscope of emotions. One turn plunges you into sorrow so suffocating that there's no way to draw the breath you need to live. Another turn, and you're laughing so hard you fear you might be losing your mind, but you don't care because it's a reprieve from the pain. It's a series of moments lived on the knife's edge of uninterrupted, overwhelming feelings—some so crushing that if you weren't neck-deep in them, you'd swear no human could survive. But here you are, living it every day, for days on end, praying for relief. Then, just as quickly, begging for it to never end, because it only stops when your person is gone.

"Do you need anything, baby?" Mom asks.

"Can I get a cold washcloth for my head? It really hurts."

I head for the kitchen where we've been keeping washcloths in the fridge for June. "I'll get it." Once I get back to her, I gently place the cloth on her forehead. "Here you go, Junie."

She grabs my wrist and holds me there. "Thank you, Hope."

"Anytime, Junie."

"Hope." She pulls me closer and lowers her voice. "You don't have to be perfect all the time." There's no mistaking the command in her voice.

My legs give out, and I drop down in the chair next to the bed. This woman has cut me open in one sentence, and now my guts are exposed to everyone. "How..."

She licks her dry lips. "I've known for a long time. I thought you knew too. But I'm not sure you do, so before I go, I want you to know that we love you—job, no job, PhD or no PhD, greasy hair and all."

"Even Grace." I try to make it a light quip, but I don't think I pull it off.

"Especially Grace," June says and releases my wrist.

A small sob pushes up my throat. "I'll try to remember that."

"Don't try. Do."

I stand and touch my lips to her forehead over the bruise that still stains her beautiful face. "I'll endeavor to *do*, Junie."

Babe and Clay are the first to arrive. Babe, who looks like she just received the worst news of her life, goes immediately to June's bed. I move out of the way so that she can get to June. She takes my place in the chair next to the bed and drops her head to the mattress. "It can't be time. I'm not ready."

"I know, but I am ready, Babe." My dying sister feels

around until she lands on Babe's back. "You're going to be alright."

Babe's turned her head, her cheek resting on the bed. "I won't." If Babe were standing, I imagine she would stomp her foot.

June chuckles. "You will if you do what I've taught you. I'm not going to be around to fight your battles, so you have to do that yourself. Don't take any shit, Babe."

"Okay." As declarations of strength go, it's a pitiful attempt, but it seems to pacify June.

Grace and Joy come in at the same time. They make a beeline to me. I've moved away from June's bed, in case she decides she wants to spill more of my deepest darkest fears for the whole family to hear.

"What happened?" Grace asks.

I shake my head. "I don't know. She told Mom that it was time."

"But she was fine when we left," Joy says.

"She still seems fine, but I don't know what to expect. She's been dying for weeks now." I look behind them. "Did you bring the kids?"

Grace shakes her head. "We thought we should see what was happening first. They're at Joy's house with Carrie."

"We asked her to come hang out with them," Joy says. "She brought her pillows in case she needs to stay the night—she can't sleep without them, since she started menopause."

"I hear that," Grace says.

"She wants to help." Just then my phone buzzes in my pocket. I pull it out and see Carrie's name. "Speak of the devil." I tap the screen to open my text app.

*I'm praying for y'all. Keep me posted.*

I text back.*Thank you. I will.*

"Joy and Grace," June calls.

They go to her. "We're here," Joy says.

"You know I've never asked y'all for anything," June begins.

"That's absolutely not true," Grace contradicts her.

Joy is nodding before Grace finishes her sentence. "You ask us for stuff all the time. The other day, you asked us to TP the Fowlers' house."

Grace crosses her arms. "Last week you asked us to clean out your car so that everyone else wouldn't see what a disaster it is after you're gone." Her voice betrays her on the last word.

June waves her hand in the air. "Those things aren't important. This is."

Grace's hands go to her hips. "Fine. What do you want now?"

"You could be nicer," June says. "I am dying."

Grace looks away from June, and I can see her swallow several times. She's fighting a truckload of emotions, just like the rest of us, and using irritation to cover it up. "You're right. I'm sorry."

Joy takes June's left hand, playing with the solitaire diamond ring on her finger. "What do you want to ask us, June?"

"I need you both to drop this stupid thing with Jimmy Jenkins. He's not worthy of either of you. He's hurt you both and continues to hurt you. If I could, I'd kick his ass right now for how he's played you both. Promise me you'll let this go and be friends."

The anticipation in the room is as thick as the tears clogging my throat.

We're all looking at Joy and Grace, but they are purposely not looking at each other. Finally, their gazes collide. The war of emotions playing out on their faces would be funny if it were any other situation. It's plain to see that they do not want to agree to June's request.

My admiration for June just went stratospheric. She's diabolically genius. How can they deny her dying wish? Tricky, tricky girl.

"I agree," Joy says.

"Fine. I do too," Grace agrees.

"Good. Now hug."

Grace looks horrified.

Joy sits on the bed next to June, careful not to jostle her. "Don't push your luck, little sister."

"That's fair." A satisfied smile spreads across her pale face.

"Don't look so smug either," Grace says.

June giggles groggily. "I'd say I've earned a small amount of smugness. This must be how God felt when he got to Sunday during the creation week."

"June Elizabeth," Mom scolds. "I think that might be blasphemy."

"It's okay, Mom. Me and God, we're just fine."

# Chapter Thirty-Eight

Aaron enters the room in a way I did not expect. Instead of rushing in with the same urgency my sisters had, he wanders in like a child lost in a crowd, searching for anything familiar, anything to ground him and give him directions back to a life that isn't possible anymore.

But June is his beacon, leading him to his destination.

Once he sees her, he goes directly to her.

My sisters move away from June's side to give Aaron room to sit with his wife. But he doesn't sit. He places one hand on each side of her head and hovers over her like he's about to kiss her. "Hey, baby."

June's smile is brilliant, or as brilliant as a dying woman's can be. "Hey."

"I hear you've made a big announcement." Unlike the rest of us, his eyes are dry.

"Yeah. I'm sorry."

He gingerly sits on the side of her bed, and thumbs away her tears. "Why are you sorry, baby?"

"I can't fight anymore."

"It's okay." He pulls her blanket so that it covers her chest but with her arms out, then tucks it there, just the way she likes it. "You've been fighting a long time."

She takes his face in her hands. "I love you."

He leans his forehead against hers. "I love you too."

Good God. How is a person supposed to survive this?

Over the next twenty minutes, we rotate from sitting to standing to going to June's bedside to say our goodbyes and declare everlasting love. The irony of worship music playing in the background while we all battle our own private hell is disorienting. If you asked any of us to do anything other than perform the basic functions of life in that moment, I doubt very seriously that we'd be able to even comprehend the request.

"Knock, knock," Stephanie, the hospice nurse, says as she comes through the unlocked front door.

I meet her as she enters the living room. "Thank you for coming."

Her blue eyes meet mine. This woman has seen some things. "That's what we do."

I nod. "Still, I'm glad you're here."

She makes her way to June and sets her medical bag down on the chair beside the bed. "Hey, June. It's Stephanie."

A smile spreads across June's peaceful face. "Hey."

The nurse pulls her stethoscope from her scrub top pocket. "Can you tell me what's going on?"

"I think it's time."

Stephanie takes an alcohol prep and cleans the stethoscope. "Okay. Let me take a listen."

While Stephanie checks June's vitals, I find myself standing alone on the edge of the room. As I look around, I see that the rest of my family is paired up. Mom and Dad stand at the end of June's bed. Clay's holding Babe like he can block the terrible truth of the moment with his body. Ian has his arm around Aaron's shoulder as they stand on the other side of June's bed. And surprisingly, Joy and Grace are next to each other on the sofa. Joy's gaze finds me, and she reaches out her hand to me in invitation. Something about that small gesture breaks me.

The tears I've banked begin to flow as I sit next to my sisters on the sofa. Joy's arm goes around my shaking shoulders. I allow myself to lean into her and let go of all restraint. I cry for the loss of June and for the loss of who the four of us will be when she's gone.

Another arm goes around my waist. I look over to see that Grace has moved to my other side, then a warm hand covers mine. Babe is sitting on the floor in front of me.

I use my free hand to wipe my nose with the hem of my T-shirt. "I love y'all."

"We know," Babe says. "We love you too."

I look at Joy, who gives me a gentle smile. "She's right, we do."

I sneak a peek at Grace. But unlike Joy's gentleness, she rolls her eyes. "Yeah, me too."

An inappropriate laugh skips around our little huddle. I lean my head on Grace's shoulder and am pleased when she rests her cheek against the top of my head.

"It looks like Stephanie's finished," Joy says.

We all turn our attention to the hospice nurse, who's noting June's vitals on her tablet.

She takes her stethoscope from around her neck and puts it back into her pocket. "June, your vitals are all normal."

"What does that mean?" Mom asks.

Stephanie smooths her hand over June's fuzzy head. "It means that it's not time yet."

"Really?" June sounds disappointed.

"Really. It is normal to have some anxiety, though. I can prescribe something for anxiety if you want."

"Can you prescribe some for us?" Mom asks.

Stephanie laughs. "I wish I could." She turns her attention back to June. "June, few things that will happen right before it's time. Most of them you probably won't be aware of, but the biggest sign for your family will be that your breathing will change. It will become shallower and faster."

June nods.

Stephanie packs up her blood pressure cuff and other supplies. "I'm only a phone call away if you need me," she says to all of us, then she leaves.

Once she's gone, we stand around looking at each other like we'd all boarded the wrong train and realized it at the same time.

What do we do now?

"Well, I guess it's not tonight." June pulls the covers up to her chin, then turns away from us all. "Y'all can go home now. I'm tired." She says it like we've shown up to a movie on the wrong night, not like we've spent the last hour envisioning a future none of us can comprehend.

"You heard her," Dad says. "Go home. I'm tired too."

Clay leaves, but Aaron, Joy, Grace, and Babe stay, *just in case.*

After a quiet round of goodnights, everyone but Aaron heads upstairs. "Hope, I can stay with her tonight," he says.

"I'm good to stay with her, Aaron. You take the bed and I'll sleep on the sofa." At his hesitation, I say, "I promise I'll come and get you at the first sign of trouble."

He grins at June's sleeping back. "Then I probably won't get a lick of sleep."

Ian shakes his head and chuckles. "I know that's right."

Aaron gives the narrow sofas a dubious look. "You promise you'll come and get me?"

"Cross my heart."

Once everyone is gone, Ian and I are left standing beside June's bed as she sleeps.

"That was intense," he says.

I huff out a laugh. "Yeah. But do you expect anything else from June?"

"Not at all. Always a troublemaker." He says it with such affection that my eyes well again.

"Always."

"I can hear you, you know," June says.

"Good," I say and yawn. "Now if you're done with the drama, I'd like to go to sleep."

She flicks her hand like a queen to her subjects. "Carry on."

I kiss her cheek. "Go back to sleep. You've got more trouble to make tomorrow, I'm sure."

"You know it," is her whispered response.

Hours later, a nightmare jerks me awake. June was on a sailboat, and I was running along the shoreline, trying to catch up with her. Every time I got close, the wind would propel her farther away from me. Even after she was well out of sight, I couldn't stop running.

I sit up and push my hair from my sweaty face, trying to get my bearings. It takes a while for my heart to return to a normal beat. When I'm sure I won't faint from too much adrenaline, I get up from my makeshift bed on the sofa to check on June, with the memory of the dream still tangled in my mind. Relief replaces the adrenaline as soon as I see her chest rising and falling.

The tumors in June's lungs make each breath sound like someone slowly releasing air from a balloon. I involuntarily inhale deeply, trying to breathe for her. I would do this forever if it would help, but it won't.

I sit in the chair next to her bed and take in every feature of her face. My beautiful, brave sister. How have we gotten here so fast? I want to shake my fist at God and scream "Why?" until I get answers, but none are coming. We're not getting our miracle. I'm not sure I even believe in miracles anymore, but I would've taken the one Mom and Babe have been convinced we'd get. It's all so unfair.

She'll never see her forty-first birthday.

She's going to die.

And there's nothing I can do about it.

The tears aren't a surprise, given the nightmare and the night we've had, but the intensity is alarming. My body shakes with racking sobs. I try to stifle my hiccuping gasps but can't. The sorrow is stronger than my will to stay quiet. I rest my head on the side of her bed and give myself over to the helplessness. Thankfully, the strength of June's medication makes it nearly impossible to wake her.

The tears continue until there's no moisture left in my body. I'm a teary, snotty mess. I dry my face on June's bedcovers, stand, and gently kiss her forehead, memorizing the feeling of her warm skin on my lips.

I move to the kitchen to get a bottle of water to replenish all the fluid I've lost. The fridge is full of dishes covered in plastic wrap and foil. People have continued to love us with food. A huge bowl of banana pudding is between me and the water. There's no room to move it due to the overcrowding. I maneuver it out and hold it in the crook of one arm, then grab the closest bottle of water. Then I go to replace the dessert, but I can't seem to let it go.

I don't want to let it go.

In fact, I've never wanted anything less in my life.

Before I can talk myself out of this ill-advised decision, I close the refrigerator with my hip, grab a spoon, and slide to the floor with the water and pudding.

The first bite tastes like sin and freedom. "Oh, my God!" I yell. My mood instantly improves the minute the sugar hits my system. So this is what I've been missing out on all these years? Why have I deprived myself of such joy? At the moment, I can't think of one good reason why.

One bite leads to ten.

I'd be appalled at my lack of control if I cared anymore.

My sisters, who are spending the night in case something else happens with June, rush into the kitchen and find me sprawled on the floor, elbow-deep in banana pudding.

"Hope, is everything alright?" Babe asks.

"Yep." It's hard to speak around the vanilla wafer lodged in my mouth. "Why are y'all up?"

"Joy heard you yell and woke us." Grace ties the belt on her robe. "You good?"

"Dandy." Without looking up from the dessert in my lap, I reach up, yank open the silverware drawer, and grab a handful of spoons. "Join me."

They sit with me, and I place the bowl on the floor between us.

Joy dips her spoon into the pudding. "Wanna tell us what's going on?"

"This isn't like you at all," Babe says with a full mouth.

"Yeah, when's the last time you had a bite of sugar, let alone a gallon bowl?" Grace asks.

"I've tried to fix this." I wave my spoon in the direction of the living room where June is still sleeping. "I've tried to reason it out, and nothing's made me feel better." I shrug and shovel another spoonful into my mouth. "So I thought I'd eat about it and see if that works."

Grace scoops up a generous helping. "Makes perfect sense to me."

Joy holds up her utensil. "Here's to eatin' our feelin's."

We click our spoons together. "Here's to eatin' our feelin's," we echo.

The only sounds after that are lips smacking, spoons scraping against the bowl, and moans of pleasure as we drown our sorrows in custard.

I know I'll pay for this tomorrow. Grace is right. I haven't had this much sugar in forever. But for right now, there's no place I'd rather be than with my sisters on this kitchen floor, eating this bowl of banana pudding.

# Chapter Thirty-Nine

"Help me, Hope!" June cries. "Please, please, please help me, Hope!"

My name being screamed is a refrain that's played with increasing frequency over the last few days. I wonder if she could sense this was coming, and that's why she tried to will herself to death three days ago. It's horrible to watch. Thankfully, it's not all the time, but every time June turns to me for help and I can't because she's exceeded her allotted dosage of pain medication, it digs a groove in my heart that I know will be there for the rest of my life.

Now isn't one of those times. "Hang on, June. I'm getting the morphine." I suck a full dose of the pain medication into the syringe. I don't give her a choice of a smaller dose. Judging from the way she's writhing in agony, I don't think she'll mind.

"You're giving her that whole syringe full?" Babe, who does mind, asks.

I move past her to get to June. "Yes."

"That's too much. She's going to get addicted."

I stop midstride and turn on Babe. "I hope she does. I hope

she's as high as a kite and feeling no pain for these last few days. She at least deserves that mercy." I should probably feel bad for snapping at Babe, but I don't.

June can no longer swallow pills, so we're having to give her meds sublingually. I hold the syringe filled with morphine to June's mouth. "Here you go, Junie." She opens her mouth and I administer the medicine under her tongue. "You should feel better soon."

The effects come quickly. She's not completely out of pain, but it subsides enough that she's not screaming my name anymore.

Babe crosses her arms over her chest. "You didn't even ask if she wanted the full dose."

"I did. I want it all," June mumbles between moans of misery.

I resist the urge to shake my little sister. "She shouldn't have to suffer, Babe. It's senseless and cruel." I glance at Mom and Dad for backup, but they stay silent, which only increases my aggravation.

Babe and Mom's fear is that June will be a drug addict when God heals her. But I'm pretty sure if He can rid June of this monster disease, a little thing like a morphine addiction would be child's play to cure. I admire their faith, right up until it causes June suffering.

I know they understand that concern is irrational, but not one of us is thinking rationally right now. It's the only reason I haven't completely lost it on them, but it's been a near thing.

Babe buries her face in her hands, then looks up at me. "You're right." Her eyes are as tired as mine and she looks just as disheveled, though it does appear she's washed her hair recently. I still haven't made it to that chore yet.

I nod, then head to the kitchen to rinse the syringe. I brace my hands on the side of the sink. It's literally one thing after another.

*Hope, what do you think we should do about June not eating?*

*Why are you giving her that medication, Hope?*

*When do you think it will happen, Hope?*

Hell, I don't know. I barely know my own name right about now.

I've spent years wanting my family to prize my intellect and competence. Now that they're turning to me for every answer, it's heaping anxiety on top of anxiety. Be careful what you wish for.

Too much stress over too long a period of time has made my chest feel like a pressure cooker about to blow. I can feel it, but I try to breathe through the stress.

"Hope, do you think your family would like Italian or BBQ for dinner?" A hapless Ian wanders in from outside. "The girls June coaches want to bring food tonight. I told them—"

I shove off the counter and round on him. "I. Don't. Care." The words fire from me. The stunned look on his face is almost enough to rein me in, but not quite. "BBQ, Italian, a burrito from the convenience store..." I hold my hands up in front of me, warding him and everyone else off. "I don't care. Ask someone else."

"Okaaay." He doesn't look offended, just a little confused, and a lot concerned.

The concern is what triggers the tears. I will not do this here. I grab my purse and head to my car. There's no plan. I simply have to get out of the inferno for a while.

As soon as I'm in the car, I dial Carrie's number.

"Hi—"

"Carrie, I'm coming to your—"

"I'm not available. Leave a message after the tone—"

I end the call and throw my phone into the passenger seat. Fresh tears stream down my face. What good is a best friend if they're not around when you're falling apart?

I drive aimlessly for I don't know how long, tears pouring from my eyes. It's probably not safe, but neither is staying at the house where I can feel years being peeled from my life, and the chance I'll blow up at an innocent bystander is 100%. The car rolls past the hardware store, the elementary school, the diner, and Cuttin' Up.

I immediately whip a U-turn and before I know what I'm doing, I'm parking and climbing the steps to Cuttin' Up.

I push through the door and am greeted with the smell of perm solution, coconut shampoo, and mildew. Heaven.

Patty's doing someone's hair and has her back to me, but shouts, "Welcome! How can we help?"

When I don't answer, she turns to me. I must look as bad as I feel because she says, "Oh, my Lord, baby girl." She holds her arms open and I stumble into them. "Sweetie, tell me what's wrong. Did June...?"

I shake my head. "No. My..." I sob. "My hair is dirty, and I don't have the energy to wash it."

"Lovey baby." She strokes my back. "Hush now, I'll take care of you. You head over to the washing bowl, and I'll be right with you. I'm almost done with Lois here."

I peek over Patty's shoulder and see that Lois's hair is nearly done. Or at least it looks like it is. I don't think it could get much higher, and there's enough hairspray to shellac a boat.

I do as I'm told, making a quick stop at the bathroom. The pink and black tile on the wall is the same as it was when I was a kid and came with my grandmother. I immediately feel better. I splash water on my splotchy face, then dry it with paper towels. The person I see in the mirror bears only a vague resemblance to the woman from a couple of months ago.

My olive skin has a sallow tint, my green eyes are deep set with dark circles under them, and my auburn hair is lifeless, with strands of gray streaked through it. The tight bun on top of my head does nothing to add animation to my face.

By the time I get to the wash bowl, Patty is waiting for me. She's turned down the lights and changed the country music that was playing when I walked in to something soothing and melodic.

I situate myself in the chair with my head back. By some unspoken agreement, we don't speak. Patty warms the water in the bowl, then begins to wet my hair. She lathers twice. The scrubbing feels better than anything has in a long time, until she begins to massage my scalp, neck, and temples during the conditioning phase. That takes this from feeling nice to a true religious experience.

She takes her time, not rushing me or the moment, as the fibers of my muscles slowly uncoil. The entire thing is a gift I didn't know I needed.

When she's finished, she wraps a towel around my head and leads me to her chair, where she adds product and gently combs out any lingering tangles. Still, we don't speak. Finally, she asks, "You want the Patty Special?"

What is the Patty Special? No clue.

Do I need the Patty Special? Not at all.

Am I getting the Patty Special? You better believe it.

I've lost the ability to speak, I'm so zoned out, all I can manage is a nod. But then a thought hits me. "I don't want it cut."

Her strong hands press and knead the muscle in my neck and shoulders. "The Patty Special doesn't come with a cut."

"Okay." This woman could lead me to join a cult and at the moment, I'd happily follow.

She turns the chair away from the mirror so the blow dryer

will reach the plug. Once my hair is dry, she asks, "Sweetie, you ready to talk?"

I shrug. "There's not much to say. I think it all just got to me today."

"Oh, honey, I understand that. When my Stan was sick, before he passed, I was a basket case. It's cruel that you have to make decisions and do things when you're barely hanging on yourself."

"That's it exactly."

"Your family should take some of the burden from you, sweetheart."

I turn my head so she can see my face. "They do. They're great. It's mostly my fault. I try to do too much."

"Well, darlin', then you're a gem. I hope they all know that."

I wince at a pulling sensation at the top of my head. "We're all doing the best we can."

I've lost track of time, so when she pronounces me done and I check my phone, it's been two hours. I feel like a different person. When she turns the chair to face the mirror, I see that I look like a different person too. In fact, my shoulder-length locks look remarkably like Lois's did, and like half the women in Bonedalia.

My hair is brushed away from my face and back-combed on top to form a bump at the crown of my head, then sleek straight until the ends, which kick up like cancan dancers on parade. It's the ugliest thing I think I've ever seen, and I love it.

In fact, I love everything about Patty and this place. If I could, I'd move in and live the rest of my life here.

"What do I owe you?" I ask when we get to the front of the salon.

She gently takes my chin in her hand. "It's on the house, baby doll."

"No, I couldn't—"

"You'll hurt my feelings, shug, if you don't let me do this for you." She puts her finger to the side of her nose. "Remember, I lived the hell you're living now. You can pass it on at some point."

Another round of tears threatens, but I gulp them back. My arms go around her broad shoulders. Her returning hug is bone-cracking. "Thank you, Patty. You really saved the day."

"Aw, honey bear, that's what we do at Cuttin' Up. We save the day."

Once in my car, I check my reflection in the visor mirror. Yep, still a back-combed helmet. There's no telling how much shampoo it will take to rid my hair of the hairspray, but none of that matters now. The only thing I care about is the softness of the muscles in my neck and shoulders and the lightness in my heart.

My phone buzzes with a text from Mom.

*If it's not too much trouble, June was wondering if you could grab her a blue Gatorade on the way home.*

You can almost hear my mother's trepidation in making the request. I can't say I blame her, given how I stormed out of the house.

*Absolutely.*

I pull out of the parking lot and immediately know that I will not be going to the Shop and Save. I might appreciate what Patty did for me, but this hair looks truly heinous, and the grocery store will be far too crowded for the Patty Special.

The parking lot of the drugstore has only a few cars, so I whip in. The store is as empty as the parking lot. Thank goodness. I make my way to the cooler to grab June's beverage, which I'm convinced she won't drink.

An argument on the aisle next to me catches my attention.

"Aunt Marjorie, you promised to buy me anything I wanted."

Marjorie? Could it be Marjorie Fowler?

My suspicions are confirmed when I hear Aunt Marjorie's voice. "Jewel, I've already ordered you those $300 boots."

Wasn't Jewel the name of the niece my sisters were talking about in the cheerleader story?

There's a sniff that only a teenager can make, followed by, "When you asked me to try out in place of Samantha, you didn't put a time limit on how long you had to buy me what I wanted, and I want these lipsticks."

"Shhh, keep your voice down," Marjorie whisper-yells. "Fine. I'll get you the lipsticks, but this is the last thing."

"Thank you, Auntie." The sour syrup note in Jewel's voice indicates that this will in fact not be the last thing she extorts from Marjorie.

"You're welcome. Now come on, we'll pay for them at the pharmacy when I get my prescription."

As soon as I see them move to the back of the store, I rush to the self-checkout then to my car, electricity zinging through me at this tasty bit of gossip that's fallen into my lap.

It's an effort to drive the speed limit home. I make it in record time. Gravel flies when I skid to a stop in the parking area in front of my parents' house.

I nearly break my neck getting into the house.

"Hope? Are you alright?" Mom asks.

"I'm great." My response is breathy and a little manic. I turn to my sisters, who are all around June's bed. "Y'all are not going to believe this!"

# Chapter Forty

"Why do you look like Dolly Parton's younger, less endowed sister?" Joy asks when I enter the living room.

"You've got the helmet, where's your motorcycle?" Babe asks, then slaps the hand Joy raises

"She got the Patty Special." Grace laughs, which causes everyone else to laugh, including me.

I shrug. "When in Rome?"

Babe holds her phone up like she's going to take a picture.

I stare her down. "Don't you dare!"

She laughs. "Fine. What are we not going to believe?"

"You were right. You were all right." I'm practically bouncing out of my shoes.

"About your hair being hideous? We know," June slurs.

I hang my purse on the back of one of the kitchen chairs and go to stand beside her bed. "How do you know? You can't even see me." I'm relieved to see she seems better than she was before I left.

June gives me a drunken smile. "I too have been a victim of

the Patty Special. It wasn't pretty." She makes a rolling motion with her hand. "Go on. What are we right about?"

"Oh, my gosh. I was at the drugstore and overheard—"

"What the hell happened to your hair, Hope?" Dad, who's just come in from outside, interrupts.

"Patty Special," the other five members of my family say in unison.

A rusty chuckle rolls from his lips. "Patty Patton strikes again." He pats my upper arm sympathetically as he walks past me to the kitchen. "It was bound to happen if you stayed here long enough."

"It's true, honey," Mom adds. "And it doesn't look that bad."

"It's horrible, Mom, but that's not the point." I look to my sisters again. "I overheard Marjorie Fowler and her niece Jewel in the drugstore arguing over whether Marjorie was going to buy Jewel these lipsticks she wanted."

"So?" Grace says.

"As stories go, that one sucks, Hope," June adds unhelpfully.

"Marjorie didn't want to buy them because she's already bought Jewel some really expensive boots." I raise my brows waiting for them to put it together. They don't. "Oh, my gosh, y'all. Marjorie bought her the boots and ultimately the lipsticks because Jewel reminded her she'd tried out for cheerleader in Samantha's place!"

"You heard her say those words?" Grace asks.

I cross my arms over my chest, a little embarrassed at how pleased I am to have confirmed their idle gossip. "Sure did."

Babe shakes her head. "I knew it."

"That bit"—Joy glances over at Mom—"um, witch."

"Di. A. Bolical." June's head is on her pillow, her eyes are closed, and she's grinning like a loon.

"She is." I look around at my sisters. "So, what are we going to do about it?"

We? I've lost my mind.

The four of them look a little confused.

"Do about it?" Joy asks.

"Yeah, now that we know for sure. What are we going to do?" I can't seem to help myself. I'm all in on whatever revenge plan they come up with.

"We aren't going to do anything," Grace says. "It's enough that we know. And believe me, that kind of knowledge is power in this town."

I should be grateful that Grace is trying to rein me in, but I'm mostly annoyed. "No. We need to do something. Tell 'em, June."

She shakes her head. "Grace is right. This is information best kept to ourselves until we need it, and we don't need it now."

"But... I thought... Never mind."

Babe smiles encouragingly, but it kind of comes off patronizing. "You did good, though, Hope. It is juicy information."

I can't understand why they're not out for blood, then it hits me. Simply knowing the gossip satisfies them. The truth itself isn't the point. It's having the knowledge. The gossip is its own reward. Stinging heat marches up my neck and spreads over my cheeks. "I'm going to..." I point toward the front door. "I'll be right back."

I push through the front door, sucking air deep into my lungs. The exhale comes as I drop down onto the porch swing. For several moments, I'm not sure what to feel.

Embarrassment, for sure. Lord, I practically yelled, "We ride at dawn!" The absurdity teases a chuckle from me. The chuckle turns to a giggle, followed by gut-splitting belly laughs.

What did I think we were going to do? Round up the Fowlers and publicly shame them?

This town. These people. They're lovable in their ridiculousness.

My phone buzzes with a text from Carrie.

*I saw I missed your call. What's up?*

I quickly type.

*I was having a good, old-fashioned come undone, but I'm better now.*

Her response is quick.

*Oh, no. Are you okay?*

My fingers move across the keypad.

*I'm good now. I got the Patty Special.*

She sends back.

*I NEED A PIC.*

I hold the phone up, snap a pic and send it to her.

Her text pops up on my screen, and I laugh.

*OMG!!!* 🤣🤣🤣

"Hope?"

I look up to see Ian making his way to the porch from the RV.

"It's me."

I send Carrie one last text.

*Gotta go. I'll call you tomorrow.*

"I... um... your hair." He seems to be at a loss for words.

I go to flip my hair with my hand, but it doesn't move. "It's a long story."

He chuckles but looks more uncomfortable than I've seen him look in a while. "Do you have a minute to talk?"

"Sure. But first, I'm sorry for biting your head off earlier."

He waves off my apology and pulls a chair over to sit across from me, elbows resting on his knees. "I've been thinking about all the things you said to me that night at the hospital."

I scrunch my nose, something else I probably need to apologize for. "Yeah. That was a bad night. I could've handled that better."

He doesn't say anything, only stares at the ground between his splayed legs. When he raises his gaze there's a depth of emotion there that I haven't seen in a really long time. "You were right."

"What?" His admission catches me completely off guard.

He repeats himself. "You were right."

"I was?"

"Yes. I'm guilty of it all. I treated you like shit. I took your independence and lack of confrontation as permission to do as I wanted." He shifts his gaze to the fields beyond the house. "I didn't see it for what it was, survival. I taught you to behave that way, and then I held it against you."

This is so out of left field that I have no idea what to say. So I settle for, "Okay."

He rubs his teeth over his bottom lip and examines his boots. When he turns his attention to me, there's a resignation in his eyes. "I tore us apart, Hope. I did that. I see it now." He scrubs his hand over his head. "Jesus, I let you down in every way possible. I'm a bastard. No wonder you can't trust anything I say as truth." It's clear from the pain in his expression that this is a new revelation to him. "I'm sorry—so damn sorry. You didn't deserve my selfishness." He stands and slips his fingers into his front pockets and shrugs. "You don't have to say anything. I just wanted you to know."

I shove down the ingrained instinct to absolve and rescue him and shield him from anything hard. "Thank you. Can I ask what brought this on?"

The question startles a laugh from him. "First, it's way past time that I made things right. Second, in light of what's going on in there"—he juts his chin in the direction of the house—"I don't want to leave anything unsaid. When you said to make decisions based on what you will and won't regret, well, I would regret not saying those things to you."

"We both made mistakes and didn't take care of what was precious. We can't go back and fix what happened with us, but there's something precious inside that house that we can take care of." I stand and open the front door for him. "After you."

# Chapter Forty-One

The next morning, June wakes and tries to sit up. "Hope, help me."

"Help you what?"

"I need to get up." She reaches for the railing of the bed.

"Get up?" I can't help the incredulity in my voice. "Like out of bed?"

"Yes. I'm healed."

"Hallelujah," Mom whispers behind me.

"Somebody, help me," June yells, though it sounds more like a kitten wailing.

"Okay." I look at Babe, who shrugs, then comes to help.

I release lower the bed railing, then take June's hand. "Babe and I have got you." I put my other hand behind June's back and help her sit, while Babe helps move her legs over the edge of the bed. "Can you sit by yourself?"

"Yes. I told you I was healed."

"Alright." I hold my hands up but don't move too far away. Babe stays close too, in case June really does try to stand on her own. Because the reality is, even if by some miracle she's been healed, she's so weak from muscle attrition and lack of food that there's no way she could stand on her own.

"Are you sure about this, June?" Babe asks.

"Yes, I'm sure." She's emphatic, but she doesn't immediately try to stand. "I'm just gettin' my bearings."

"Junie, how do you know you're healed?" Mom asks, and I can hear the hope in her voice.

"God told me last night."

"Did he?" Babe asks, and now I can see she and Mom are swimming in the same hope-filled pool.

"Yes," June says, but she's still not making a move to stand.

"Do you want some help?" I ask.

She shakes her head. "I got it." She blows out a breath like a weightlifter about to deadlift 300 lbs. and shimmies her skinny butt to the edge of the bed until her feet touch the ground. "One." She places her hands on the bed next to her hips. "Two." Then leans forward. "Three." With her limited strength, she pushes her body up. Nothing happens. She tries once more. Still nothing. She teeters and almost falls to the side, but Babe catches her. "Well, shit. I guess I dreamed it."

I kneel in front of her and place my hands on her knees. "Sounds like a great dream."

"It really was."

I can hear Mom and Babe crying behind me. "Wanna lie down now?"

Her chuckle sounds like dry, cracked earth looks. "I think I should before I fall over."

I help her back into the bed without Babe, which means I can't get her back into the right position.

Grace and Joy come in then, and we try to get her situated but can't move her without hurting her.

"Go get Dad," I say to Babe.

She goes to the backyard and comes back with our father in a few minutes.

"Dad, can you get her under the arms and pull her up so her head is on the pillow?" Joy asks.

"Help me, Dad. These weaklings can't do it," June teases.

"I've got you, Junie." He stands at the head of the bed and places his hands under her arms. "Ready?"

"Yes."

"Here we go." He pulls, and June yells out, but she's in the right place in the bed. Dad comes to her side. "I'm so sorry I hurt ya."

"It's okay." She shrugs. "It's just the way it is. I love you."

He takes her hand. "I love you too."

"I know."

"Good."

He turns to leave, but June doesn't let go of his hand. "Now tell my sisters you love them."

Dad chuckles uneasily. "Huh?"

"Tell my sisters that you love them," June says emphatically.

He shakes his head, looks down, and says, "I love y'all."

"No." June still refuses to let go of his hand. "Tell each one of them like you mean it. Because I know you do mean it, Dad. They need to know it too."

I've never seen a man look more uncomfortable in my life. Red splotches cover his cheeks, and he keeps making a sound between a laugh and a cough.

The awkwardness doesn't stop with my dad. My sisters are acting weird too. Grace makes an inappropriate joke that Joy laughs too hard at, and if Babe shuffles her feet any faster, she'll be dancing. My bones and muscles have turned to stone. I look like a totem pole with daddy issues.

"Tell 'em, Dad," June whispers.

"I love you, Babe." The words are clipped like the keys of a typewriter.

"I love you too, Dad."

"I love you, Joy." The cadence isn't quite so rigid, but it still sounds like he's trying to speak a foreign language.

"Love you too."

I glance over at Mom, who's standing by the bar, clutching a dish towel, with tears running down her cheeks.

Dad turns to Grace. "I love you, Gracie."

Gracie? I've never heard the man call her Gracie, but regardless of how unfamiliar the words are, they seem genuine.

She jerks her chin down and mumbles, "You too."

When it's my turn, Dad hesitates for a second, and that slight pause cuts my heart in two. I've always known I wasn't his favorite person, but I did assume he loved me. In the blink of that silence, I wonder if I've been wrong.

"Hope..."

"Yeah, Dad?"

"I love you." He holds my gaze. "I'm proud of you."

I hear the words, but I have no point of reference for where they fit into my narrative of our relationship. I've told myself the same story for as long as I can remember, and it sure as hell wasn't that this man, who I've never really known, was proud of me. Something like sunshine glows through me. The little girl deep inside me wants to run through the streets singing, *my daddy is proud of me*. I wait to feel embarrassed about that, but I don't at all.

He looks around the room. "I'm so damn proud of all of you." He swallows several times. "I know that if it weren't for your mama, I probably wouldn't have a relationship with any of you, and I'm sorry for that."

"That's really good, Dad," June says and pats his arm.

He glances back at her and grins, even though she can't see

him. "It was always easy with June, probably because she wouldn't leave me alone, but it shouldn't have been up to you girls to come after me." It's like once the words start, he can't stop. "I should've shown up for you. I'm gonna do better." He puts his other hand over June's. "I promise."

"I'm proud of you, Dad," June says.

He kisses the back of her hand, then releases it. "I'm gonna head back outside." He leaves through the back door without looking back.

No one says anything for more than a few heartbeats.

"Well, shit," Grace says. "Who knew he had it in him?"

June grins and snuggles into the pillow. "Me."

# Chapter Forty-Two

"Oh, my God, June! Do you remember when you threw yourself onto the hood of my car, in nothing but a towel?" Joy's friend Pam asks around huge guffaws.

"It's burned into my memory, like a bad dream," June says dryly.

Today's been a pretty good day for June, which means it's been a pretty good day for us too. In this season of life and dying, she is the kite and we are the tail. We go where she goes, until the day comes when we can't.

I try to shove the heavy weight of that inevitability away. "Wait," I say. "I don't know this story." I glance at Chloe, who's sitting next to me. She and Carrie are helping me pick pictures of June for her funeral. A job I hoped I'd never have to do. "Have you heard this one?"

She shakes her head. "I don't think so."

"It's my favorite June story," Pam says, scooting to the edge of her seat. "Joy and I had just turned sixteen and gotten our driver's licenses. So of course, our favorite thing to do was ride around."

"Oh, the days of driving up Hamilton Street, around the square, back down Madison Street, turning around in the 7-Eleven parking lot, then doing it all again," Grace says.

"For hours," Joy adds.

"It was the highlight of the week," Carrie adds wistfully.

"Sounds boring," Chloe says.

"Kind of like scrolling social media for hours?" Joy asks.

Chloe gives her mother a look that only a fourteen-year-old is capable of making.

Pam holds her hands up to get our attention again. "Anyway, Joy and I were about to go riding around, and June had come in from basketball practice." She turns to June. "How old were you?"

"Twelve."

"That's right. And she asked if she could go with us." Pam tries to continue but starts laughing again.

"I said yes," Joy adds.

A dry laugh rattles up June's throat. "I was so excited. I asked them to wait so I could shower, and they agreed. I run and jump into the shower. But while I'm in there, I start to think that they agreed a little too easily. So I grab my towel and run into the living room, only to see these bitches getting into Pam's car."

"When she burst out of the front door, I shifted into reverse," Pam says.

Joy picks up the story. "The next thing we know, June throws herself onto the hood of the car and holds on where the front meets the windshield."

"But did they stop?" June asks. "No, they did not. They were yelling at me to get off, but I wouldn't let go. So that heifer"—she points in the direction of Pam—"put it in drive and kept going. I'm buck naked, except for the towel, and she drives all the way to Madison Street with me hanging on for dear life. When she stopped at the stop sign, I had to admit defeat."

"But that's like a quarter of a mile," I say.

"Yeah, try walking that quarter of a mile in nothing but a scrap of terry cloth and barefoot."

I look from Joy to Pam. "Y'all didn't give her a ride home?"

Joy laughs. "No."

"That's so mean," Chloe says, but her offense on June's behalf loses credibility when she laughs.

"You should've seen your grandmother's face when I came through the front door," June chuckles.

"I was appalled that Joy and Pam had done such a thing," Mom adds.

One side of June's mouth kicks up. "And I milked that for everything it was worth. How long were you grounded for, Joy?"

"A month."

"I'll take that win any day of the week and twice on Sundays," June says.

Joy looks at me, Carrie, and Chloe and motions toward June. "You see why we left her, right?"

Chloe giggles.

Carrie snort laughs.

I hold up my hands in surrender. "Don't make me pick sides."

June winces in pain when she tries to adjust herself in the bed. "Yeah, because the dying girl always wins."

Joy rolls her eyes. "Always trying to work the angle."

Ian comes into the living room with a fresh glass of water for June. "It wouldn't be the last time she went somewhere in a towel."

"Ian Hall, I swear I'll get out of this bed and kick your ass if you tell that story," June says sluggishly, but she's grinning like an idiot.

Mom looks from Ian to June. "Do I want to hear this?"

Babe, who's already laughing, says, "No."

"Come on, Bug, confession is good for the soul," my ex says.

June waves her hand. "Fine, go ahead."

Ian sits down in the chair next to June's bed and takes her hand. "I'll hold your hand while I tell it because we're probably both going to get in trouble once I'm done."

"You're probably right," she slurs.

"One Saturday night, I'm at home alone, when I get this phone call from Buddy Albert, sayin' that this one here"—he tilts his head toward June—"is three sheets to the wind at this party, and that I should probably come get her because she's about to fight some girl from Hawkins."

I scroll through my memories but come up empty. "Where was I?"

"You and Carrie had gone to that antique show down in Round Top." He sucks his bottom lip between his teeth. "This is why I'm probably gettin' in trouble. I never told anyone what happened."

"Snitches get stitches," June slurs.

"What she said." His eyes crinkle at the corners when he grins. "Anyhow, when I get there, I see Bug in her robe and her hair wrapped in a towel with this girl twice her size pinned up against the wall."

"What?" I'm not sure why I'm surprised. June is known for stories like this one. "Why were you in your robe and a towel on your head?"

"Why were you at a party with a robe on and a towel on your head?" Chloe is clearly appalled.

"I'd just gotten out of the shower when one of my friends called to say this girl from Hawkins was messin' with my boyfriend at Buddy's party. I was pissed. First of all," she says, but the morphine makes it sound like *fistofall.* "I didn't even know there was a party. And second, you don't poach my man."

"Which boyfriend was that?" Grace asks.

She waves the question away. "I don't remember. We'd only gone out a few times."

"You got into a fight over some boy you'd only gone out with a handful of times?" I ask.

"Youdon'tpoachmyman."

"Thankfully, I got to her before she could throw the first punch," Ian says. "I grabbed her around the middle to lift her away from danger because that girl was only biding her time until she could get a clean shot at Bug."

"Yeah, and you gave her one," June says. "As soon as you pulled me off of her, she pounced."

Ian rubs his jaw with his free hand, amusement shining in his eyes. "She was quick."

"Yeah, she was."

"Next thing I know, June is kicking and screaming while I'm holding her."

June grins. "I was showing all my business to everyone. That was the unfortunate part."

"OMG." Chloe is clutching her pearls.

"Oh, *that* was the unfortunate part?" I ask.

"Chloe," June says

"Yes, Aunt June."

"I'm goin' to give you a piece of advice that will serve you well."

Chloe sits up straight, like she's waiting for wisdom from on high. "I'm listening."

"Always, and I mean always, throw the first punch if you've got an opening."

Chloe makes a show of deflating back against the sofa, but

there are tears in her eyes, and I know she understands that this moment is precious.

Everyone is laughing, and it's not a polite, June is dying so let's laugh at her stories laugh. It's a *we desperately love everything about this woman* laugh. It's not lost on me that June has never conformed to life's expectations. She's never tried to be perfect. Her whole life she's dared people not to love her, warts and all. I admire the hell out of her for that.

"I don't think I ever thanked you for coming to my rescue, Ian."

Ian kisses the back of her hand. "Anytime, anywhere, Bug."

Mom comes over to the hospital bed and kisses June's forehead. "You are something else."

She sighs at the touch of Mom's lips on her skin. "I've had a good life."

Mom smooths her hand over June's head. "You have, baby. It's just not been long enough."

"Mom."

"Yeah, honey?"

"Thank you."

"For?"

"My good life."

## Chapter Forty-Three

That night, Mom, Dad, my sisters, Clay, Aaron, and I are all in our usual spots in the living room. Joy and Grace seem to have taken June's request to get along seriously, because lately they always end up on the same sofa together. Clay is in one recliner, and Dad's in the other. Mom is in her rocking chair, situated close to June's bed. I'm on the other sofa, and Babe and Aaron are at June's bedside.

And Ian, who knows?

"Does anyone know where Ian is?" I ask as casually as possible.

I honestly don't know what he's doing when he's not helping in the kitchen. What I do know is I'm keenly aware when he's not around and inexplicably comforted when he is.

That's probably a problem.

But if it is, it's one for another day.

"He's gone to our house," Aaron says. "June wanted that old, beat-up sweatshirt she always wears."

"It's not beat-up. It's well-loved," June argues. She's been more lucid and talkative tonight than she has been in days.

Aaron grins and kisses her fingers. "June wanted that well-loved sweatshirt she always wears."

"That's better." Two lines form between her brows. "What's taking him so long? It feels like he's been gone a long time."

"You're right." Aaron checks his phone for the time. "It's been more than an hour."

An uncomfortable pinch shoots through my chest.

Is he alright?

Did he get a flat tire?

Was he in an accident?

I walk out onto the porch and call him.

He picks up on the fourth ring. "Hello."

He sounds horrible, and that pinch becomes a stab.

"Where are you?"

The only thing I hear is his breath coming through the phone.

"Ian. You're scaring me. Where are you?"

"I'm at June's."

"Oh, okay." I'm relieved that he's not in a ditch somewhere, but he still sounds off. "Are you okay?"

"I can't, Hope."

"Can't what? Find June's sweatshirt? Did you look in ”

"No. I can't come back." His voice breaks. "I walked in here, and it smells like her perfume. Her makeup's in the bathroom. Her shoes are by the door. And she's never coming home. I know that. But being here, seeing all her stuff... I can't go back there and watch her die." He barely gets the words out because of his tears.

I open my mouth, ready to rattle off the litany of indictments that I've used to describe his character for the last ten years. But the accusations die before they can form, because he's right. It is too hard.

I close my eyes and lean against the wall. "I know," I say quietly. "You're right. It is too hard. I don't want to do it either."

I hear him release a shaky breath. "I'm sorry—"

"I need you."

"What?"

I let out my own wobbly breath. "I need you here, Ian. I don't think I can do this without you. I've never told you that before. But I do. I need you here with me."

There's no sound from the other end of the call, not even his breathing. Finally, "Okay." His voice is rough. "I'm on my way."

Twenty minutes later, Ian walks into the house with June's sweatshirt. Red, puffy eyes betray the calm he presents as he hands me the sweatshirt without a word.

"Look what Ian brought you, Junie." I help her put it on.

She pulls the hood up and snuggles into the sweatshirt. "Thank you, Ian."

"Anytime, anywhere, Bug."

The smile I give him fits comfortably on my face. I do an internal check and am surprised there's not an ounce of resentment or disappointment to be found, only gratitude and an acceptance that we're all just doing the best we can.

He nods, then looks away, like any more eye contact and his resolve to ride this out with us will crumble.

A baseball game plays on the TV, but nobody's paying much attention.

June's been in a sour mood for the last hour, and it has nothing to do with her cancer or the fact that she's in her last days of life. No, she's mad because we just found out the Fowlers won the trophy for best yard display for homecoming.

"I can't believe they won," she says for the twenty-fifth time.

"I know. It chaps my hide too," Dad, who's not taking it any better than June, says.

"Don't worry, y'all'll get 'em next time," Clay says from the recliner. As soon as the words are out of his mouth, his eyes go round, and all the color drains from his cheeks. "I'm... Ugh... I didn't mean..."

"It's fine, Clay." June dismisses his fumbled apology. "I won't be here for the next one, but y'all better show up for the Christmas Parade and help Dad."

Out of my periphery, I see Aaron drop his head to June's bed.

June runs her pink-tipped nails over his scalp. "I'm serious. He can't do it by himself, and I have a legacy to protect."

Clay clears the tears from his throat. "I'll be there, June."

"I'm countin' on ya, Clay."

"I swear," he says with all the sincerity of a man pledging himself to God and country.

A knock on the door prevents June from eliciting vows from the rest of us.

"I'll get it," Joy says. "Oh, hello. Come in."

She reenters the room with Colleen Fowler and her husband Henry trailing behind her.

"Colleen?" Mom tries but fails to hide her surprise.

Mrs. Fowler rushes to Mom, arms spread wide, and engulfs her in a hug. "Oh, Marie. I can't imagine. This must be agony."

Surely I'm imagining the accusation in her tone, like somehow June is purposely hurting my parents by dying.

But then Colleen releases her hold on Mom and says with a helpless shrug, "Adult children."

Yep. No mistaking the indictment.

"Um, what brings you two by?" Mom asks, ever polite.

Mr. Fowler moves to June's bedside and holds his hand out

for his wife. "We, of course, wanted to express our love and concern for your family."

"Of course." The words coming out of Dad's mouth are so dry they could be used as kindling.

Colleen places her hand over her heart. "That's not all. We wanted to give this to you, June." She reaches into her giant purse, pulls out a gold trophy, and presents it to June.

June doesn't react because, of course, she can't see what's happening.

"Um, June?" Colleen's irritation that she didn't get the reaction she expected comes across loud and clear. "Oh, my goodness, I did hear you'd been struck blind." She takes my sister's hand and curls her fingers around the trophy.

Struck blind? This woman. She may as well just come out and say that God cursed June. "She wasn't—"

"You poor thing," Colleen continues.

June frowns. "What is it?"

"It's a trophy for you, sweet June," Colleen croons.

"For what?" June asks.

"For... Well... For being you." Colleen curls a stray hair that's fought its way free from her tight bun behind her ear. "And also, it didn't seem right that we would win the biggest competition of the year and receive our trophy without you having... something."

"Is that a bowler on the top of the trophy?" Clay asks.

"Yes," Colleen says. "It's one of Henry Junior's old trophies. I thought since June is blind..."

"Alright," Grace says, standing. "That's enough of—"

Mom clears her throat and shakes her head at Grace.

The Fowlers are lucky. Being told off by Grace isn't something that leaves a mark. I should know.

"Um... enough excitement for the night." Grace course

corrects. "Thank you for coming, Colleen and Henry, but June needs to rest."

"Of course," Colleen says and turns to leave.

Henry, however, lingers by June's bedside, his eyes moist with tears. He reaches down and pats her arm. "Take care, June."

"Thank you, Henry," she says.

"Henry," Colleen snaps.

"Coming, dear." He turns and hurries after his wife.

It's quiet as a church for several minutes after they leave.

"Did I just get a pity trophy?" The offense in June's voice is comical.

"That's what it looks like," Joy says.

"Oh, hell no." She tries to hold the trophy up, but the plastic thing is too heavy for her to lift. "Get rid of it. I can win my own damn trophy. Also, I don't want anything that used to belong to Henry Junior. There's no tellin' where it's been. I've heard stories."

Ian goes to June's bedside. "What do you want us to do with it?"

"Throw it in the tank for all I care."

He takes the trophy. "Anytime, anywhere, Bug."

# Chapter Forty-Four

"I feel like we should say something," Joy says as we make our way to the dock overlooking the tank behind Mom and Dad's house.

"Fuck the Fowlers?" Clay offers.

We all laugh.

"You're lucky Mom stayed in the house with June," Babe says.

Except for Mom, the rest of us came to carry out June's last wish.

"How about..." Ian lifts the trophy into the air. "For June," he roars, then hurls the trophy into the water.

"For June!" we all scream at the top of our lungs.

I don't know who starts crying first, but once the first person starts, we all fall apart and no one can stop. Misery rolls off us, wraps around us, and binds us together.

Aaron drops down into one of the chairs on the dock. "How am I going to do this?" It's not just a question. It's a plea from a husband, a man who's only loved one woman and is about to lose her.

No planning or knowledge or preparedness can protect you from this kind of pain. I've tried. And I'm still standing in the middle of my broken family and am as shattered as they are. Losing someone you love wrecks you in every way possible. Nobody gets out of it without scars.

Clay grips Aaron's shoulder. "I don't know, man, but you don't have to do it alone."

Aaron's big hand covers Clay's, and a big tear rolls down his face

"Aaron!" Mom yells from the house. There's an urgency in her voice that's unmistakable. "Aaron, come quick!"

We all take off toward the house.

Not yet.

Not yet.

Not yet.

Aaron's already at June's side by the time I get into the house. "What is it, baby?" he asks her.

Tears are running down my sister's face. "I can see."

"What?" I ask. "Are you sure?" Stupid question, but given the incident when she dreamed she was healed...

"I'm sure."

Babe drops down onto the bed next to June. "How?"

"I don't know. It just happened." She wipes her face with the blanket, then narrows her eyes. "Is that my necklace?"

Babe covers the pendant with her hand. "Yep, she can see."

"Baby, look at me," Aaron says.

The sun shines in June's smile when she turns her head to Aaron. She runs her hand down the side of his face, from temple to jaw. "Hey, you. You're wearing the T-shirt you were wearing when we met."

He blinks his wet lashes and swallows several times before he speaks. "It's my lucky shirt."

Her left hand joins her right as she cups each of his cheeks.

"I'm so glad I get to see your face one more time. It's the best face."

Aaron doesn't say anything but turns to kiss her palm.

June drags her gaze from her husband and looks at all of us. "I'm glad I get to see your faces, too."

"How'd this happen?" Dad asks.

"I don't know. One minute I couldn't see, and the next I could."

Grace bends over her and stares into her eyes like she's inspecting an interesting bug. "Is your vision blurry?"

"No. And you're in my bubble." She pushes Grace away playfully.

"It's a miracle." It's a statement of fact for Mom.

And looking at June right now, I have to agree. How many people get to witness an honest-to-God miracle? She was totally sightless fifteen minutes ago, and now she's not.

Mom pulls me away from June's bed. "Do you think we need to call the hospice nurse?"

"I don't think so."

Two little lines form between my mother's brows, a sure sign she's irritated. "I think you should. She's clearly getting better. She's had two really good days, and now she can see. I think God is healing her. I don't want to give her any more of that horrible medicine if she's being healed. There's no reason."

Oh, my poor, sweet Mama. The absolute conviction that the Almighty is giving her the miracle she's been begging for is a knife to my broken heart. "I'll call her, Mom."

"Thank you." The lines are gone, but the hope that's taken up residence in her expression is far worse than her being mad at me.

"I'm going to step outside to make the phone call," I say and gesture to the front door.

She nods and goes back to June.

I make my way to the front porch to call Stephanie, but I already know what she's going to say.

I've read everything I can get my hands on about end-of-life care, and this is exactly what is described as happening. It's called the rally, and it almost always comes hours to a couple of days before death.

A sick, sour mixture churns in my belly. How do I tell my mom the miracle that she thinks she's getting is actually June preparing to die?

# Chapter Forty-Five

The dream yanks me upright in bed, gasping and disoriented. I grab my phone to check the time. Two thirty a.m. I try to grab the threads of the images that were playing in my sleep, but they're gone. The only evidence of their existence is the thump, thump, thump of my heart behind my ribs.

My pulse is on overdrive when I make it downstairs to get some water. I stare out the kitchen window while I drink, at the RV parked in the drive. I can't believe he's lasted this long.

I thought for sure he'd turn tail and run after the first week, but he's stuck it out, no matter how hard it's been. And it's so damn hard. I'm not sure what we would've done without him.

The Ian I lived with for the last ten years would never have made the sacrifices he's made over the last month. But is this crisis-induced caring, or has he really changed? The softness I feel toward Ian is confusing and not something I have the mental or emotional bandwidth to dissect.

"Who's there?" June whispers.

I set the glass down and go to her. "It's me." I keep my voice quiet too, so I don't wake Aaron, who's sleeping on the sofa.

"I hurt." It's little more than a pitiful whimper.

"Have you had any meds since we all went to bed?"

"No."

"Okay, I'll be right back." I find the medication log, where we track her doses and the times they were given. It's not that I don't trust June to tell me if she's had medication, but she loses track of time and what she's been given. Honestly, so do we. Keeping up with all her prescriptions and dosages is a full-time job.

I fill the oral syringe with her dose of morphine and return to her side. "Here you go."

"Hard to swallow."

"Turn your head toward me. I'll squeeze it in slowly, and we'll let gravity help us." It takes several minutes, but we get the medication down her throat. "Want some water?"

She shakes her head.

I sit next to her on the bed. "Can I do anything to help?"

"Hold my hand?"

"I can do that." I take her frail hand in mine. "It's crazy how good your manicure still looks."

"It does?"

"Yeah. It's grown out some, but those pink nails are still sassy."

By the glow of the night light by her bed, I see her smile. "Good. I want to go out looking sassy."

I force out a laugh because if I don't, I'll cry, and I don't want to put that on her.

"It's almost time, isn't it?" There's not an ounce of fear in her question.

I trace the veins on the back of her hand. "I think so."

She grips my hand tighter. "Me too. And this time it isn't because I'm just tired. My body is telling me it's time."

It's my turn to nod. Any words I might say are dammed behind the weight of what I know is coming. I will live the rest of my life without this amazing person. Our sister group chat will now only consist of four names and not five, and my defend-you-till-the-end person will be gone.

"How are you so brave, June? I think I would be terrified, but ever since you decided to stop treatment, you've been so calm."

She licks her dry lips. "I just know you can't control what happens to you. You can only control your reaction. This isn't me being brave, it's just me controlling my reaction to something that I can't change."

Just when I thought I couldn't admire her more than I do, she says something that rocks the entire foundation of my world. "You amaze me, little sister."

"What are you going to do about Ian?"

The subject change is so jarring that I laugh for real this time. "What?"

"He still loves you." Her voice is quiet but strong.

I press my cheek to my shoulder to catch a stray tear. "What makes you say that?"

She snorts. "Why do you think he's camping in the front yard?"

"He's doing that for the family. Because he loves you."

"Come on, Hope, really? You can't see that it's all for you?"

I adjust my position on the bed. "I hadn't... I don't know."

"Also, he told me."

"He did?"

"Yes, but that wouldn't matter. Talk is cheap. It's more that he's stayed and continues to show up, even though you gave him no encouragement." She shrugs, but she's so weak that her frail shoulders barely move. "Don't get me wrong. I understand. He's been a jackass. He all but abandoned you, but I believe he knows it and wants to change." Her fingers tighten around mine. "Will you at least think about what I said?"

I don't answer immediately. She's not simply putting the request to me as a sister, it's her dying wish. I can't lie to her. It's too important. "I'll think about it."

Her grip lessens around my fingers, and she grins. "I like the power that comes with dying."

I laugh. "Yeah, you could probably get just about anything you want right now."

She exhales, and her whole body relaxes as the morphine takes effect. "I have everything I want. Nobody could have had a better life than me. Goodnight, Hope. I love you." Her breathing deepens, then she's asleep.

I straighten her covers and kiss her forehead. My tears fall on her face, and I wipe them away with the tips of my fingers. "I love you too, June."

# Chapter Forty-Six

At six a.m., I give up any thought of restful sleep and get out of bed. I've barely slept since my conversation with June.

I'm halfway down the stairs when I hear it. The breathing change the hospice nurse told us would begin before the end. My feet barely touch the ground until I make it to the living room. Then they stop abruptly.

Aaron is standing over June with the lost child look I've seen on his face a million times over the last couple of months. He's staring at her as if he doesn't know who she is. Like his wife was replaced by a foreign creature while he slept.

"Aaron?" I ask, not wanting to spook him, because he looks like he's battling his fight-or-flight instinct, and flight is winning. He turns to me, and it takes a minute for comprehension to register in his eyes.

"Hope?"

I go to him and guide him into the chair next to June's bed. "When did this start?"

"About an hour ago." He's not looking at me. It's clear he's staring down the barrel of a future that doesn't include June. "I tried to wake her, but she won't wake up."

"Did you give her any medicine?" We have medication to help reduce the secretions that are causing the loud rattling coming from June's throat.

"Um... No."

June makes a sound that is only heard on death's door, and Aaron jerks his head around to her.

I abandon my attempts to get information. He's not capable, and I don't blame him. I find Stephanie's name in my contacts and call her.

"Hello."

"Stephanie, this is Hope Hall. We woke up this morning and June—"

"I can hear her. I'll be there as soon as I can."

"What do I do in the meantime?" I try to sound competent and in control, but I'm pretty sure I don't pull it off.

"Have you given her any medication?"

"She had morphine at two thirty. That sound... It's awful."

"I know, but she's not in distress. Her body knows what to do and is doing it." Her kindness might be my undoing.

"Okay."

"You can give another dose of morphine and the medication for the secretions, which will help relax her body. This is all normal and natural, Hope. It's part of the dying process."

I nod, then realize she can't see me. "'Kay." I disconnect the call, head to the kitchen, and call Grace.

"Hey, what's up?" Sleep weighs her words down.

"It's June. Her breathing is different."

"Different how?"

"You know. Like death breathing."

"I'm on my way."

"Will you call Joy and Babe? I hate to ask, but I need to get June's meds and then I have to wake Mom and Dad."

"Sure. How's Aaron?"

I glance over at Aaron. He hasn't moved. He's still in the chair, still staring at June. "Bad."

"We'll be right there."

I give June her medication, which basically consists of squirting it under her tongue, then tilting her head to let gravity help get it down. It's horrible. Another thing that I know will haunt me long after this terrible time is over.

I go back to the kitchen to put the syringe in the sink and call Ian,

"Hey, I was about to head in." He sounds more awake than Grace did.

"Good. I think it's today." How many times can I be expected to say June is dying? It's unbearable.

His sharp intake of air is his only response, then the line goes dead. Within seconds, he's pushing through the front door. Long strides eat up the distance between us. He doesn't touch me, but the look he gives me tells me he's there if I need him. "What can I do?"

"Go see about Aaron. He's not okay."

"Done."

I close my eyes, take several steadying breaths, and prepare myself to go tell my parents. But when I come around the bar to head down the hall, I see Dad frozen in the same spot I was standing in a few minutes ago.

"What's wrong with her?" he demands, but I can tell he really doesn't want the answer.

"She's—"

"June!" Mom shoves past Dad and rushes to June's bed. "Why is she making that noise?"

"She's..." I try again. "She's dying, Mom. This is what happens. Remember what Stephanie told us?"

"Where is Stephanie? She needs to do something." The desperation rolling off my mother nearly smothers me.

"She's on her way, but she told me what to do."

"You're not a nurse." Her tone slaps me in the face, but I'm not offended. Her daughter's dying. She's entitled to a few swipes.

"Mom," I say with all the gentleness in my soul. "Stephanie's not going to do anything. That's what hospice care is. There's no lifesaving intervention. This is what June chose."

There's no answer, but her tears of surrender tell me that she understands. She sits next to my sister and clasps her hand. "We're here, Junie, and we're not going anywhere."

Dad has made his way to June's bed by now. He stands behind Mom and places his hands on her shoulders.

Mom scoots her chair as close as she can to June's bed, but it must not be close enough because she pulls away from Dad and crawls onto the bed to lie down next to June. Body-wrenching sobs wrack her small frame as she whispers unintelligible words of love and tells my sister how brave she is.

Dad collapses into the abandoned chair. and stretches his arm out to cover Mom and June. He drops his head to the bed, and weeps like he might never stop.

I don't think I ever understood the true meaning of anguish until right this very minute. My parents are lost to it, and there's nothing any of us can do to help.

My sisters, Clay, Max and Chloe come in, and we all surround June's bed.

"I don't understand," Babe wails. "She was so much better yesterday. She could see. I thought..."

"We all thought she was getting better," Mom says.

I don't correct her. I didn't, and I doubt Grace did either. I knew what it was, and I don't know which is worse, being blindsided by this morning's events or knowing they were coming sooner rather than later. It's all horrible.

"Knock, knock," Stephanie says as she lets herself into the house.

"In here," Ian replies. His face is red and wet with his own tears.

"I'm so sorry, y'all," Stephanie says with all the sympathy in the world. How does she do this day in and day out and still keep her humanity?

I press the heel of my hand to my wet face. "Thank you."

"I'm going to take June's vitals and do a little exam, but from what I see and hear, I think you all know where this is headed, right?"

We all nod.

Mom, who's gotten out of June's bed goes to Stephanie and takes the woman's face in her hands. "You take good care of our girl."

Stephanie places her hand over mom's. "Like she was mine."

My mother's chin quivers and she nods, then goes to my dad. She buries her head in his chest as he wraps his arms around her.

They made this incredible person, and now they have to watch her die. I can't think of anything that could be worse in this whole world.

Stephanie gets to work, and when she tries to get June's blood pressure with the little machine she usually uses, nothing registers. "I'm going to have to do this the old-fashioned way." She pulls out a blood pressure cuff connected to a hose with a dial and pump attached. Several attempts are made before she says, "Ah, there it is." She looks up at us. "It's very weak. It won't be long."

Babe clings to Clay like she'll fall to the ground if he doesn't hold onto her.

Ian is standing next to Aaron, who's still sitting in the chair beside June's bed, but it's clear that if Ian moved, Aaron would not be able to sit upright alone.

Joy, Grace, the kids, and I are holding onto one another, standing at the end of June's bed.

I don't know how long we stand there, maybe another hour, while June's favorite worship music plays. We watch each breath as they get farther and farther apart, until finally one becomes her last.

"Is that it?" Babe asks.

"I think so," I say, and am shocked to hear my voice is steady.

"No." Babe cries and falls into Clay.

Grace and Joy wrap their arms around Max and Chloe as they all fall completely apart.

It's over.

The thing we've dreaded has happened, and it's as horrific as I ever dreamed it would be. And still, there's a beauty in what we've just witnessed that I don't know if I'll ever be able to describe to anyone who hasn't also witnessed it. We bore witness to June's life and her death because we love her.

Mom leans her head on my shoulder. "I hope she knew how much she was loved."

I wrap my arm around her. "She did, Mom. And she loved us right back."

With tears pouring from her eyes, Mom leans over and kisses June's forehead. "I loved you first, Junie. I loved you first."

# Chapter Forty-Seven

Shortly after our final moments with June, Stephanie asks us all to step out of the room so she can get June ready for the funeral home.

We all congregate on the front porch.

"It was so peaceful," Mom says. She and Dad are sitting on the porch swing. "Wasn't it peaceful, Russ?"

He slips his arm around her shoulder. "It was, Marie. Real peaceful." They both wear the exact same shell-shocked expression, and my heart breaks for them all over again.

After that, no one speaks. Each of us left to our own private pain.

I pull out my phone and text Carrie.

*She's gone.*

Those two words change everything about me. The fiber of my being is no longer the same because she's gone.

I look around the porch at my family, and gratitude for each of them fills my heart. Then I notice that Ian isn't with us. Panic quickly pushes gratitude to the side.

Where is he?

Did he leave?

If he left, is he coming back?

The RV is still parked in its usual place, so I slip away quietly to find him. He should be here with us. He's been to hell and back right beside us.

As soon as I get to the back of the house, I see him sitting in a chair on the dock, elbows on his knees, looking out over the water. My steps falter, and I stop moving. I'm so disoriented by my desire to run to him. For so long he hasn't been safe, and now my heart is screaming *safe, safe, safe.*

I'm locked in indecision, but then he sees me, stands, and opens his arms.

Any hesitation melts away, and I'm running to him before my next thought. He covers me with his arms, and for a few precious moments, that's where I live. Safe in his embrace, where nothing and no one can hurt me. My body and heart remember this man.

"I'm so damn sorry, Hope."

I nod against his chest.

"Not just for June, though God knows how any of us will live without her. I'm sorry that I ruined us." I feel him shrug. "I don't know if there's any way possible to rebuild it." He holds me away from him to look in my eyes. "But that's all I want. To rebuild us."

"I'm not saying no, but I'm not in any shape to be making major life decisions right now, and maybe not for a while—"

"I'll wait."

"If you'll give me some time, then I think I'd like to revisit this conversation."

His smile is brilliant and so reminiscent of the man I used to know that it brings another wave of tears to my eyes. "A few weeks, a few months, a few years. Take all the time you need. I'm not going anywhere."

"Hope, Stephanie said we can go back in with June," Joy yells from the back porch.

I hook my thumb toward the house. "We should go back in."

"You go. I'll be there in a bit."

"Okay." I turn to leave, then stop. "Thank you for taking care of us."

"We took care of each other."

Back inside the living room, we gather around June and say our final goodbyes before the funeral director comes for her.

Joy angles her head and stares at June's face.

"What's the matter?" I ask.

"Chin hairs," Grace whispers.

"What?" I angle my head the same way Joy did, and sure enough, the morning sun shining through the window glistens off three curling whiskers.

Joy grabs Grace's purse and begins rummaging through it.

"What are you doing?" Grace asks.

"Looking for the tweezers." Joy withdraws her hand from Grace's purse. "Found them."

The four of us stifle a giggle.

"We can't," Babe says, and looks to me for confirmation... or permission?

I shrug. "I... She did say..."

Grace bumps Babe out of the way. "She said she'd haunt us if we let her go to her grave with chin hair." She yanks the grooming tool from Joy's hand. "Give me those tweezers."

# Chapter Forty-Eight

We laid June to rest today.

Words I never thought I'd say. Even with all of my pragmatism, at the core of my being, I never thought we'd ever be without her.

But here we are.

Whoever said that preemptive grief is in some ways worse than grief after the fact was an idiot.

It was me. I was that idiot. I miss that woman. She was blissfully unaware of what it's like to walk someone you love to the end of their life.

June died last Saturday, so we waited until this Saturday to have her funeral so all of her teacher friends and students could come. Seven days without her has felt like an eternity, and yet I have a lifetime to live without her.

There's a movie where Drew Barrymore wakes up every morning with no memory of the day before, unaware that her life has changed. That's how I feel. Every morning there's this split second of time where I forget that June is gone and that our lives will never be the same.

I love that moment.

But then reality crashes in, and the rollercoaster ride we've been on for months begins again. It's exhausting.

We're all at the end of our physical and emotional capacity, and yet somehow we continue on. It's one of life's mysteries how the human spirit can endure so much pain and still function.

The outpouring of love has sustained us, but that too is draining. Thank God for Carrie running interference for us. She and Jack have been our rocks this week. Even now, she's in the house making sure Mom and Dad are taken care of and not overwhelmed.

Last night at June's viewing, hundreds of people waited in line for a couple of hours to hug our necks and tell us how much they loved June. It was precious, but I could barely string two words together afterward.

The funeral was brutal, but I expected that. What I didn't expect was how funny and uplifting it would also be. Pastor Hal really understood June, and that came across in what he said about her, especially that she chose faith over fear. And of course, per June's request, when Tupac's "Picture Me Rollin'" played, everyone cracked up laughing. Leave it to June to bring the party, even in death.

I've escaped the crowded house full of people who love us and dangle my bare feet over the side of the dock. The summer heat has warmed the water, and it soothes a small part of my broken pieces.

"Hey, want some company?" Joy says from behind me.

I turn and see Joy, Grace, and Babe, the same lines of grief and exhaustion etched into their faces that I know are on mine. "Pull up a seat."

They slip off their shoes and sit next to me. We don't speak.

The only sound is the lapping of the water around our legs and the faint voices from inside the house.

A turtle pops his head up from under the water. I watch as his four little legs paddle him to the shore, where three more turtles are sunning on the rocks.

"I told Jimmy not to come to the funeral, and that we're done," Joy says without preamble.

"I did too," Grace adds.

"Y'all did?" I ask, trying to sound as neutral as possible, but I don't think I succeed.

That's confirmed when Joy chuckles and says, "I did. And you can stop pretending you don't care."

I grin and kick my leg out, and water arches in front of me. "How'd he take it?"

"Like he takes everything, like it was no skin off his back." Joy says.

"Same," Grace adds.

I'm relieved that neither of them sounds too upset about their decision. "One thing you can say about ol' Jimmy, he's an uncomplicated man."

"I did notice that he wasn't at the funeral, but I thought it was because he didn't have any cut-off shorts nice enough for the occasion," Babe says, and immediately adds, "I'm sorry. That was—"

"Accurate." Grace laughs. When Joy joins in, I can see June's smug smile.

We're quiet again, each lost in our own thoughts. One of the sunning turtles slips from the rock with a plop into the water.

"I'm pregnant." The words come out of Babe's mouth like a bucking bull out of the chute.

"What?" I ask.

"How far along?" Grace yells.

"You're what?" Joy shouts.

Babe grins and ducks her head. "I'm twelve weeks pregnant."

"Twelve weeks? Why did you wait so long to tell us?" Joy asks.

Our baby sister shrugs and looks out over the water. "June knew. I told her about a month ago. It was our last secret."

Grace swipes at a tear on her cheek like it personally offends her. "That's so great, Babe."

I wait for the familiar feeling of loss and envy that always accompanies a pregnancy announcement, but it never comes. The only thing I feel is genuine joy for my sister. "Congratulations, Babe. Clay must be over the moon. I'm surprised he could keep the secret this long."

"Right?" Grace says, then looks at Babe. "Does he know?"

She laughs. "Of course he knows, and it killed him not to say anything, but he understood why I wanted to wait."

"So what's going to happen with you and Ian?" Grace asks me matter-of-factly.

"I don't know." I shrug. "I guess we'll have to see. Whatever happens, it'll be okay."

"Wow. That's a very un-Hope-like response," Joy says. "No plan? No definite way forward?"

"What about work?" Babe asks. "Did you ever hear back about that professor job?"

I take a breath. "I got it and turned it down."

"What?" Joy sits up. "Why?"

"Because June needed me. And I needed to be here." I shrug. "It was the right choice."

Grace stares at me. "The Hope I knew six months ago would never have done that."

"Yeah, well." I watch a hawk fly overhead. "That Hope also thought she could control everything. Turns out you can't."

It's scary as hell to release the death grip I've always had on life, but it also feels really right. "A very wise woman once said, 'You can't control what happens to you. All you can control is your reaction to what happens.' That's my new motto for life."

I've spent my whole life trying to control the outcome of every situation. If things went badly, that meant I'd done something wrong. But these last few months have taught me you can do everything right and things still may not work out. You can lose your marriage, your job, your sister. And you can still show up. You still have a good life.

A choked sob comes from Babe at the reminder of June's words. I slip my arm around her shoulder.

"We didn't get our miracle." Her voice cracks.

Joy dabs with the hem of her dress. "I think the ten years we had with her was our miracle, Babe."

The sun behind us projects our four silhouettes onto the water in front of us.

Four.

Not five.

A vivid reminder of our new reality, and my heart breaks all over again.

"What are we going to do without her?" Babe asks.

"I don't know," I answer as my tears fall freely.

"What did you say before, Hope?" Joy asks. "The next thing? I guess we just do the next thing."

Grace stands and straightens her skirt.

"Where are you going?" I ask as I dab my cheeks with the heel of my hand.

She dries her feet and slips them back into her shoes. "My version of the next thing."

Joy pulls her feet out of the water and laughs. "And what's that?"

"The Fowlers are out of town, and toilet paper's on sale at the Shop and Save." Grace grins. "Y'all comin'?"

We only hesitate for a moment, then the three of us are drying our feet and grabbing our shoes. Babe steadies herself on my arm as she slips hers on.

I touch her tiny baby bump. "Hey, little darlin', let me tell you about your Auntie June..."

# Epilogue

It's been a year today since we lost June.

A year learning to navigate a new normal, where sorrow is braided into every day, even the good days. Because joy didn't cease to exist after June died, but it is different now.

Everyone knows that death is hard and losing someone you love is unbearable, but what no one tells you about is the reality of living without your person. The haunting silence after everyone leaves, after the meals stop showing up, and the phone calls to see how you are become fewer and fewer.

Some days you're so unbearably sad that you don't even recognize yourself in the mirror. Those days are hard, but you expect to feel that way. The trickier days, for me, are the ones that have a vague resemblance to normal. Days when I go through my hours without breaking down, or times when I get things done without losing my train of thought because grief has stolen my capacity to focus. Most people would think the good days would make me happy, but they mark another step away from life with June.

But no matter how hard it was to watch June die, or how hard this year has been, I don't have any regrets. That was what I hoped I'd feel once June was gone, and it's a comfort to know I accomplished that.

Today we've gathered at Mom and Dad's to celebrate her and us for making it through a year without falling apart as a family. We're all at different points in our healing journey. None of us is whole, but we're trying.

A warm arm slides around my shoulder, and soft lips press against my temple. "Hey."

Ian.

He's still around. The counseling we both insisted on hasn't been easy. We've both had to take responsibility for the problems with our marriage. We're taking it one day at a time. No wedding plans, no promises we can't keep, just showing up for each other the best we can.

"How are you?" he asks.

I lean into him. "Horrible. How the hell do you think I am?" The response has become our litmus test as to how we're really doing. If we answer any other way, we know the other is struggling that day. It's weird, but it works for us.

He kisses my temple again, and I can feel his lips curve into a smile. "I feel the same, in case you're wondering."

"I know."

"Hope, can you grab this platter of burgers before I drop it?" Mom asks as she makes her way to the dock, followed by Max and Chloe, who are both carrying dishes of food.

Ian relieves her of her burden. "Here, let me."

"Aunt Hope, can you take the ketchup from under my arm. I'm about to drop it," Max asks.

"I've got it."

"Thanks."

I turn to Chloe. "Have any condiments that need rescuing?"

"No. I'm good."

Everyone places their dishes and platters on the table. "This all looks delicious, Marie," Ian says.

"Believe me, I wished for you this morning when I was trying to get everything organized." She hugs him. "I'll never be able to thank you enough for what you did for us when June was in hospice care."

The flush that colors his face is familiar. Mom has thanked him at least fifty times for all he did. "I've told you that you don't have to thank me. It was nothing."

"It was everything," I say, and mean it. Ian taking care of my family when we couldn't take care of ourselves is the most romantic thing he's ever done for me.

He nods, but I can see his discomfort, so I change the subject.

"Carrie texted this morning to say she's thinking about us today."

Moisture glistens in my mother's blue eyes. "She texted me too." Mom dabs at her eyes with a tissue she pulled from her pocket. "She is precious. She'll randomly text me funny memories of June. I hope she knows how much that means to me."

"She's the best." I grab a few pickle slices off the garnish plate and hand one to Max, who promptly pops it into his mouth, and offer one to Chloe, who declines. "Is Aaron coming?"

Mom folds the napkins she brought with her from the house. "Yes, he texted and said he's on his way."

"How is he?"

"He's okay. It's different for him. She was the love of his life. We all have each other, but he doesn't have her." She shrugs. "I'm not sure how to help, except to be available if he wants to talk."

"I've been checking on him," Ian says. "Your assessment is pretty accurate. He's getting by, but it's gonna take time."

The strand of sorrow that's woven into every part of my life yanks a little harder at the thought of Aaron alone in the house he shared with June. He'd often say that June was the perfect woman for him. I can't imagine his pain and loss.

I steal another pickle slice. "Where are Joy and Grace?"

"They had a meeting this morning with Lee Edwards, the new athletic director at the high school, about June's scholarship." She checks her watch. "They should be here any minute."

Over the last year, Joy and Grace have developed a scholarship program for female athletes at Bonedalia High School. June's death has given them a reason to bury their differences and work together on something important to our whole family. The best news is that no one has seen hide nor hair of Jimmy Jenkins in more than a year. Good riddance.

"Give me that baby," Mom shouts and holds out her hands.

Babe is making her way across the lawn with six-month-old Misty June in her arms. Clay's not far behind, loaded down with baby paraphernalia like a sherpa on a Mt. Everest expedition.

Babe hands Misty June to Mom. "She's been crying for her Gran all morning."

"Well, of course she has. She's my little punkin', aren't you, baby girl? Give Gran a kiss."

Misty squeals in delight, grabs Mom's face with her pudgy hands, and plants an open-mouth kiss on Mom's chin.

We all laugh, grabbing the little girl's attention. She smiles like she gets the joke and flashes two little teeth behind her lower lip.

The day after Misty June was born, Babe sent Clay home to rest. Grace, Joy, Chloe, Mom, and I spent the day with her and the baby in the hospital. It was a precious time filled with so much joy for the newest James girl, and also sadness for the James girl who wasn't there—joy braided with sadness.

"Clay, you need some help with that?" Ian asks.

"Can you grab the bouncy seat?"

"You've got it." Ian picks up the thing that can best be described as a piece of equipment. "Where would you like me to put it, Babe?"

She gestures to a place next to the table. "Right here is fine."

"Don't hog that baby, Marie," Dad yells as he, Joy, Grace, and Aaron make their way to the dock. "I heard she needed some spoilin' and I'm here to do it."

"Who are you and what did you do with our father?" Joy asks.

"Right?" Grace agrees.

"Y'all leave him alone," Mom says and hands him the baby.

"They don't bother us. Do they, Misty June?" Dad blows a raspberry into his granddaughter's neck. Her carefree giggles fill the air, and I swear I can see June in her sweet smile.

Aaron moves next to Dad, grabs Misty June's foot, and leans over to kiss her forehead. "Hey, sweet girl," he whispers.

That small expression of love causes heat and pressure to push against my eyes. Not just grief for June, but something else too. For years, seeing babies only reminded me of what I'd never have. But Misty June doesn't feel like loss. She feels like hope.

"Let me have her, Dad. I'm going to put her down for a nap inside," Babe says.

"All by herself?" The indignation on my dad's face is comical.

Clay waves a white box in the air. "We've got a camera. We can watch her from out here."

The little family disappears into the house.

Aaron juts his chin toward the shotgun hung on the rifle rack under the covered patio of the dock. "Russ, are you still seein' snakes?"

"We saw a big one a couple of weeks ago while we were fishin', didn't we, Grandad?" Max says.

"Yeah, ugly sucker. Lucky for him, he kept his distance." Dad grabs a beer from the cooler. "It's kind of late for 'em, but I don't like to be out here without my shotgun in case one decides to get friendly."

"And we appreciate that, Grandpa" Chloe says.

She, Max, and Clay have become my dad's co-conspirators in the Fowler feud. They did whip the Fowlers' ass at Halloween and at every other competition this year. June would be so proud.

Babe and Clay rejoin us, monitor in hand.

"That was fast," I say.

"She's a good sleeper," Babe says.

"She is," Chloe, who has become Misty June's favorite babysitter agrees. "All you have to do is put her in her sleep suit give her the paci, and put her in her crib,"

"Did I tell you she said Dada the other night?" Clay asks. "I'm pretty sure she's advanced." Love and pride roll off him in waves.

Babe shakes her head. "I carried her for nine months, birthed her, got up in the night to breastfeed her, and the first word she says is Dada. That's one of life's true injustices."

Clay wraps his arms around her. "What can I say? I inspire greatness."

She laughs and gives him a quick kiss. "Shut up, you idiot."

"Y'all find your spot," Mom says. "The food's gettin' cold."

We all take our places at the table. Once we're seated, Dad takes his can of beer and says, "It's been a long year and a hard one, but it hasn't all been bad." He motions to the monitor. "We've got our sweet Misty June, and we have each other." He clears the emotion from his throat. "I've been thinkin' that every day we live without our Junie is how we honor her. I think she'd be proud of us." He raises his beer. "For June."

There are tears in everyone's eyes as we all raise our glasses. "For June."

The food, drinks, conversation, and tears flow easily. It's the most natural thing in the world, and I think my dad is right. June would be proud of us.

"How's your job, Hope?" Joy asks.

I swallow the gooey, creamy potato salad I just put in my mouth. "It's great."

"Where are you working again?" Aaron asks.

"I'm working with the Dallas Independent School District as the Literacy Initiatives Director. I work with teachers to find out why students aren't reading, then we come up with a plan to fix it."

"I think that's wonderful, honey," Mom says.

"It is," I agree. And I mean it. No marble halls or distinguished faculty titles. Simply showing up where I'm needed. I think June would approve of that too.

Clay points toward the water. "What's that?"

"What?" Babe asks.

"That shiny spot in the water. I think somethin's floatin' out there," Clay says.

We all get up and move toward the edge of the dock.

Grace shields her eyes from the sun with one hand. "I can't tell what it is."

Babe lowers her sunglasses. "Neither can I."

"Oh, my Lord," Joy yells. "It's the Fowlers' trophy."

"It can't be," I say.

Ian squints toward the water. "It is. The cheap thing floats."

"Oh, my word," Mom says. "June would hate that. Russ, we need to get that out of there and throw it away."

The ch-chck of a shotgun being racked fills the air. We turn and see Dad aiming at the trophy. "I got it, Marie." Then he yells, "For June." And blows it out of the water.

"For June," we all cry.

***

## Book Club Questions

1. Hope begins the novel believing that doing everything "right" should lead to a successful, stable life. How does the story challenge her ideas about control, success, and happiness?

2. The James sisters are loud, messy, and deeply connected. Which sister did you relate to most, and why?

3. June often uses humor and irreverence to cope with fear and pain, while Hope tends to rely on control and restraint. How do their different approaches to difficult situations shape the emotional impact of the story?

4. June faces her circumstances with a very specific kind of courage. How did her journey affect the rest of the family—and you as a reader?

5. Family dynamics are at the heart of this novel. How do the sisters show love differently, even when they're in conflict?

6. The novel suggests that you can't control everything, no

matter how hard you try. Do you agree? How does that idea show up in your own life?

7. What does "coming home" mean for Hope? Has your definition of home ever changed?

8. Were there moments when you felt frustrated with Hope or her choices? What would you have done differently?

9. The story explores grief, but also resilience and second chances. What message did you take away from the ending?

10. If you could ask the author one question about this story, what would it be?

***

## The Story Behind The Summer That Changed Us

This story came from my sister Joni. From the last months of her life, from the way our family laughed when we probably shouldn't have, and from the thing I needed to do after she was gone.

I wrote it all down — the real story behind this novel, the moments that made it onto the page and the ones that didn't, and what it meant to turn the hardest thing I've ever lived through into the best thing I've ever written.

But I wasn't the only one writing.

Other members of our family have also written down

their thoughts on that time and how much Joni meant to them.

I'd like you to have all of it.

Sign up for my newsletter and I'll send you *The Story Behind The Summer That Changed Us* — my personal essay about where this book really came from, along with pieces written by the people who loved Joni. Click Here to Get The Story.

*You'll also be the first to hear about new releases, behind-the-scenes news, and whatever I'm up to next. No spam. Just me, showing up in your inbox when I have something worth saying.*

**Not ready to leave small-town Texas?**

I've been making readers snort-laugh for nine years with my small-town romantic comedies set in Texas, full of big personalities, slow burns, and happily ever afters that are swoon worthy.

**Fair warning:** they are not this book. They're romances, which means there's a love story at the center and it gets worked out by the last page. They're also a little spicy, which means things get worked out in other ways too.

If that sounds like exactly what you need after everything the James family just put you through, start with ***Running From a Rock Star***, Book 1 in the ***Brides on the Run*** series.

Read Running From a Rock Star

# Also by Jami Albright

Brides on the Run

Running From a Rock Star

Running With a Sweet Talker

Running From the Law

Running After a Heartbreaker

Running Out on The One

Other Books By Jami

Homecoming King

Duke-ing It Out

Happy New You

# About the Author

Jami Albright is a born and raised Texas girl, a multiple award-winning author, and co-host of Wish I'd Known Then... For Writers—a podcast with over 500,000 downloads dedicated to helping authors navigate the craft and business of writing. Her small-town romantic comedies have reached Amazon's Top 100 and built a devoted readership across nine years of publishing.

She is also a wife, mother, grandmother (Coco), and in a former life, an actress and comedian.

Jami lives in Texas, roots loudly for the Houston Texans, and believes puppies are the answer to most of life's problems.

Jami loves to hear from readers. You can reach her at:

https://www.jamialbright.com/contact

www.ingramcontent.com/pod-product-compliance
Lightning Source LLC
LaVergne TN
LVHW091253150826
845673LV00006B/1400

* 9 7 9 8 9 9 6 1 1 3 8 0 4 *